Her fingers closed lightly around his biceps and traced down his arm to his hand.

"We haven't known each other very long, but I think of you as a friend, Josh. You've helped me so much. I just want you to know that if there's anything I can do to help you, I'm here."

Josh pulled her close so she wouldn't see the sudden flood of emotion he felt. She had no idea. If he told her the truth, she would go—should go—running far away. "Thank you," he managed to say.

"I mean it." Mickie's words vibrated against his chest. The feel of a warm body against his. The scent of her hair. The touch of her hands as they skimmed around his waist to link together, holding him in place. For a moment, all the confusion and regret and pain faded away. Being with her felt like stepping out of a shrieking wind and into a quiet moment of peace.

"I know," he whispered in her ear. "Thank you."

She leaned back to look up at him. He couldn't meet her gaze. Instead he focused on her lips. Pink. The lower lip fuller than the top. Pretty. He wondered what it would be like to kiss them.

"Josh," she said.

He kissed her.

Whatever she wanted to say, he didn't want to hear.

Dear Reader,

Welcome back to The Cleaning Crew! We'll be leaving beautiful Charleston to follow Josh to Columbia, SC, where he is setting up a new Crew. DeShawn is there to help him get the new branch up and running.

I was eager to write Josh's story because he is, in many ways, much more damaged than Sadie. He's just better at hiding it. In spite of everything, he's a nice guy and deserves his happily-ever-after.

Mickie is the young single mother next door. She has secrets of her own. She and I also have one big thing in common: nursing school. She is clinging to the hope that once she becomes a nurse, she can stop running from her past and provide a good life for her son. Attending nursing school is extremely stressful and I was able to share some of my insane study/coping mechanisms with her. Hint: index cards.

It was a tall assignment to get Josh, who is terrified of family and commitment, and Mickie, who has serious trust issues and comes with a toddler, together. They are both rather mule-headed but also people with a lot of love to give. They just need to learn to accept love.

I hope you enjoy their journey.

Janet Lee Nye

JANET LEE NYE

Boss on Notice

ISBN-13: 978-0-373-61016-7

Boss on Notice

This edition published by arrangement with Harlequin Books S.A.

For questions and comments about the quality of this book, please contact us at CustomerService@Harlequin.com.

Printed in U.S.A.

Janet Lee Nye is a writer by day and a neonatal nurse by night. She lives in Charleston, SC, with her fella and her felines. She spends too much time on Twitter and too little time on housework and has no plans to remedy this.

Books by Janet Lee Nye

HARLEQUIN SUPERROMANCE

The Cleaning Crew

Spying on the Boss

Other titles by this author available in ebook format.

In dedication to all the romance writers who helped me, cheered me on, gave me critiques. I'm not going to name names because every person I talked to, every workshop I attended, every book I read, gave me a little bit of knowledge and insight. Thank you all.

CHAPTER ONE

THERE WAS A kid in his kitchen. Not a regular kid but a baby-size kid. Josh stopped in the doorway and stared at him. The kid, in blue shorts and a white shirt with a sailboat on the front, stood a few feet from the sliding glass door that led to the patio. He was rubbing the bottom of his nose with the back of a fat little hand, staring at his own reflection in the glass and scratching his bottom with the other hand.

"Uh...um, hey? Who are you?"

The kid's eyes opened wide as he turned to look at Josh. He pulled the hand away from his nose and a string of snot followed, stretching long and low, before dripping down onto the floor. The kid stood there, mouth moving, looking too startled to speak. Josh put his hands up like, "okay, okay, it's good, we'll figure this out," but it was too late. The kid's face crumpled into something that resembled a boiled troll's seconds before an ungodly screeching wail began.

What the hell? This kid could give an ambulance siren some competition. Tears began to run down his face and he shuffled his feet in a kind of awkward dance.

"Hey. Hey. It's okay," Josh said, taking a step forward and extending a hand, not knowing if he was supposed to extend the hand. "Sorry. You scared the sh— You scared me." He gave his best shot at a friendly smile.

How it was possible for the screech to get louder, Josh did not know, but, yep, the volume shot straight from ambulance siren to aircraft-taking-off territory. Josh glanced around the small apartment. He'd left the sliding glass door to the back patio open to air out the kitchen after he'd accidentally set fire to a bag of microwave popcorn. The screen had been pushed open. The kid had wandered in. Which meant that whoever the kid belonged to was out there, somewhere. Okay, this was a problem with a solution.

"Hey, come on," he said. "Let's find your mom."

Josh took a few steps in the direction of the door but the kid didn't follow. Nope. Not that easy. What the kid did was fall over on his butt and…get louder? Was that even possible? Yes, it was.

Josh started to cover his ears, then forced himself to let his hands fall back to his sides. How did parents deal with this? He tried a smile. Made what he hoped was a comical shrug. What did they do on *Sesame Street*? There had to be some kind of kid code, a universal sign for "all is cool," but hell if he knew it. "Where's your momma, little guy?"

The shriek seemed to have maxed out, but now there was a bubble of snot expanding, expanding...from one of the kid's nostrils. At the point Josh thought surely it was going to pop, the snot bubble shrank back down when the kid remembered to breathe. Then, it began to grow again. *Okay, really?* The thing about snot bubbles was— How do you look away? Josh felt his own face going red. A train wreck of a house he could handle. That was all in a day's work. Nasty grout that needed scouring, a floor that hadn't been mopped in months, greasy kitchen grime—all that he could put right with or without the rest of the Crew. But a wailing kid? There were people for that. Parents. Again, he gave it a try. "Hey, little guy, your mom? Where?" Nope, not going to be that easy apparently.

He crossed the kitchen, put his hands under the kid's armpits and lifted. He turned his face to the side so he wouldn't get puked on and could at least spare one eardrum. That snot bubble was an issue, too, now about a big as a bubble in a Hubba Bubba gum ad. He slid the screen door to the side and walked outside holding the kid as far from himself as possible. Wasn't there a character in an *X-Men* movie that could knock down brick walls with his superpowered scream? This kid could be that guy.

He crossed the small concrete patio and stepped out into the grass, already feeling the weight of the kid in his shoulders. He looked both ways. There were four apartments lined up. Two duplexes and a parched strip of St. Augustine grass between the two buildings. What he did not see was anyone that could help.

"Hello?" he said.

Now the kid was kicking his legs and wiggling in Josh's grip. He caught a couple of baby-shoe kicks in the ribs. Geez, put this kid in martial arts, he'd be dangerous.

"Ian?"

Josh turned toward the sound of the voice. Frantic. Female. Mom? Could this be Mom? Ian screamed and wiggled and blew more snot bubbles. *Please, God, let that be his mother.* A woman snatched the baby from his hands. She sank down into the grass, clutching the baby. Petite, young, blonde. When she looked up at him, as if still wondering what to think, he saw the panic in her eyes. Blue eyes, pupils wide, shining with tears.

"Oh, my God, Ian. Ian, baby. Don't ever scare Mommy like that ever again."

She hugged him and kissed his face. Josh wanted to look away when the snot bubble popped right on Mom's cheek, but if she even noticed, there was no sign of it. *Okay, yeah, maybe moms don't care, but gross!* Josh shifted his feet in the grass and stuffed his hands in his back pockets. "Uh. Sorry. The sliding glass door, on my patio, it was open, he wandered in. I think I scared him."

She stood, keeping the boy clutched tight against her. "He… Wait, what? Oh, God." She looked at the boy, shook her head and then looked back at Josh. Tears welled at the bottom of her eyes. She ran a hand through her hair, brushing it back, and let out a great big breath. "Thank you. Oh, Ian. Don't do… Don't scare me like…" She cleared her throat, turned her head, seemed to compose herself. "I didn't realize our back door was unlocked," she said. "I went in the other room for one second and…" Her face went pale and Josh could see in her eyes all of the nightmare scenarios that were playing out in her head. She hugged Ian to her. "Thank you. He's not getting out of my sight again." She looked at Ian. "No, sir, you are not."

"At least now I know where to return him. I'm Josh, by the way. Josh Sanders."

She jiggled the baby to her hip and held out a free hand. "Mickie Phillips. Nice to meet you."

"Moving in?" He tried to look her over with being too obvious about it. Her laser focus on the child in her arms helped in this regard. She was busy finger-brushing his messy hair and cleaning the snot off his cheek—*finally!*—with a tissue that seemed to have materialized out of thin air. Was that some kind of secret mom power? She looked like she might be halfway through her twenties. Slim, but he could see the strength in her, in the way she held that boy. Good cheekbones, cute nose. Blond hair and ice-blue eyes. Dang. She looked like she could have some Viking shieldmaiden in her gene pool. There was a slight trace of an accent he couldn't place, but it wasn't Southern.

"Yeah."

"Welcome to the neighborhood. Let me know if you ever need anything."

He said it as he was already turning around and starting to walk back to his place. The spot on his arm where her hand had brushed him tingled with a little rush of heat. Cute little blonde? Maybe. Cute little blonde with a baby? Oh, hell no. He and babies did not mix. Would not.

Once he got back to his place, he slid the glass door shut and made sure to lock it behind him. He washed his hands at the kitchen sink in case there were any lingering baby germs.

Well, that had sure been something. He snagged a paper towel, wiped his hands dry. Ice-blue eyes… He glanced toward the patio. *Nope.*

Popped open the fridge but surprisingly, nothing had magically appeared there that could be properly considered food. Jars of mustard, mayo. Some bologna maybe a smidge past sketchy. Bottles of water. Why was he hungry all of a sudden? Blonde. Blue eyes. He scooped up his motorcycle helmet and made a beeline for the door.

The thing about it was that Columbia didn't feel like home yet. He felt like a visitor. Still felt like it was all temporary. He missed Charleston more than he'd thought he would. He missed Sadie and the guys. He pulled the cover off his restored '68 Harley Sportster. So, he'd kill a couple of hours exploring the town, see if he could work this out. Maybe pick up a few groceries—or, let's be real here, take-out—and come back to get ready for the next day.

As the bike rumbled out of the small parking lot to the street, he caught a glimpse of blond hair turning the corner. He turned in that direction. Mickie. She was walking briskly down the street, pushing the baby in a stroller. He lifted a hand as he rode by, but she didn't see him. Maybe that was okay. Maybe that was better. He gunned the accelerator, hit the road, twisted and turned through the maze that was this strange new place.

Blond hair, blue eyes, hey, come on. Geez.

Look around you. USC. The statehouse. Liberty Tap Room and UFO, like he'd ever get up and sing karaoke. At least having a bike meant he could find parking somewhere, maybe. That was different from downtown Charleston. And even this was only the tight little downtown area. Never mind all the outlying areas he hadn't ventured out into yet.

This was a much bigger city, sprawling out into a confusing jumble of suburbs. The move had come sooner than expected. Josh was running the expansion of Sadie's all-male cleaning company, the Cleaning Crew. The plan had been to run it out of Charleston for several months before committing to a move. But the client list had grown more quickly than expected. He was gaining more respect for what Sadie had built. Between hiring employees and making sure clients understood that house cleaning was the only service provided, he was currently only one of two guys doing the cleaning. Add in all the paperwork and he was pretty sure Sadie was a freaking genius and a saint for never having throttled anyone, at least not anyone that Josh knew of.

He rode until he remembered that he was hungry. That popcorn was supposed to have been breakfast. Hey, the Five Points shopping district was straight ahead. Starbucks to satisfy the immediate urge for caffeine and something solid, maybe a bagel, with a follow-up at the Food Lion for some grown-up shopping. He did exactly that. After he finished, the grocery store was right there.

He grabbed as much as he could fit in the saddlebags on the bike and headed home. The ride home put his head straight. That was a lot easier now that there was food in his stomach. When he turned into the duplex, he saw her again.

Mickie. She was pushing the stroller. A bulging backpack was strung across her shoulders, while shopping bags dangled from the stroller handles and a cardboard box balanced on top of the handles. Wait, why? Moving in like that? From where?

He shook his head as he pulled around back, parking the bike on his patio. *None of your business, man. You need to get into those applications. Find some guys.*

A couple of hours later, there she was again, pushing the baby stroller, loaded down with shopping bags. What was she going back and forth for? Didn't she have a car? Could she only carry small bits at a time? Kind of like him and his saddlebags when he wasn't driving the SUV? He stepped out on the front porch.

"Do you need some help?" he asked.

Her cheeks were pink and there was a faint

sheen of perspiration on her forehead. It was well over 90 degrees. Hello, South Carolina summer. The baby...boy—wasn't there another word? Toddler!—looked toasty, also.

"No. I'm fine." There was slight emphasis on the *fine*. A *back off* emphasis.

He hesitated. Because she clearly wasn't fine. She was hauling stuff with a baby in this heat. That didn't seem to be fine to him. He shrugged. Not his problem. "Okay. But if you need help, I'm right here. Ask."

She nodded as she pushed the stroller over her doorstep and closed the door. *Whatever. I offered.* A minute later, he heard her door open and close again. He frowned at the sight out his front window. She was heading off again, empty backpack and empty stroller. Well, the kid was still in there. He stood there for a long minute. *She doesn't want your help, dude. Let it go.* He let it go.

Until she repeated the process. He opened his front door again. "Hey. Wait up."

She stopped on the sidewalk and turned back to him. "I've got this."

"I'm sure you do. But I've got an SUV. Might cut down on the number of trips you have to make."

She let go of the stroller to lift her hair off her neck as she contemplated him. He hated that his offer of help had to be considered with such a concern for safety, but that was the world today. "I told you my name. I'm Josh Sanders. I can call references for you right now. I want to help. I can't stand watching you run back and forth in this heat with the little guy." He reached into his back pocket and pulled out his phone. "See, I'll call my boss. Sadie Martin." He tapped through, hoping Sadie would answer. She did. He put the call on speaker and moved closer to Mickie.

"Hey, Josh, what's up?" Sadie asked. He couldn't get over how happy and relaxed she sounded. Love was agreeing with her.

"Hey. Listen, I've got my new neighbor Mickie here and she needs some help moving her stuff. Tell her I'm a good guy."

"He's a great guy, Mickie. Let him help. Don't let him cook for you, but let him help you move heavy things."

Mickie smiled but was still shaking her head. "You could be anyone," she said.

"But I'm not," Sadie said through the speaker. "I'm Sadie Martin. I own the Cleaning Crew down in Charleston. Josh is my number-one guy. He's up there getting our second location started. You can look us up online. He was the only person I trusted on this planet to do that for me. Let him help you move some boxes."

"I really do have an SUV," Josh said. "If you

CHAPTER TWO

SHE COULD NOT believe she was doing this. Getting in a car with a strange man. Worse, putting her baby in a car with a stranger. She looked at him, looked him right in the eyes, trying to gauge if she could trust him. He didn't try to convince her. He held her eye contact and gave her a smile that seemed to say "I understand."

They made it happen. Somehow, awkwardly. She wrestled the car seat in place in the backseat. Once she had it in and secured—even tugged on the seat a few times to make sure it was strapped in correctly—she lifted Ian out of the stroller. "Up, big man," she said and Ian climbed in, squirming around as she buckled him.

"Go! Go! Go!" Ian said. He slapped both hands together each time he said it.

"Yeah, we're gonna go, go, go," Mickie muttered under her breath as she shut the back door and climbed up front into the passenger's seat. *Hopefully not to our most gruesome end.*

Josh smiled at her from the driver's seat. "All set?"

"Sure." She leaned against the door and closed her eyes. Tired. She was so damn tired. Of every little thing being an obstacle. Of keeping a smiling face and happy voice for Ian. Of hiding the tears and her fears from him. None of this was his fault. The car didn't move and she opened her eyes.

"Where are we going?"

"Oh. Yeah. That'd help, huh? That garage a little ways down on Devine Street. Next to the Jiffy Lube?"

He dropped the car in Drive and pulled out into the light Sunday traffic. "You lived at the garage?"

"No. My car is at the garage."

Actually, her car was dead. She should have been grateful that it decided to pop its transmission out onto the road so close to her new place, but still…this was the new place that she couldn't afford anymore since the job she'd counted on had crapped out. Then the car crapped out. She rubbed her eyes. *It'll be okay. You have some left in savings. The apartment is on the bus line. You'll find another job.* She twisted in her seat to look at Ian. He was passed out. Poor baby. This guy must think she was the worst mother in the world, dragging him around in the heat.

"How old is he?" Josh asked.

She looked over at Josh, this strange man.

Cute, but really? From the way he'd carried Ian out of his apartment that morning, a sight she'd giggled long and hard over once her fright had diminished, she knew he had zero to no experience with children. Good-looking, with curly, black hair, and a bit shaggy, but that was okay. Blue eyes. No rings on his fingers, she could see that as he held the steering wheel. And they were nice hands. Strong-looking hands. She looked away. "Almost two," she said.

"Oh."

Silence followed. So much silence that when he hit the turn signal, it startled her. "Why did you ask?" she asked as they pulled into the garage's parking lot. She pointed to her poor dead car, parked to the side.

He shrugged. "Aren't you supposed to ask things like that about people's kids?"

Instead of answering, she unhooked her seat belt and opened the door. She glanced back at Ian. He was still sleeping. Good.

"I'll leave the AC running," Josh said. He pulled the parking brake, slid out, popped open the back hatch.

Mickie frowned. Part of her was screaming to not leave Ian alone in a running car, but what else could she do? She left her door open just in case she had to jump in and save him. Her eyes scanned the parking lot as she walked to her car and unlocked the back door and the trunk. Everything she owned in the world was crammed in there. Well, everything that would fit anyway. She'd left some furniture behind. Well, hey, it wasn't like it had been Queen Anne antiques. Mostly Wal-Mart and sidewalk-salvage, chipboard, snap-together stuff. Hey, you could afford what you could afford. She reached into the backseat and hauled out a box. She'd replace it. *Right. With the money from the job that you, oh, yeah, no longer have.*

"All of it?" Josh asked as he started moving boxes from the trunk of her car to his SUV.

"Yeah, everything that will fit. Guy here told me he was having the car hauled to the junkyard in the morning whether I had my stuff out or not."

"What a dick. Seriously?"

She nodded and swallowed down the lump in her throat. Yeah, the guy had been a dick. But he'd given her two hundred dollars for the corpse of her car and a day to get her stuff out. She could sleep on the floor. She could eat ramen noodles. But Ian needed real food and the money, well, that would get it for him. It took a depressingly short amount of time to move everything out of the car.

"Where's your furniture?" Josh asked as they got back in his car.

She felt her cheeks burn hot. “It’s coming,” she lied. There was nothing coming. She couldn’t afford to rent a U-Haul. She certainly couldn’t afford a moving company. It wasn’t like they were family heirlooms. She hoped the next tenants would have use of it, maybe for kindling in the fireplace when winter began to make its way south.

She and Josh didn’t talk at all on the ride back to the apartment. That was actually something Mickie was very grateful for. She was exhausted and worried and seemed to be constantly on the edge of tears. She needed to get settled and get some sleep and regroup. She’d be fine. She needed a moment.

“Hey,” he said.

She jumped at the soft whisper and the gentle touch on her arm. The seat belt tightened against her. Damn. She’d fallen asleep? In a strange car? With a strange man? And her baby in the back? She twisted to look over her shoulder. Ian was still asleep. Josh had driven across the grass and had backed the SUV up to her front door.

“Wow,” she said. “Oh, my God. Sorry. Must be my naptime, too.”

She blew out a breath, got herself together. *Wow.*

Then she climbed out and got the car seat unhooked, not even bothering to take out Ian. She manhandled the entire thing out of the SUV with him in it. Josh was there and he took it in one hand. "I've got it. Open the door and you can get him settled. I'll bring all the stuff in for you."

"You don't have to. I can get it. I'll let you know when I'm done and you can move the car back."

He stayed on the front porch, leaning in to put the car seat inside the front door. "Now, that isn't going to happen. But if you don't want me inside, I'll move things to the porch and you can take them from there."

She opened to her mouth to protest. *Stop it. Stop it, Mickie. He's being a normal nice guy. Stop treating everyone like the enemy.* "I'm sorry to be so..." So what? She didn't know. Scared? Bitchy? Suspicious?

"Cautious? Don't worry about it. I understand."

He walked off and opened the hatch. Mickie watched for a moment the way that the muscles of his back shifted against the fabric of his T-shirt, how his biceps flexed as he lifted boxes. A flutter of warm appreciation for a gorgeous male body tried to come to life deep in her belly. She turned to Ian, snorting out a hard laugh at her stupidity. *Because a man would make all this better. Right. That's what got you into this mess, Mickie. A good-looking, sweet-talking, nice-acting man.*

JOSH MOVED THE boxes to the porch and let Mickie carry them deeper into the apartment. Most of the boxes looked old, like they'd been used and reused and kept together with duct tape. She was cagey about letting him in and he could understand that. She was a young mother. Living alone, it seemed. Well, alone except for Ian. Which had to make it even more difficult. There was nothing he could do or say to put her more at ease other than try not to make it worse.

As he set the last of the boxes down inside the door, she came over and pushed it out of the way with her foot. He glanced inside. She'd moved them all into the empty living room. His eyes went back to her. She leaned against the door frame with one hand on the doorknob. Her khaki shorts and black T-shirt were streaked with dust. She pushed a hand through blond hair that looked like a fall of silk and looked up at him with ice-blue eyes. She was very pretty. And very young. And had a kid.

"Thank you for letting me help you," he said. "This means I'm all caught up on my good deeds for at least a week."

She smiled and he felt something within him warm at the sight. "Thank you for insisting. I'm sorry if I was treating you like you were a creep or something."

"Understandable." He stuck his hands in his

back pockets as he searched for something else to say. He wanted to keep looking into those eyes, wanted to ask about those distant shield maiden genes. Where was she from, where was she going? Then, he noticed the dark smudges beneath those eyes. She'd fallen asleep on the short ride home. Tired, right. She was exhausted, and he could respect that. "Let me know if you need anything else," he said.

Back in his own place, Josh powered up the laptop. He could still hear her moving around. Strange that he'd never noticed the sounds of the previous tenant. She was clinking glassware, opening and closing cabinets and making other assorted unpacking thumps and bumps. She seemed to be alone, not only living alone with the little guy, but also alone in the city. *She's not alone, dude, she has a baby. You know, those miniature humans that you don't have any contact with?* He shook his head. *Get it together, man.*

He had a lot to do tomorrow. There were three interviews for new Crew members, two client interviews and four actual cleanings to do. He skimmed through the calendar. Good. All regular cleanings, all in apartments, so that should be easy. It was a straightforward business model: hot guys cleaning house. It had worked for Sadie down in Charleston and he was here to make it happen a second time, in the state capital. He loaded the addresses into his phone and Googled them to look at the map and get a sense of the locations. His phone rang and Sadie's name popped up on the screen.

"Did you save your damsel in distress?" she asked.

"Yeah, thanks."

"How you doing up there?"

"Good." He gave her a brief rundown of Crew business.

"I meant *with you*, Josh," she said when he finished. "How are *you* doing?"

"Good. Starting to not feel lost every place I go. I found a yoga studio that seems like it isn't just a place to go look pretty. Still looking for a dojo."

He sat back and rubbed a hand through his curly hair. And a barbershop. He needed to find one of those. Yoga and meditation were akin to breathing. He couldn't go without, not for long. Not if he wanted to stay himself, the self he could stand. And while he was perfectly able to practice at home, there was something about being in a class, about being pushed past his limits, that he needed. The dojo? Well, he'd been studying martial arts since he was twenty. Yoga for peace of mind and karate for discipline—the two things that kept him sane. That kept him functional.

"Is she pretty?"

"Huh?"

"Your new neighbor. Is she pretty?"

He laughed. "Now that you're disgustingly happy in love, you want to hook up everyone you know?"

"You should try it. It's awesomely fun."

"She has a kid. A little kid. A baby-size kid."

Sadie didn't say anything but he could hear her breathe. She let out a slow sigh. "I wish I could hug you."

"I don't need a hug. I need some pointers on the behavior contract."

Yeah, that. The behavior contract. The Cleaning Crew, as a business model, provided a superior cleaning service and nothing else. But Sadie had found that some clients' understanding of this simple fact was at times fuzzy. Hot guys, right? It wasn't surprising where some people's minds went. A false allegation in the company's early days had frightened her. Now she required clients and employees to sign a contract that essentially said "keep your hands to yourself."

"What's the problem? It's pretty straightforward."

"Some clients are taking it as condescending. Like we're saying they won't be able to control themselves around a good-looking guy or something."

"Huh," Sadie said. She paused for a moment. "There may be something to that. It's not everyone, is it? Just a few here and there?"

"Yeah. I started being way more careful in how I explained it after that. It's helped some."

"All right. Keep me posted. If it gets to be a problem, I guess I could drive up and get them signed."

"I guess." But he didn't want her to do that. If this was going to be his branch, his company to grow, then he had to find a way around this. He figured that it was the newness of the idea here in Columbia. In Charleston, the company had been established long enough that new clients knew about the contract, knew about the expectations Sadie had for them and the guys. It was still in the titillation phase here. A hot guy vacuuming your rugs? Giggle and drool. He heard Jules, Sadie's fiancé's niece, in the background, yelling for Sadie to come look at this *right now.* "I'll figure it out. Go. Give Jules a hug from me."

CHAPTER THREE

MICKIE STARTLED AWAKE on her blanket bed on the floor. Sunlight streamed through the windows. How long had she slept? She scrambled up to her feet. More importantly, why had Ian slept so late? He usually woke her at the butt crack of dawn. She crossed the hall and found him sitting quietly on his own blanket bed with a book. Naked. She followed her nose to the dirty diaper tossed on the rug. Awesome. She added a trip to the Laundromat to her chore list for the day.

"Good morning, sunshine," she cooed.

Ian looked up at her and smiled that goofy baby smile that always melted her heart. He held up the book. "Pat! Pat bunny!"

"We'll pat the bunny. But first, let's get you cleaned up, little man."

The second order of business, after bath, book and breakfast, was to find a job. While Ian ate, Mickie sipped coffee and browsed through the local listings. Nursing school wouldn't start for two and a half months. She'd have to rely on her savings while she was in school, but right now?

Right now, she needed to work. The job that she'd had lined up—a nurses' aide at the hospital affiliated with the nursing school—had been perfect. The pay was good, the hours were good and there had been access to the onsite day care center and valuable experience to put on a résumé. But at the last minute, the day-shift position had been changed to a night-shift position. Which wouldn't have been a problem except the day care wasn't offered overnight.

"Square one," she said to Ian. "Not like we haven't been back here before, huh, buddy?"

"One!" he shouted. He handed her a Cheerio.

"Thank you."

"Whelk!"

Tears burned at her eyes as she watched Ian return to his breakfast. What was she doing? Dragging him willy-nilly along while she tried to get her shit together. Jumping and running at every bump in the night. She took a deep breath and swallowed the lump in her throat. This was it. Hopefully their last stop. She had two years to go and then she'd have her nursing degree. Once she had that, she'd have financial security. Right? Then they could stop. The two of them, her and Ian, they could begin to put down some roots and find some sense of normal. But first, she needed a job. And affordable day care.

She shook her head. *Sitting around feeling*

sorry for yourself isn't going to help a thing. Get to the Laundromat. Maybe there'd be some places along the way she could stop and put in applications.

An hour later, she was pushing the stroller out of the door, with duffel bags of laundry dangling from the handles. She had her backpack strapped on and an entirely too grumpy Ian strapped in the stroller. He didn't want to go wash clothes. He wanted to read *Pat the Bunny* for the ten jillionth time. She paused to secure the swaying bags. The door of the apartment next to hers opened and a flicker of annoyance darted through her. *Please don't be Hot Guy offering to drive me again.* She hated people offering to help her. It was stupid, she knew, but it made her scared. As if they could sense her vulnerability and weakness.

"All right, thanks for stopping by. I'll let you know once the test results are back."

She glanced over. Hot Neighbor Josh was shaking hands with a hot stranger dude. Hot Stranger Dude nodded. "Thank you for the opportunity."

Mickie frowned at this exchange, then shook her head. *None of your business.* She tested the balance of the duffels and shifted the backpack.

"Hey, neighbor," Josh called.

She tried not to look, but how could she not?

He was too good-looking. That black curly hair and the blue eyes. His shoulders, his chest, his arms… He was built but he didn't try to show it off by wearing a shirt two sizes too small for his body. She bit her bottom lip, felt it slip back into her mouth as she watched him. Those jeans. Levi's. Straightforward workingman's jeans. Nothing fancy. She felt warm in all the wrong places.

"Hi," she said.

Short, sweet, to the point. *Get out of here before he offers you a ride.* She pushed the stroller but he met her at the sidewalk. He squatted to look at Ian.

"Hey, little man. What big adventure are you off to today? Going to break into a few more houses?"

"Go! Go! Go!" Ian shouted back.

"Sounds like a plan."

"Sorry," she said. "Shouting seems to be the only volume he has these days."

He stood and smiled at her. "You guys always seem to be on the go."

"Yep. That's us. Busy, busy, busy."

He looked at her. Then at the duffels. Then at the street. He rubbed his jaw, the stubble there making a faint scratching noise that went straight through her. She squared her shoulders.

"Yeah. I should get back to work."

Work. *Whoa. Wait.* What was it that lady had told her on the phone? He was here setting up a cleaning business. She could clean.

"You're hiring?"

He gave her a look. A half smile. "Yeah, but…"

"Can I apply? I don't have any experience other than cleaning my own house. But I'm a fast learner. And I'm not afraid of hard work—"

"Mickie," he said, cutting off her babble.

"What?"

"We are an all-male cleaning company. That's our gimmick. Good-looking guys cleaning your house."

"Oh." She was too disappointed to say anything else.

"Sorry."

"It's okay. Nothing ventured and all. Well, I should get going."

She could feel him watching her as she navigated down the sidewalk to the street. *All male.* Weren't there, like, discrimination laws about stuff like that? She tried to get angry about it but she couldn't seem to think around the echoes of the scrape of his fingers against the stubble. Her own fingers twitched on the stroller handles. She'd like to run a finger over that stubble.

"Oh, for the love of Pete. Stop it," she said to herself. She took a deep breath, held her eyes shut for a second and told herself to let it go.

You've got way bigger things to think about. Shut it down.

"Momma?" Ian was staring up at her with that curious look in his eyes. Down the street, there was the traffic, always the sound of people coming and going, on their way to work, to school, off to keep the world running. She needed to get back to being a part of that. But why, exactly?

Oh, yeah. Money. Bills. Being the grown-up.

She laughed and leaned over to look down into Ian's dark eyes. "Your momma is crazy, baby man, you know this?"

"Go! Go! Go!"

Yeah, we're going. Going and going and going. I hope we get there eventually.

ANOTHER DAY PASSED, and there she was again. That was the thing about living right next door to someone. Sometimes, they blended into the background. Other times...hmm. Well, Josh was still figuring that out.

He watched as Mickie pushed the stroller down the sidewalk. Yesterday he'd been about to tell her that he had a washer-dryer combo in his apartment but her back-off vibe had been so strong he thought it best to wait. Besides, he had two more applicants coming in for Cleaning Crew interviews and then he had to do three actual cleanings this afternoon by himself. One of the Charleston guys, Aaron, was coming down two days a week to help with the heavy days, but he needed to get some local, full-time help—and fast. He couldn't keep up with the cleanings and the processing of all the new clients for too much longer. Not all on his own, at least.

He pulled up the next interview's application. Problem was, most of the guys were thinking the job was a shortcut to getting laid. Sadie had warned him that there would be ten crap applications for every one good possibility. And, as well, there were the applications that frankly startled him. One of the guys had finished law school. Another cited boatloads of business management experience. He wondered what their stories were there. As much as he understood the need to work, he also had to take the business into consideration. You wanted someone who'd stay with the company long enough to at least get good at it. Employee turnover was expensive. That was why Sadie invested so much in providing a quality work environment for her people. Hire the right people and then treat them right. That's return on investment.

His phone vibrated on the tabletop. Speaking of... "Hey, boss," he answered.

"I'm sending you a present," Sadie said.

"Oh?"

"Indeed. It should be there in a few minutes."

He glanced at the front door. “Care to enlighten me any further?”

“Nope.”

She ended the call and he stared at the phone. “Huh.” Who was this woman with Sadie’s voice and what had she done with Sadie? Or, rather, what had Wyatt Anderson done to his hard-as-nails boss? Wyatt. He wondered how he was doing these days. That had been a time, finding out who he was and what he was up to. But he’d made things right, and Josh had to give him credit for that. He returned to the applications.

Not five minutes later, he rose to answer a knock on his front door. It was a pretty distinct knock. Firm, confident. An I’m-here-to-get-it-done kind of knock. Josh knew who owned that knock. “DeShawn!”

“Josh,” he said. The two of them bumped fists before DeShawn said, “Come on, man, give it up,” and went in for the hug. Just a quick old-friends-who-share-a-story kind of hug. They were good like that.

“Shut the hell up. Are you my present? I thought you were heading to the army.”

DeShawn had been a part of Sadie’s Crew in Charleston almost as long as they’d been the Crew. His laid-back, amiable personality had made him a client favorite. His attention to detail and ability to hustle had made him a Sadie favorite.

"I am, but I'm not insane. I'm not doing basic and officer training in Georgia in the summer. I'm yours, full-time, until the end of September."

"Hallelujah." Josh pulled DeShawn in for another one-armed, back-smacking hug. "This is perfect. I've reached a tipping point here."

"Just tell me what you need."

The two men sat at the dining room table that passed as Josh's office. "I've got twenty clients, fifteen of which are weekly cleans. I have Aaron coming up on the weeks we've got all twenty due. I'm doing the every-other-week cleans by myself but it's not leaving me enough time to screen applicants quickly enough. And I'm getting behind on my client interviews."

"Okay. You hired anyone yet?"

"I've got two I think are going to do well. I don't know how I'm going to train them."

DeShawn leaned back. "I guess this is where I come in. Run me through the clients and I can start training as soon as they are hired."

"Ah, man, I gotta thank Sadie. This solves all my problems. I'll get these guys on the payroll. You can take one, I'll take the other. That'll free me up for interviews. I don't know how Sadie did all this."

"She had you. Now you got me."

JOSH ENDED THE day feeling much less stressed than he had been that morning. He'd gotten the two best applicants hired. He and DeShawn had gone through the cleanings in half the time it would have taken him if he'd done it alone. Finally, some of the crushing anxiety lifted off him. He could almost see it float up into the air and pop like a bubble. Boom, done. Maybe he wouldn't screw this up entirely. Maybe he could make this as successful as the Charleston location. He scrolled to the picture of Sadie scrunching up her nose at him on his phone and tapped the call icon.

"Did you like your present?"

"Yes. Thank you. It was perfect. I really appreciate you sending him my way."

"Not a problem. You needed help. Your client base is growing, Josh. I can see it. A little more every day. This is happening, for real. You're making it happen."

"Yeah, it's been crazy. I don't know how you did it."

"Easy. I had you, Josh. Don't forget that. I didn't build this alone. You were with me from the beginning. And it took us a year to reach the level you've reached in a month. Don't be afraid to slow your client acceptance until you've got the employees trained to handle it. You are right on budget."

"Except I'm not making a profit yet."

"We didn't expect that you would be. The losses aren't crazy, though."

"What does that even mean?"

"You know," she said, and then laughed. The confident, caring laugh of someone who'd made it work, and was happy to help others do the same. "I actually have no idea. Lena told me. She said it's good and not to worry. So I don't worry. And I don't want you to worry, either. Just keep doing what you're doing."

"Well, if Princess Lena says it's okay," Josh said and let out a laugh of his own. It wasn't quite laced with that same full-bodied confidence, but more of a laugh that said, "Okay, I'm getting there, but damn if I know how it's happening."

"Will you two give it a rest already?"

Josh laughed again. That sounded like the old Sadie and hearing that brought back the old Josh. Funny how that happened. The thing was, he didn't really have a problem with Lena. She was Sadie's best friend and accountant. He liked her well enough to have her manage his money. She hadn't made him quite as rich as she'd made Sadie—hey, she's the boss—but he was happy with his nest egg. The bickering was done more out of habit that any real animosity.

When he'd first met Sadie, she and Lena had

been friends for several years. Josh was like the new baby in the family that takes the attention away from the middle child. Lena did not like sharing Sadie with him in the beginning, but they'd reached a détente of sorts over the years.

"I have something important to ask you," Sadie said.

"What's that?" Her pause was long enough to send a thread of worry winding through his gut. "Sades? Everything okay?"

"Yeah. I just don't want to cry. But, okay. Here goes. Will you give me away at the wedding?"

"Give you away?" He echoed the words, stunned.

"Yeah, you know. Walk me down the aisle?" Her voice dropped and wavered with the tears she didn't want to shed. "If Abuelito was still alive, I'd ask him. You know you're the brother of my heart, Josh. There's no one else."

"Of course," he said. He looked around the room and for a second, everything felt strange, unfamiliar. Wait, what was happening here? He shook his head and brought his attention back to the phone.

He wasn't sure why the request had hit him like it had. It was no secret that neither he nor Sadie had any real family. They were both products of the foster-care system and had been turned out on the streets at eighteen. Sadie's half brother had found her and she was slowly building a relationship with him. But Josh was her brother of choice. Just as he thought of her as his sister. His big sister. His fingers played over the keys of his laptop and a file opened.

"Are you sure?"

"Yes. I'm sure." He forced a laugh. "It's just so grown-up. Real. Family stuff. Things we thought we'd never have."

"I know," she whispered. "It's a good thing, little brother. Our family is growing. Getting stronger. And you'll always be my brother. Always."

His throat closed painfully. "Always."

After he ended the call, he opened the file. His little sister. The one he'd lost. She'd been adopted away from him. At two, she was young enough, cute enough and not as scarred by their ordeal as he was. The file was pathetically small. Lists of reunification websites. His own notes. Names of social workers he'd spoken to over the years. Random bits of memory. The memories of a five-year-old.

Her name was Kim. He'd called her Kimmie. Her birthday was in the summer. Her hair was dark and curly, same as his. But he couldn't remember what color her eyes were. Strange the things he could remember, the things that he couldn't. Memory was the strangest thing ever, the way certain things would just be there, for no reason, and other things he couldn't find in his head no matter how hard he searched for them. She had called him "Yoss." He remembered that.

He clicked open another file and stared at the artist's sketch. He looked at the picture of his memory of his sister and tried to remember. Really remember. Was this truly how she looked? Or was it just some phantom his mind had created over the years? He closed the files. Put his hand to his chin and rubbed, trying to sort it all out.

He opened a browser on his laptop and pulled up his post on the adoption-reunion website. Nothing. Same as the last three years. Next, he scanned through the new posts hoping to find anything that might give him some hope. Nothing.

He leaned back in the chair. Spun his phone around in a circle. He had a new idea, one that had just occurred to him. Spying? Investigating. Who did he know who did that? Mmm-hmm. That was the thing. He did have an ally in this search, didn't he? *Do it. Before you talk yourself out of it.* A moment later, he was pacing around the small kitchen and scrolling through contact numbers.

"Wyatt Anderson."

Resisting the urge to claim an accidental butt

dial, Josh leaned against the counter. "Hey, it's Josh. I've got a question for you."

"All right."

Wyatt sounded surprised. Probably because he was used to dealing with Sadie, who never asked anyone for anything. And if Josh was being honest with himself, he didn't, either. He had to force the words out.

"I have a younger sister. We went into foster care together. She was adopted and I never saw her again. Can you help me find her?"

It hurt worse than he thought it would. Saying it out loud. Sadie knew. But Sadie was different. She understood. He paced around the kitchen, unable to stand still. His heart rate picked up but there was a light feeling filling his chest. It took him a moment to figure it out. He was excited. Hopeful. Things he hadn't felt in quite a while.

"Wow. Okay. Just hold on. Let me grab a pen. All right," Wyatt said. "Tell me everything you know. Adoptions are hard because family court records are sealed but I can check it out. See what I can come up with."

"Thank you. I really appreciate it. Whatever your normal rate is..."

"Shut up, Josh. You're family. Now tell me everything you remember."

After going over the details he knew, he tried

to return to what he was supposed to be doing. Cleaning Crew work. Now that he had DeShawn, he could start to move forward. Get the two new guys trained. More clients. Then more guys. He worked out a schedule for the coming week and as he did, he heard a thump and a wail through the thin walls of the duplex. Ian must have wiped out.

He heard Mickie's voice. Not the words but the smooth, lilting tones of comfort. It was a nice sound. He regretted the job thing. She was clearly in a bad spot. No job, no car and a baby. But he admired her grit. She wasn't complaining or whining. She was just moving forward, doing the best she could.

Wait. The laundry thing.

Mickie had Ian in her arms when she opened the door. He clung to her neck and waist like a little barnacle. "Sorry, did his crying bother you?"

"What? No. I mean I heard it but that's not why I came over. Is he okay?"

"Tried to climb the kitchen counter and learned a lesson in gravitational pull. What's up?"

She shifted the baby on her hip and he peeked at Josh. He pointed to his forehead. It was sporting a red spot. "Owie."

"I see that. You'll be okay. You're a tough guy."

"Tuh?"

Josh flexed his arm, making the bicep pop. "Strong."

"Stong?"

Josh laughed and looked to Mickie, who was looking at his arm with unmistakable appreciation. A warm flood of desire washed through him, cooled by a dart of fear. *No way, dude, she's got a kid.* "Yeah, I was distracted this morning but I meant to tell you that I've got a washer-dryer set up over at my place. You're welcome to use it. Save you some time and money."

Her gaze met his. Gone was the soft appraisal. Now he was looking at a woman with a chip on her shoulder. She looked like Sadie did when you offered to help her with anything. Like it was the greatest of insults.

"Thank you for the offer," she said. "But we've imposed on you enough."

"You haven't imposed at all. Listen, I've been here. I've been on my own since I was eighteen. No family. It's hard. So, if you want to use the washer, let me know. That's all I'm saying."

And why was he even bothering? Obviously she didn't want his help. Obviously he was insulting her. He lifted a hand to wave at the baby. "See you around, little man."

"Wait."

He turned back. Her cheeks were stained with

pink and her expression held a sad mix of hurt pride and desperate need.

"Thank you," she said.

He dipped his head. "You're welcome."

CHAPTER FOUR

SHE WENT OVER the numbers again. Leaning back in the kitchen chair, Mickie let out a long sigh. There was nothing else to do. She'd applied at four places the day before. Two waitress jobs, a boutique and, the most desirable, a day care center. She could bring Ian to work with her. But she was running out of money and could not dip into her savings. That was to live on while in school. The rent was due and she needed groceries and more minutes on her phone.

The problem was, she discovered later while wandering the streets with a grumpy Ian in his stroller, pay phones were becoming extinct. She finally found one on the USC campus, not far from where she would be studying nursing come fall.

She plugged coins into the slot while preparing herself for the subterfuge. The ploys and the hiding and the lies that made up her life now. Already the tears were stinging. Her mother answered on the second ring.

"Hi, Auntie Em. It's me."

Code names. Fake addresses. Lies and constant fear.

"Dorothy! How wonderful to hear your voice. How is…everything?"

"About the same. Did you get the pictures I sent you from my vacation?"

Pictures of her grandson, whom she'd only held once. Mickie covered her face with a hand at the memory of her mother whispering in baby Ian's ear. *I love you, I love you, I love you, MeMe will always love you.* And then they had fled.

"Yes. Thank you so much. Everything looked so wonderful. I love to see all the places you go. I just wish you would travel by here someday."

"Me, too. I will. Someday. I don't have much time, but I was wondering if you could send me some more of those greeting cards you make. Everyone just loves them."

Greeting cards meant prepaid debit cards.

"Of course I can. How many do you need?"

"Three? Four? Whatever you can."

"I'll send them today. Give everyone kisses for me. I love you all."

"I love you, too." The word *Mom* slipped from her lips when she'd hung up. When it was safe. She pressed her forehead to the handset, fighting back the tears and the exhaustion and the loneliness.

"Mama. Mama. Mama."

Ian's chubby arms waved at her. Up. He wanted up. She scooped him from the stroller and hugged him tight. "It's almost over, baby love. I'll be done with school in two years and we'll be all set. We'll buy a real house and a car and you can have a dog. And all this will be over."

That put some steel back in her spine. Over. Safe. Secure. Before Ian was old enough to know they'd once been this poor and desperate. Now that she had some extra money on the way, she felt some of the tension leave her.

"You ready for some lunch? Yeah? Okay. Let's go eat."

While Ian ate his lunch, Mickie filled the duffel bag with laundry. She considered Josh's offer to use his. She was tired. Tired of walking. Tired of dragging things from here to there, towing Ian along behind her. She shook her head. Nope. *Take it to the Laundromat. You've let him get too close already.* She took a quick minute to gobble down her own lunch and got Ian cleaned up. He loved the Laundromat anyway. Loved watching the clothes tumble around in the front-load washers. And there were usually some older women there who showered Ian with attention. She shouldered the duffel with a sigh and strapped Ian into his stroller. If only everything didn't have to be so hard.

MICKIE WAS HEADING down the sidewalk as Josh slowed down to turn into the driveway. Pushing the stroller with the heavy bag across her shoulders, she was going in the other direction so she didn't see him. He parked the car and climbed out. She had that same duffel the other day when she went to the Laundromat. *How much laundry did she go through?* Hurrying to the sidewalk, hoping to catch her and offer the use of his washer again, he realized it wasn't that she went through that much laundry, but that she couldn't carry it all that far.

"Damn it," he muttered. She had turned the corner, out of hailing distance. "Damn it." He considered getting back in the car and going to find her. She'd had to have turned at the first corner to be out of sight so quickly. Walking back up the sidewalk, he shook his head. The way she'd reacted to his offer? If he drove around to find her now? She'd be livid. *Let her have her pride, man. It's probably all she has.*

It bothered him, though. He rummaged through his supply of frozen dinners and ripped one open. *None of your business. You offered.* Punching the correct number of minutes on the microwave, he hit Start and leaned against the kitchen counter to wait. He couldn't shake the image of her marching down the street, head high, pushing the kid in his stroller and that heavy bag slung across her back.

The microwave beeped and he pulled out the steaming plastic tray, cussing as the heat singed his fingertips. He put the tray on the table and grabbed a fork. He was beginning to suspect Mickie possessed more than Sadie's reluctance to accept help. Sadie hadn't built a successful company without an iron will and the strength to push ahead against all odds. Mickie seemed to have that same strength.

He was finishing up his meal when Aaron wandered in with Travis. "Dude," Aaron said. "Do you know how much crap and salt is in those things?"

Josh got up. "Yes. What are you guys doing back so soon?"

"We need to resupply and make a report," Aaron said. He gestured at Travis with his thumb. "Client this morning was pushing the boundaries but he deflected it perfectly."

Frowning, Josh looked over at Travis. He tilted his head, raised an eyebrow. This was something they took very seriously. "Travis," he said. "Do I need to talk to her?"

"I don't think so," Travis said. He took a step backward, dipped his head down, shook it. Put his hands up like it wasn't a thing. "She backed down immediately. Apologized."

"What was the name?" Josh asked with a sigh. He'd have to flag her account. He drummed out a beat on the tabletop with his fingertips. "Before you leave, I'm going to need both of you to write up exactly what was said and what happened."

Aaron nodded. "I know where the incident-report form is. We'll use the computer in the testing room."

"Okay. I'll get the report together and forward it to Sadie this afternoon. We'll see what she says."

As they left the kitchen, Josh grabbed a bottle of water. He knew what Sadie was going to say. Most of it would consist of blistering profanities. They'd had an incident in the early years when a client accused a Crew member of inappropriate behavior. She'd made it up to try to get him fired for not reciprocating, but it had scared Sadie. Why did people have to act this way? Did high school ever end? Not for some people, apparently. The reason that it hit Sadie so hard was because the Crew was her family. She felt responsible for them. The behavioral contracts had been born from that incident.

Now it was his turn to feel that pressure. To protect his Crew. He might have to tiptoe around this a little more delicately than Sadie would. Sadie could be direct and no-nonsense with another woman. He'd have to be more diplomatic about it. *Crap. Why can't people just behave?*

MICKIE LISTENED, IN the dark, wrapped in blankets, on her bed of foam padding. She'd woken out of sleep, as much sleep as she'd been able to manage, by a panicked thought. Had Ian cried? A steady bang on the front door sent her heart racing even faster as she scrambled to her feet and ran out the bedroom door toward Ian's room.

"Fire department!" The two words came in one big burst of sound, accompanied by another quick round of pounding on the door.

Fire? She scooped up Ian up, still in his blanket, and carried him to the living room. There, she could see the pulse of red lights and she could hear the rumbling of engines. She opened the door just as the firefighter was about to knock again.

"What's happening?"

"Gas leak in the next duplex over. We're temporarily evacuating until the line gets shut down for repairs. Shouldn't take more than a couple of hours."

"Oh, okay."

Great. She slipped on the flip-flops she kept by the front door and carried Ian outside. The firefighter directed her to a spot down the street where she could see other residents huddled together. *At least it's summer and not raining.*

"Mickie," a voice called from the side of the street.

She turned toward the voice. Josh. He was sitting cross-legged in the grass, looking as cute as ever. Even relaxed on the grass, those shoulders—damn. She walked over, said hey and tried to ease herself down near him, but ended up losing her balance and falling flat on her ass. Ouch! At least she cushioned the plop down for Ian, who was still asleep in her arms. Not an easy armful. Ian was getting bigger every day and hauling him around wasn't easy. He'd stirred as her butt hit the ground, but thankfully it wasn't too much.

"Shhh. Go to sleep. It's okay," she murmured to him as she rocked him in her arms.

"Nice night to get kicked out of bed, huh?" Josh asked. His hair was a bit messy, but in a sexy way, like he'd just been stirred out of a nap on the sofa. She imagined… Wait, no!

"Ugh. Tomorrow morning is not going to be pretty," she said. She was already imagining all the things she had to do tomorrow and how much more pleasant they'd be without any sleep. "Do they have any idea how long it's going to take?"

"Someone from the Red Cross just got here.

Said they have emergency shelter for people with no place to go."

"Is it going to be that long? Where is it?"

He shrugged. "I didn't ask. If it's more than an hour, I'll call DeShawn, go to his place."

"Oh."

"You have some place to go? To take the kiddo?"

She shook her head, pressing her lips together. *Awesome. Another thing she'd never thought of. What to do in an emergency.* She could barely take care of them when everything was going perfectly. She shifted Ian in her arms and fussed with his blanket. When the fear and the shame hit, it was like a slow trickle of cold in her gut, dead center, that spread outward and upward, all through her. She hated not knowing what to do next. Because she was supposed to know. She was the mom. And, yet, here we are. *Don't cry. Do not cry in front of him.* Whether she meant Josh or Ian, she wasn't sure.

She blew a breath out. There was a throb in her temple now. If she wasn't careful, she'd end up with a whopper of a headache on top of it all. That's help. That'd just be the icing on the cake.

"Hey. You okay?" Josh asked. "You want me to get the Red Cross guy so you can talk to him?"

His voice, warm and low, full of concern, should have comforted her. Really, it should have. But it only made her feel worse. Because she was the worst mother on the planet. What would happen? What if the apartment burned down? What if there was a flood? Or a tornado? What if she got sick? What would happen to Ian? How would she take care of him? It struck her, all at once, just how precarious this plan of hers was. Make it to the start of nursing school, power through, come through the other side financially solid. Who actually thought that was going to work? And the thing was, she hadn't just put herself in this position, she'd put her son in this position, and that was indefensible.

She turned her face away from Josh, curling forward to rest her cheek on the top of Ian's head. There were bad thoughts piling up in her head and she knew—she *knew*—that she had to let that bad talk fall away. She couldn't let that plow her under, that big mudslide of bad. "No. I'll talk to him if it's going to take much longer."

Take care of the immediate problem. The one that's right in front of you. Okay, great plan. How, exactly?

"I'm sure DeShawn would make room for all of us," Josh said. "If it came to that."

A small shuddering laugh escaped her lips. Oh, God. Not just alone with Josh. Alone with Josh and his buddy? No. *Just, no.* She hugged Ian against her. "We'll be okay."

This is where you are. On the street with a stranger offering to take you and your son to an even stranger stranger's house. Giving in to the heavy weight of guilt and shame, her constant companions these days, her shoulders slumped. Looking at the ground beside her to make sure there were no fire-ant mounds there before running her hand across it, she gently lowered Ian to the grass and took a moment to make sure he was covered with the blanket because she could feel Josh's gaze on her back. She shook out her aching arms. *He's getting so big.*

"Can I ask you something?"

She bit back the profane remark that rose to the tip of her tongue. She was too tired for this. *He's a nice guy. Don't take it out on him.* "You can ask."

"I saw you going to the Laundromat the other day," he said, instantly horrifying her in fifty thousand different ways by this observation. Then he doubled down by adding, "Please use my washer and dryer. It's right there. I barely use it. If you want, just let me know when you need it and I'll leave the back door unlocked so you can come and go while I'm out working."

The thing about it was...he looked so innocent and guileless when he said it. Just sitting there on the grass, like it wasn't a thing, waiting for a response.

"What does it matter to you?" she said, brushing a loose strand of hair away from her eyes. She started playing with her whole mess of hair, wishing she'd grabbed a scrunchie on her way out the door. They were everywhere in her apartment: on the dresser, on the sink, on the floor, behind the sofa. Every time she cleaned, she'd find at least half a dozen and have no idea how they got where she found them.

He huffed out a burst of air in such obvious exasperation that she looked over at him. He was grinning at her. "You don't know this," he said, "but you are so like my boss, Sadie, that it isn't even funny."

She glared at him, glad for the spark of anger that burned out her feelings of failure. "And what is that supposed to mean?"

He held up a hand and began ticking off fingers, one by one. "Stubborn, mule-headed, prideful, wouldn't ask for a glass of water if she was on fire. Should I continue?"

"Why not?" she said. "You still have a thumb to use." But she turned away before he could finish, making sure to flounce her hair. She turned back to him and scrunched up her nose. "You act like those are bad things."

"No, not bad," he said. "Just unnecessary at times. Why are you dragging yourself and Ian to the Laundromat a couple of times a week, in this heat, spending the money when you can walk next door and do it for free?"

"Because nothing is for free, Josh. You know that."

That made him shut up. After a few minutes, a firefighter made his way down to the small crowd. "Okay, everyone can return to their homes. The leak is secured. The gas is off until the repairs can be made but the property owners told me that only the heat is gas-powered so you shouldn't be impacted at all."

"Other than dragging us out into the street in the middle of the night," Mickie grumbled. But she said it under her breath because it wasn't this guy's fault and that was one thing she always hated—the way people would attack the easy target, the person who just happened to be there, trying to help. She stood, lifting Ian as she did. Gosh, he was heavy.

"Let me carry him for you," Josh said.

"I've got him."

"Mickie."

She stopped at the tone of his voice. She was

feeling just a hitch past irritated and bordering on perturbed at this point. "What?"

"Let someone help you, for God's sake. You don't have to do everything alone."

She stared at him. "Yes. I do," she whispered.

He stepped closer. "No. You don't." He held out his hands. "Let me carry him back to your place."

"You don't even know how to hold a baby."

"It's easier when they aren't screaming and blowing snot bubbles at me." He stood, grinning at her with his hands still extended, conceding her point, but still not backing down. Still wanting to do what he could do. The grin faded. "Please, Mickie."

"Why?"

"Because I was alone for a long time, too. I get it."

Why are you being like this? Because you trusted a man once before, that's why. But she was so tempted. A washer and dryer! Right next door. No more two-hour trips to the Laundromat twice a week? She drew in a breath. "Okay."

His smile returned. "Okay?"

"I'll use your stupid washer and dryer. But only because it means so much to you. I'm perfectly capable of taking care of myself."

"Of course you are. Now, give me the baby."

She handed Ian over to him. He looked mildly

afraid and awkwardly maneuvered the sleeping toddler in his arms. But he figured it out and looked over at her. "Dang. He's heavier than I remember. How do you lug him around all day?"

"It's called being a mother."

CHAPTER FIVE

HIS PHONE WAS like a mosquito in a dark bedroom; the minute you thought it'd flown away, it buzzed again. He would have turned off the sound but he was waiting for a couple of calls he couldn't miss. Josh tried to ignore it, tried to concentrate on the young man sitting across from him. His application had looked good and he had some experience. His father ran an industrial cleaning company. They went into office buildings at night and cleaned. Dean had helped out over the summers while he was in high school. He seemed like a bright guy and he knew Sadie would approve.

The phone jittered on the table. He glanced down. Sent it to voice mail.

"This all looks great. I'll get you started on the testing now. After I get the results and talk to your references..."

"There's a woman at the door," Travis said, pointing over Josh's shoulder.

Josh twisted to look. It was Mickie. And the baby sleeping in his stroller. She had a duffel bag hooked over a shoulder. He held back the grin. It had been almost a week since the night she'd let him carry Ian back to her front door. He'd been letting her have her space. Like a head-shy puppy, he knew she'd run if he even looked at her funny. As he stood, she began to shake her head and step back.

"Sorry," she said as he slid the door open. "It's a bad time. I'll come back later."

"No, come on in."

"You sure?"

"If you don't, I'll wake the baby."

That earned him a twist of her luscious lips and a raised eyebrow. "You wake the baby and I'll leave him here with you."

He pushed the door open wider. "See? Now you have to come in. For Ian's own protection." He turned away and motioned to Travis. "Come on, I'll set up the testing programs for you."

He had the testing room set up in the second bedroom. As he got Travis settled part of him was listening to Mickie humming slightly off-key as she started the washer.

"Your phone is buzzing," she called out.

"What's it say?"

Pause. "Unknown number."

"Ignore it."

He turned back to Travis. "There are two tests. They are both fairly long, about a hundred questions each. After the first is done, the second should load automatically. Let me know if it doesn't. Bathroom is across the hall if you need, there's no time limit. Get me if you have any problems or questions."

"It buzzed two more times," Mickie said as he returned to the kitchen. She stopped, turned, looked back and met his gaze directly. "Both unknowns so I ignored them."

"Thanks."

"If it's okay, I'll just leave the duffel here. I've got another load."

"That's fine."

As she worked the stroller out the back door, she said, "Thanks again."

"No problem."

He watched her leave, a little dizzy with the whirl of desire he was feeling. Part of him wanted to put an arm around her and help solve all her problems, while the other wanted to lift her up on the washer and step between those legs and…

The phone buzzed and the doorbell rang. Shit. It was DeShawn on the phone. And at the door was his next applicant, early for his interview. Of course. So, while the interviewee cooled his heels on the couch, Josh talked DeShawn through getting the behavior contract signed with a touchy client. Mickie came and went, doing an exaggerated tiptoe across the room that made him smile.

When she came back next, he was on his third interview. Travis was finishing up his testing, applicant number two was beginning his test and Josh was about to take a hammer to the phone. She gave a quick wave and began to fold the laundry from the dryer. Josh found it hard to fully concentrate on his interview with the motion of her body and the sway of her long hair in the periphery of his vision. The phone buzzed again. He reached out, but Mickie scooped the phone off the table.

"The Cleaning Crew, this is Mickie. How may I help you?"

Josh's mouth dropped open for a second and he snapped it shut. What the heck was she doing? And good God, where did that phone-sex voice come from?

"Yes, ma'am. Thank you so much. Mr. Sanders is in a meeting right now. If you'd like to leave your name and number, I will have him get in touch with you for an estimate."

She made a writing motion with her free hand. Josh handed her his pen. She snatched a page of a résumé off the desk and began to write. When she hung up, he lifted his hands, palms up, not quite sure how he felt about it. "What are you doing?" he asked.

She smiled and reached across the table to steal one of the stacks of yellow legal tablets he liked to use for to-do lists. "Paying for the laundry," she said.

She maneuvered the stroller into the living room and came back to gather her clean clothes in her arms before returning to the living room. Josh turned his attention back to the poor guy who'd just had his interview interrupted at least a dozen times. He'd deal with Mickie in a minute. When he was done. She knew nothing about his business. She should not be answering phones and dealing with customers. *True,* a part of him said, *but is it worse than sending them to voice mail?* And he couldn't ignore how much more smoothly he got the interview and testing done without the nagging buzz of the phone. An hour later, he shut the door as the last of the three finished. Mickie handed him the legal tablet.

"This column here," she said as her finger traced down the page, "is people who want an estimate on cleaning services. This one was guys looking for information on applying. This was your boss, I think. Sadie, right? She's your boss?"

"Yeah," he said. She'd answered—he skimmed the list—ten phone calls. Ten people who got a person to talk to, not a voice mail. "What did Sadie want?"

Hell, he really did wonder. Sadie was adamant about maintaining a professional demeanor at all times. What was she about to say about him letting his next-door neighbor take calls?

"Well, she was a little surprised when I answered," Mickie said. She smiled, as if recalling a private joke. "But I explained. She said I had a great phone voice. Said to tell you it wasn't urgent, she was just checking to see how you were doing. Oh, and to call her back at your convenience."

"Thanks."

She tucked a lock of hair behind her ear and smiled. A real smile. A pleased-with-herself smile. It lit up her eyes like sunshine glinting off glacier ice. Something in him warmed at the sincerity in that smile. He couldn't look away from it. Didn't want to look away. Anything to keep that warmth spreading like a balm over aches he didn't know he had.

"Mamamamamama!"

Ian's demand for attention doused the warmth with icy reality. She had a kid. A baby. She'd want a father for Ian. The one thing he was never going to be.

"Shhh, Ian. I know it's time for lunch," Mickie said. Her fingers were warm as she briefly touched his arm. "Thanks again for letting me use the washer and dryer."

"Sure. No problem. Anytime."

The words fell out of his mouth because his mind was churning. The touch, that smile. The kid. The old fears. And a completely preposterous idea was trying to surface. No. He tried to push it away, but it held its ground.

He needed a secretary. Mickie needed a job.

A tight huff of laughter tore from his throat. "Great idea, Josh," he said aloud. Have her in here all day, every day? No. Just no.

An hour later, he'd returned all the phone calls, set up appointments to meet with the potential clients, redirected the applicants to the online application page and successfully managed to not call Sadie back. Mickie, however, stayed on his mind. One of the most important things the Cleaning Crew looked for in an employee was initiative. You see a problem or a need, you take care of it. Mickie had done just that. Plus, she knew she didn't know enough about the business, so she limited herself to merely taking messages. Common sense.

Sure, common sense and initiative. And that hair he'd like to get his hands in. Those lips he'd like to taste. Eyes he'd like to drown in. And a kid. He stood and paced to the fridge. *You need food. You are not thinking straight. You should be running as fast as you can. She and Ian deserve way better than the likes of you.* Yet one phone call later, he was knocking on her back door.

"Is everything okay? I got you in trouble, didn't I? I'm so sorry. I was just trying to help." The words poured out of her the moment she opened the door.

"No. Wait. What?"

She put a hand over her heart. "You look so serious. I thought your boss was mad."

"No. Um. That's not why I came over," he stammered. He took a deep breath. *Get it over with.* "Do you want a job?"

The play of emotions across her face brought back that feeling of warmth. A blink as she took in the words. Surprise as the meaning set in and a moment between the surprise and the huge smile that almost broke his heart. A moment of relief so immense that even he felt the weight of it lifting.

"Yes! Really? Are you serious?"

"Yes. I need office help. It'll be cash under the table. Answer phones. Run the computer testing for the applicants. Stuff like that."

"Yes. I can do that. Just show me what to do and I'll do it."

He smiled, unable to not return the joyous grin on her face. "Okay. Come on over around nine tomorrow and we'll get you started."

"Yes! I'll be there."

Then her arms were around him, squeezing tight. Her cheek pressed against him. Whoa, wow. Could she feel the way his heart jumped when she did that? Without consent from his brain, his hands slipped around her shoulders. She seemed so tiny, as if he could wrap his arms twice around her. He should step back. He should not be doing his. Instead, he dipped his head to take in the scent of her hair.

"You don't know what this means to me," she said as she pushed away.

His arms felt cold and empty without her there. He pushed the thought away. "I think I do," he said. "See you tomorrow."

He walked back to his apartment with a smile. That had felt good. Helping her. Remembering his own relief when Sadie had offered him a job after she'd found out he was fresh out of the foster-care system, he shook his head. He wouldn't have hired himself back then. He'd been angry and stupid. But Sadie had seen something in him. And now he was just trying to pay it back.

MICKIE SPUN IN circles across the kitchen floor and scooped Ian out of his high chair. "Mommy has a job, baby man! A real job!"

She danced them around the kitchen to the tune of "Mommy's got a job," giddy with the release of the ever-constant worry. Thank God.

Now she could focus on what she needed to do before school started in the fall.

"Everything is falling into place, Ian. Pretty soon, we'll be sitting pretty. A new car. A house of our own. Everything."

She put Ian back in his chair and sat across from him. "Got a lot to do this afternoon. Call the day care and see if I can get you in now instead of when school starts. Grocery store. I need to go through my clothes and find something to wear on a job."

She began making a list. She loved lists. Their orderliness. The satisfaction of crossing off things done. As the emotional high of the sudden appearance of a job dissipated, she became aware of another feeling coursing quietly through her. It took a while to recognize it. Lust. Her long-lost sex drive decided to show up now? For her new boss? Not a good thing.

The spontaneous hug was something the old her would have done. The new Mickie wasn't so touchy-feely. And yet… It had been like hugging a tree. Solid, hard muscle had met her arms. *So, you hugged him. So what? You were happy. Surprised. It was a hug.* And he'd hugged her back. The low-grade desire flared up like a sunspot. Hot. Bright. His hands hesitantly skimming across her shoulders. Even if she could rationalize that away, there was no explanation for the brush of his cheek against her hair.

The pen fell from her inattentive fingers and skittered off the table. She scrubbed her hands across her face. *No. Just no. Don't care how warm and squishy he makes you feel. Absolutely no men.* She lifted her face to watch as Ian picked through his Cheerios. She could see enough of his father in him to always remember. He had his father's dark curls and light brown eyes. She'd trained herself over the years to only see Ian, but now she needed the reminder. No men. Someday. When she would know…

"Stop it," she hissed under her breath. She stood, her legs feeling wobbly from the sudden wave of memories. Too far. She deliberately took a deep breath and let it out in a slow stream. Her insides went cold and a humming filled her head. Turning, she made her way to the stove, where she reached up into the high cabinet and found a plastic vial. Letting the panic prickle along her nerves, she focused on breathing. Air in. Air out. *You aren't wasting a Xanax on this. Focus.*

"Mama! Fins!"

"You sure did finish it all." She put the pill bottle away and shut the cabinet. She crossed back to the table and lifted Ian from his chair, ignoring the close call. She'd not had a full-out panic attack in over a year. "How about a field trip, my little man? See if you can go play with some friends tomorrow?"

Hugging Ian tight and burying her face in his soft curls, she willed the tears back. What she really needed was her mother's arms around her. She needed to talk to her. But that was something she never dared risk again, and that was that.

JOSH LOOKED SURPRISED when she tapped on the back door at exactly one minute to nine the next morning. She watched as he tossed the dish towel he was drying his hands with over his shoulder and popped the door open.

"Where's Ian?"

"I got him in early at the day care where he'll be when I start school."

"You could have brought him."

"No. It's good for him to be around other kids," she said, putting her bag down on the kitchen table. She smiled at Josh. "And for me to get out of mommy mode for a while."

"Now I'm going to have to raise your pay to cover day care," he said, half-kidding. He was kidding, right?

"Josh. You don't have to do that. You've been so kind to us. A job is more than enough."

She stared up at him. His eyes were warm and a half smile lurked on his lips. Those lips that had brushed against her hair. Suddenly she was rendered temporarily incapable of drawing in a full breath. Oh, hell no. She crossed her arms and walked around him to the kitchen table. Simple. *Just don't look at him. Problem solved.*

Except it wasn't. He came to stand beside her. Close beside her. Now she could smell him. Ivory soap and man. He bumped his arm against hers in a friendly gesture.

"Listen, I've been there," he said in a low voice. "Alone and just needing a lifeline tossed. Sadie did that for me. If I can help in any way, big or small, I'm only paying it back. Okay?"

Tears clogged her throat and her vision went blurry for a moment before her warning system began wailing. *Do not look vulnerable. Do not look weak.* She straightened and smiled up at him. Wondered why he'd been alone. No, she couldn't think of that right now.

"Thank you. Now, I can only work until school starts in the fall. Is that going to be okay?"

"That's perfect. By then, I should have enough people trained to take over the office work myself."

"So, show me what to do."

SHE WAS SMART. Josh noticed that immediately. He began with the Cleaning Crew philosophy and what his expectations were for both the crew and the customers. As he began outlining her responsibilities, she took a yellow legal tablet and began taking quick, efficient notes. A page for what to tell prospective customers. Another for what to tell applicants. When he showed her how to set up the personality testing, she asked to take the tests herself so she would be better prepared to answer questions. He found himself wishing he could hire her permanently.

He also found himself wishing he could smell her hair again. Now he was wishing she'd brought Ian. That way, there'd be a messy, noisy reminder of why he needed to rein in his hormones. He had to get away from her.

"I'm going to get some work done. You're on telephone duty."

Through the morning, as he tried to get his inbox under some sort of control and wade through the accounting, her soft sexy voice drifted down the hall as she answered calls. Not helping his concentration. Thanks a lot, Lena. She probably made these forms as complicated as possible just to screw with him. A grin crossed his lips as he thought of Sadie's best friend and financial manager. She was just as big a part of the Crew's success as he was and she knew it. He couldn't hate on her too hard.

At noon, he wandered to the kitchen thinking about taking Mickie out for lunch. He stopped at the sight. The smell of Sharpie ink hung heavy in the air. She had a pile of file folders on the table and the stack of papers he'd dropped in the bottom drawer of the empty file cabinet. His I'll-get-to-it-eventually pile.

"What's all this?"

She smiled up at him and tucked a lock of hair behind her ear. "I got bored waiting for phone calls. I found all these loose, so I'm making files for each client." She tapped the papers. "These are your contracts, Josh. Both for services and the behavior agreement. They shouldn't be lost."

An unexpected laugh appeared at the sight of her looking at him so sweetly yet so sternly. "You're absolutely right. Thank you. It's on my list of stuff to do."

She held out a hand, palm up. "Give me the list. It's what you're paying me for."

"Later. Now it's time for the first-day-of-work tradition of going out to lunch on the boss."

"Go out? For lunch? Like a real grown-up?" She clasped her hands to her cheeks. "I'm not sure if I remember how to do that."

"I'm pretty sure it's one of those riding-a-bike kind of things."

He had planned on a quick run up to Subway, but seeing her reaction made him reevaluate. "Do you like Middle Eastern food?"

"Don't know. Never had it."

"Well, that settles it. Al-Amir on Main, it is. Uh, ever ridden a motorcycle?"

"Nope."

"We can take the car if you want. Parking the bike is so much easier."

"If you have a helmet. I'd rather not splatter my brains across the street."

He laughed. "I wouldn't put anyone on my bike without one."

THIS WAS A day of firsts, it seemed. First day on the job. First time eating Middle Eastern food—whatever that was going to turn out to be—and the first time on the back of a motorcycle. Part of her was screaming-mommy horrified that she was putting Ian in jeopardy of becoming an orphan, but the other part was too busy realizing she was clinging to her new boss like a barnacle as he navigated the city streets. At a red light, he looked back at her.

"Just relax. Lean when I lean."

Uh-huh. Not a single part of her relaxed. Not with her knees clamped against his hips and her hands clenching his middle. It was all she could do to keep her fingers from playing with the ridges of his abs. Happy for the helmet that covered her face, she gave in to a wicked smile for her thoughts. For the first time in a very long time, she was having fun. And feeling like a woman. The bike went over a small bump and she bounced forward, right up against that back. She clenched harder at his waist.

"You okay back there?"

"Yeah."

No. Her heart was pounding and she was having a hard time catching her breath. She wanted to get laid. Now. By him. In the worst possible way. It had been practically since Ian was conceived. A pulling, aching need spread through her. The bike made a sharp turn to the right and she clung to him. This did nothing to help her get her mind off jumping him.

The second the bike stopped, she scrambled off while he secured it. Her trembling fingers fumbled at the helmet strap.

"Let me get that," he said. His fingers brushing against the side of her throat stoked her need to painful levels. When the helmet lifted away, a frown creased his face. "You're flushed. Did it scare you that much?"

"No," she lied. "It was exciting. I liked it."

Dear sweet baby Jesus in the manger. Stop it. Take a breath. Act like an adult. You don't need this. But she couldn't help it. It felt good to pretend for a little while. Pretend she was a normal person. Pretend she didn't have a care in the world.

By the time they were seated, Josh noticed two things. One, Mickie had stopped just inside and scanned every face in the restaurant. Two, she sat with her back to the wall. Interesting. Especially since she wasn't from Columbia and supposedly didn't know anyone here.

By the time they'd placed their orders, the flush had faded from her cheeks, but her gaze still darted to the door every time it opened. Time to do some fishing.

"Where'd you move here from?"

Her eyes met his briefly before she focused on bobbing her straw up and down in her water. "Asheville."

He waited. That was it. "You're going to USC in the fall?"

She nodded. "Nursing school."

"Really? What made you decide on that?"

She stopped bobbing the straw and clasped her hands on the table. "When—when Ian was born." She stopped and cleared her throat. Stared at her hands. "The nurses helped me so much. I admired them. And I want to help people. Like they did for me."

"That's admirable."

He let the silence play out for a stretch. He couldn't tell if she was an incredibly private person or hiding something. Something more than just being a single mother alone in a big city.

There were glimpses he'd catch. Her spontaneous hug after he'd offered her the job. That silly little tiptoe pantomime she'd done the day she came to do her laundry. But she kept that hidden behind a wall of stubborn refusal to let people close. *Which was the real Mickie?*

"What did you mean when you told me you knew what it was like to be alone?"

Her question surprised him. Her tone was softly questioning and her gaze was direct and warm. Surely she wasn't about to confide in him. He suppressed a smile as it clicked. Nursing school. She'd found a sore spot and wanted to fix it. Beneath that wall of ice or fear or whatever it was, she cared deeply about people. He wasn't sure why he'd said that to her. Even though it was true, he rarely opened that part of his life to others. But he found he wanted to know her secret. If he wanted that maybe he'd have to give up one of his own.

"I was raised in the foster-care system. When I turned eighteen, I was out on the street. Alone. No family."

Her eyes widened and filled with warmth. Usually he saw pity or discomfort in people's eyes when he revealed this. Which was why he didn't like to do it. It led to abruptly ended conversations or questions he didn't want to answer. What he saw in Mickie's gaze stunned him because he'd only seen it once before: in Sadie's eyes the day he'd answered her help wanted ad. Empathy. His surprise deepened when she spoke. Her words dropped to a husky whisper. A question not of curiosity or compassion, but one seeking knowledge.

"How did you make it through?"

He leaned forward, wanting to be closer to her, never taking his eyes from hers. "I kept moving forward. I found Sadie. She gave me more than a job. She gave me a family. That was the most important thing. I let her help me."

The moment spun out. She drew in a breath and her lips parted. Whatever she was going to say was lost when the waitress arrived with their food.

"Everything okay here?" the waitress asked, her gaze moving between the two of them.

Mickie blinked. Smiled up at the waitress. "Yes. This looks amazing. Thank you."

Josh sat back and concentrated on his gyro and let the intensity of the conversation fade. He'd planted a seed. If she needed help, hopefully she'd let him help her. Paying it back. Just paying it back.

MICKIE COULDN'T WAIT to get to the day care and pick up Ian after finishing for the day. Hurrying down the sidewalk, she couldn't quite outpace her thoughts. Josh had scared her, drawing her in like that so easily. Establishing that emotional bond. Establishing himself as a protector. She shook her head as if to dislodge the thoughts. She wouldn't fall for it again. She knew the signs now. She needed the job but that didn't mean she'd get herself entangled. Again.

When she peeked around the corner of the playroom, she was happy to see Ian laughing and playing with another little boy. The look of joy on his face when he saw her drove away all her fears. She scooped him up and held him tight.

"Hey there, baby man. Momma is so happy to see you. I missed you so much."

Pushing the stroller across campus, she spied the pay phone she'd used before. She didn't have enough change. But she wanted to hear her mother's voice. Needed. Two minutes later, an operator was asking for charges to be accepted.

"Hey, Auntie Em," she breathed. "Sorry to bother you."

"Is everything all right, hun?"

The anxiety in her mother's voice triggered her own stab of panic. She'd never called collect before. "Yes. I'm fine. Everything is fine. I'm sorry. I wanted to let you know I got a new job. Temporary but it's perfect for...my needs now."

"Oh, that's wonderful. Did you get the greeting cards I sent you?"

"Yes. Thank you. That should be enough for now."

There was so much more she wanted to say. How frightened she'd been. How stupid she felt. All her jumbled-up emotions. Ian was beginning to fuss. He was hungry and needed supper. "I miss you," she whispered.

"We miss you, too. Write to me. I love getting your letters."

After ending the call, she stared at the black receiver. The sun beat down on her and she felt heavy again. Oh-so heavy and slow. What was it Josh had said? Just keep moving forward. Yep.

"One foot in front of the other, girl."

With a deep breath and squared shoulders, she pushed the stroller toward home. *Nursing school. Job. Nothing else. Remember it's a job. He's not your friend. He's not your confidant. He's your boss. Keep it that way.*

CHAPTER SIX

SHE SLOWED AS she came in view of the duplex. There was a woman sitting on her front porch. She slowed her steps even more as she checked her out. She was young. African American. Wearing red scrubs. The scrubs required for USC nursing students. She turned Ian's stroller up the walk leading to the house. She stopped a few feet away from the porch. Where she could reach Josh's door in a hurry. "May I help you?"

The woman looked up from the book she was reading. "Hey! Yeah. I'm looking for Michael Phillips." She tucked the book into a backpack and stood. Now Mickie could see the USC nursing school emblem and her student ID.

"That's me."

The stunned look on the woman's face wasn't new to Mickie. The head shake and self-deprecating laugh was. "Dang! And here I practically had to fight a couple other girls to get you assigned to me. Was hoping you'd be some tall, dark and handsome type."

Mickie felt a small smile form on her lips. "Nope. Short, blond, girl type."

The woman put a hand on her generous hip and looked Mickie up and down. "How'd you end up with a name like Michael?"

It wasn't the first time she'd been asked the question. But she had her lie smooth as silk. "Remember that old TV show *The Waltons*?"

"I think so. John-Boy?"

"Yeah. The actress that played the mother was named Michael. And the credits listed her as Miss Michael whatever-her-last-name-was. My mom thought it was so classy and elegant. So, here I am. Miss Michael Phillips."

"Okay. That's a new one." She walked up with her hand out. "I'm Tiana Nelson. I don't have a story about my name but I'll be your mentor this coming semester. You can call me Tiana or Tee. Call me TeeTee and we'll have a problem. I tried your number a few times but you never answered."

"Sorry. I have a thing about answering unknown phone calls. You should have left a message."

"I have a thing about voice mail. Makes me babble like a fool. So I just thought I'd drop by. Was getting to leave a note. So, do you go by Michael?"

"Mickie."

Ian let out an impatient cry. Tiana leaned down. "You have a baby! Oh, my God, he's so cute. Hey, little man, what's up?"

"He's starving, that's what's up right now. Come on in."

If Tiana was curious about the lack of furniture, she didn't say anything. Mickie hurried together some food for Ian while Tiana went over the contents of a package she'd brought. Information on registration, the new student orientation, a welcome mixer, class schedules.

"Any questions?"

Mickie sorted through the papers. "Will I live through this?"

Tiana's laugh filled the kitchen. It was a warm sound. A missed sound. Mickie smiled when Ian joined in the laughter. That's what they needed. "Yeah, you'll live. Won't seem like it, but you will." She tilted her head toward Ian, sending the short curls of her hair bouncing, then turned to Mickie. "What about little man there? You have help with him?"

"I've got him in the day care. They accommodate our school schedules. Other than that, no. It's just the two of us."

Tiana nodded slowly. Now her gaze did roam the sparse apartment before once again settling on Mickie. "Well, now there's the three of us. Okay? I'm your mentor. I hope I'll be your friend. Use me."

Tears clogged Mickie's throat. Josh's voice echoed in her mind. *I let people help me.* "Okay. Thank you."

"I mean it, Miss Michael. I almost quit in my first year. I came out of a small nowhere town and didn't know what I was doing with myself. I was alone and lost. My mentor saved me." She straightened from her slump against the counter and shrugged the backpack on her shoulders. "I'm gonna let you tend to little man here. You have my number. Call me for anything."

At the door, Mickie forced herself to reach out and take Tiana's hand. She gave it a brief squeeze. "Thank you. It's hard for me to ask for help."

"But you will?"

The question was accompanied by a stern look.

"Yes. I will."

THEY HAD SETTLED into a comfortable routine. Josh spent most of his time in the testing room while Mickie kept to the kitchen table. Something had changed, but he wasn't quite sure what. On the surface, everything was the same. She was warm, friendly and efficient. But there was a bit of aloofness there. Josh shook his head. *What do you expect? She's an employee.*

"Hey," he said as he entered the kitchen. "I'm expecting a visitor in about an hour or so. Wyatt Anderson."

Mickie glanced at him briefly before returning her attention to the laptop. "Okay."

Grabbing a bottle of water, he headed back to his office space. And stopped. "Everything okay?"

"Yes. Why?"

The look of complete professionalism on her face stabbed at him. "No reason. Just checking."

Shutting the door behind him, Josh flopped down in his office chair. The look on her face. Why was that bothering him? She was an employee. *Yeah, but,* another part of him nagged, *before that she was your hot neighbor.* He twisted the cap off the water bottle and chugged it down. *Forget it, man.*

He was so focused on plowing through the never-ending paperwork that Mickie's knock on the door startled him. "Yeah?"

The door opened. "Mr. Anderson is here," she said.

Wyatt appeared in the door. "Wyatt is fine. No need to be formal."

Josh stood to shake Wyatt's hand. "Wyatt's

almost family, Mickie. The only man brave enough to attempt to tame the big boss lady."

Wyatt laughed. "I'm not even going to attempt that. Besides, I sort of like her wild."

"Okay," Mickie said with a smile. "Is there anything I can get for you? Either of you?"

"No, I'm good. Thanks," Wyatt said. He set the laptop bag he was carrying on the table.

Josh found his full attention on that bag. His heart rate kicked up several notches. After all these years. Were his answers right there? A hand on his arm pulled his attention to Mickie's ice-blue eyes. She looked both concerned and puzzled.

"Are you okay? You look…funny."

"No, I'm fine. Thanks, Mick."

After she left them, Wyatt sat and powered up the laptop. "She's right. You looked a bit panicky there. You sure you want to know this?"

"Is it good?"

"Pretty much."

Now his breathing joined in with his heart rate and both ran in hitching, erratic patterns. He felt his fingertips go numb and Wyatt's voice dimmed. He shook his head and took in several deep, cleansing breaths. Focus. Calm. Quiet. He got his breath back under control, but his heart… He couldn't contain his heart. So much sloshing around in there. Hope. Fear. Joy. Pain.

"I've got all this in a .ZIP file and I'll email it to you so you can have it. Just thought it'd be best to go over it in person."

"Okay." Josh nodded, but his full concentration was on the file that Wyatt was opening. Just like that. After all his years of searching, Wyatt had found her in days. Was he really ready for this? He pushed down the doubts and sudden fears that were urging him to tell Wyatt to never mind, go back home.

"I'll start with what I do know. Your sister's birth name was Kimberly Sanders."

"Kimmie," Josh whispered.

Wyatt hesitated and turned to Josh. "You do know what happened to your parents, right?"

"Yes. Well. Mostly. As much as I remember. Read some old newspaper articles when I got older. There wasn't much about them I didn't know already. Poor, drunk." He shrugged. "Barely a blip on the social radar."

"Okay. It appears that the two of you were separated almost immediately. You both went into emergency protective custody. As you are probably more than aware, foster homes aren't exactly plentiful and there didn't seem to be a home available that could take you both. The foster parents who took Kimberly that night are the ones who adopted her."

A lump rose up in Josh's throat and tears stung

at his eyes. He lowered his face to his hands. Wyatt's hand came down on his shoulder.

"You okay, brother?"

"Yeah." Josh cleared his throat against the thickness. "Yeah. I'm just relieved. Getting bounced around from home to home was the worst and to know she never went through that… it's good. I'm okay. Keep going."

"Adoptive family lived in Moncks Corner. Last name is Mixon. They kept her first name so she's Kimberly Mixon now."

He clicked on another file and two pictures came up. Josh leaned forward, eager to see his sister's face. She had the same dark curls he remembered. He couldn't tell what color her eyes were but they looked light. Blue like his?

"Wow. That's her?"

"That's her. First one here is a college graduation photo. This one is from the paper. It's her engagement announcement."

Josh reached out to touch the screen. His sister. Kimmie. She was fine. "She graduated from college?"

"Yes. Degree in elementary education. She's a second grade teacher. Her fiancé is a software engineer. Seem pretty happy."

Josh let that sink in. All his life, he'd worried about Kimmie. It had been his job to protect her, to watch out for her. That he'd never known what happened to her was a pain that never went away. Now he knew. Happy. Loved.

"You said there were some things you didn't know?"

Wyatt closed down the files. "I'm going to send these to you now, yeah. I'm assuming that you are thinking about reaching out to her. I mean, Sadie and her brother must have put the idea in your mind. I'll help you with that if you want."

"But?"

"I don't know if she knows anything. If she knows she was adopted. If she knows the truth about your parents or not."

Josh watched Wyatt's hands as they moved across the keyboard, sending the file and shutting down the laptop. He had been thinking about reaching out. A letter like Sadie's half brother had sent to her. Leaning back in his chair, he covered his face with his hands. Damn. She was happy. Getting married. Did she know or would he be dropping a giant pile of pain and shame into her life?

"Shit."

"Yeah," Wyatt agreed.

Josh dropped his hands. "Still, thanks, man. At least now I know she's okay. That was the most important thing. I appreciate it. More than you know."

Wyatt's hand clamped down on Josh's shoulder and gently shook him. "Josh. Look at me. You are Sadie's brother. Which in a couple of months makes you my brother. We're all we got, man. You, Sadie, me and Jules. We're a family." He stood and pulled Josh into an embrace.

"Thank you. I mean it."

"Talk to Sadie if you need to."

"Yeah. I will. You want to grab some lunch or something?"

"Nah. I've got to get back to Charleston. Call us."

As they walked to the front door, another old ghost from the past rose. "Hey," Josh asked as they stepped out on the porch. "I hate to ask, but do you think you can get the original police reports on my parents?"

"Probably. Is that a wound you want to go digging in?"

"I don't know. But I'm starting to think *want* isn't the right word. Maybe I…need to."

"I'll look into it."

"Thanks. And, Wyatt?"

"Yeah?"

"Tell Sadie not to call me about this right now."

Wyatt's laugh made him smile. "I will relay your message."

MICKIE LOOKED UP as she heard the front door close. She waited but Josh didn't come back from the living room. "Josh?" She stood and moved to the opening between the kitchen and living room. He was standing facing the closed door, his arms on the frame, his forehead resting against the wooden surface. Unease prickled down her spine. "Are you okay?"

He lifted his head. Dropped his arms. Then turned. "Yeah. I'm fine."

She took a few steps toward him. "You look like you've seen a ghost."

His eyes met hers. Some need burned in his expression, something urgent and painful. "That's exactly what I've seen."

Taking a few more steps, she reached out for his hand and tugged him in the direction of the sofa. "Sit down. Your hands are ice-cold. What's going on?"

He lifted the hand she'd been holding, rubbing his thumb across the fingers before clenching it in a fist. "I'm okay, really, Mickie."

"No. You aren't. You are pale and obviously upset. Something happened."

"You sound like a nurse."

"I haven't even pulled my nurse voice on you yet, Josh."

That got a smile out of him before he leaned

his head back against the back of the sofa and sighed. "Ever want something, Mickie? Want it your whole life? And when you get it, it only opens up another hole to fall through?"

Mickie frowned. No. She had no idea what he was talking about. She put her hand back in his. His fingers were still cold and she absently began rubbing them between her hands. It frightened her a little to see him like this. Strong, funny, gorgeous Josh? Confused and shaken? She wasn't sure she wanted to know.

"No, Josh. I don't know. Tell me."

He didn't move but his hand tightened around hers, making her aware of her movements. She felt the heat of a blush cover her face and she tried to pull away. He held on. "Don't. This feels nice."

"Josh."

He sat back up straight. He turned a little so he was facing her. "You know I grew up in foster care?"

"Yes."

"I went into the system when I was five. I had a little sister who was two. She got adopted and I never saw her again."

Horror flooded through her. Five years old. And his sister was two! Ian was almost two. She blinked, hard, trying to stop the tears.

Josh lifted a hand and his fingers brushed her

cheeks. "Might want to work on that poker face a little bit, Mickie."

"That's awful, Josh. I can't imagine never knowing."

"I couldn't, either. But now I know. That was Sadie's fiancé. He's a private investigator and he found my sister for me."

"He did? That's amazing. Are you going to try to..." Her words faltered at the look on his face. It was not a happy or relieved look. "What?"

"He doesn't know if she knows. Anything. That she was adopted. That she has a brother. That we got shipped to foster care."

"Oh."

"She's happy, Mickie. A teacher. About to get married. Happy."

"Oh."

"Yeah. Oh."

"What are you going to do?"

He patted her knee and stood. She followed. "I don't know. I really don't know."

She looked up at him. "Does knowing she's safe and happy give you any peace?"

He smiled down at her. Put his hands to her cheeks and leaned in to press a quick kiss to her forehead. It took everything she had not to respond to that touch. The touch that set off a million alarms within her. "Yes. It does."

One hard rap on the door was the only warning they got before DeShawn came in. Mickie took a hasty step back.

"Two more clients, signed, sealed and delivered," DeShawn said, holding out papers.

Mickie stepped past Josh. "I'll take those."

As she went back to her spot at the kitchen table, she gasped, suddenly aware of her own ghost. She brought a hand to her mouth. Josh said Wyatt was a private investigator. And he'd gotten into adoption records. Found Josh's sister. Found out all sorts of things about her. She crossed her arms against her chest to hide the shaking. Would it be as easy as that? No. No. It'd been barely two years.

She stood abruptly and crossed on shaky legs to the hallway. "Hey, Josh?"

"Yeah?" he called from the back room.

"Would it be okay if I left a little early? Ian had a stuffy nose this morning and I want to get him home."

"That's fine. See you tomorrow. Hope he's okay."

She barely heard his words. She had to get to the day care. She had to see that Ian was there, safe. *No. You are scaring yourself with the impossible, girl. Stop it.* But it never stopped. Not once in over two years had it stopped.

CHAPTER SEVEN

SATURDAY, SHE PUSHED Ian in the stroller to the USC campus to meet Tiana for a grand tour. The campus was bustling and she wondered what it would be like come fall and the beginning of a new semester.

"Good idea," she told Tiana after they'd walked through the entire college of nursing and settled in the air-conditioned food court. "I'd get lost in a paper bag."

"I remember my first week. I spent half my time lost and the other half convinced I'd walked into the wrong class."

"Yep. That's me."

"You're coming in as a junior, right?"

"Yeah. I did all my prereqs at the technical college in Asheville. The waiting list was so long and with hospitals going to using BSNs, I figured I'd better transfer. USC was the first place to tell me yes."

"And here you are."

Mickie looked up at the thoughtful tone of

Tiana's words. The woman tilted her head and raised an eyebrow.

"Can I ask you something?"

"That's never a good start," Mickie replied. She bent to offer Ian another sip of water. Flutters stirred in her belly. Time to tell her lies and try to keep them straight.

"Where's your family?"

The bluntness of it shocked her a little. But only a little because she was starting to realize that Tiana was a no-nonsense kind of person. She was going to make an amazing nurse. "I… They are…far away."

"Far away? Like how far?"

"Very far. Why?"

Tiana leaned forward on her arms, her dark gaze intent on Mickie's face. "I'll tell you a truth I tell hardly anyone if you'll tell me one back."

Well, there was a loaded bet. Before she could think she said, "Okay."

"I'm twenty-two years old. I have a five-year-old little girl back home with my momma right now. If you're doing the math, that's seventeen."

Mickie swallowed. "It must be hard to be away from her."

"It is. But you know what? When she was born, I looked around. Where I come from? Aren't any good jobs. The schools are terrible. And I had to decide. What did I want for my baby girl? The same old nothing? Or was I going to do something?"

"And here you are, doing something."

"Yeah. And now tell me. What are you doing? And why are you doing it alone?"

As she said *alone*, Tiana reached out and put her hand over Mickie's. The simple gesture brought a lump to her throat. *Don't tell her. Don't tell.* Along with the warning came a weight so heavy that she could barely take in a breath. She was tired. Tired of lying. Tired of being alone. Here was a woman who would understand. Who wanted to help her. *Let her help.* She glanced down at Ian. He was focused on getting the French fry she'd given him into his mouth.

"My parents wanted me to give Ian away for adoption," she lied. Inside, her guts shriveled with shame. Shame for making her parents the bad guys in this story because that was the most horrific part of the lie. Shame for lying to Tiana, who had been so honest with her and who only wanted to help. Shame at herself for being too cowardly to tell the truth.

"Oh," Tiana said, her tone oddly neutral.

Mickie looked up at her. "They aren't bad people, just…we didn't have a lot to begin with… And they thought…"

"They thought the same thoughts I had when I found out. I considered putting Lilly up for adoption. What did I have to offer her? Teenage mother. My family was too poor to even have enough dirt to be dirt poor."

"Well, we weren't that bad off, but I had to make a choice."

"And here you are."

Mickie couldn't quite look directly at Tiana. Her entire existence felt like a spiderweb of lies. She lied to her parents. She lied to Josh. She lied to Tiana. She lied to herself. She swallowed the tears. She hoped she wasn't lying to Ian when she promised him things would be better. "Here I am," she said.

"It'll be all right," Tiana said.

It wasn't her words, but the absolute confidence in her voice that made Mickie finally look at Tiana. "How do you know that?"

"Because you're here. Doing it. You made it this far. If you were going to quit, you would have done it by now."

BY THE TIME she got home, it was well past Ian's nap time and he was letting her know about it. It started with the cranky little cries, yeah. That was just the start. But when she tried to put him to bed, he cranked up into full meltdown mode. She was walking around the kitchen with him, bouncing him and patting his back while the shrieks assaulted her eardrums. Ought to make teenage girls do this for a couple days, she thought. Better than any sex education class out there. What next? “Come on, baby boy,” she said, bouncing him up and down in her arms. *Shake those bubbles out, shake it all out, calm it down.*

She caught a glimpse of something at the sliding door and jumped back, clutching Ian. Josh.

The hell, dude? She walked over, feeling the stress run off her, and she slid the door open. “Sorry,” she said, not sure why.

“Is he okay?”

She stopped bouncing and the wails increased in volume. “Missed his nap time. Now we’re all paying for it.”

“Hey, little man,” Josh said. “Little man. People are going to think your mother is taking your favorite toy away.”

Ian turned his head, crying cut off midscream. He rested his cheek against Mickie’s. She could feel his hiccupping sighs as the tantrum subsided. Leaning back, she looked at his face. Snot and tears. Lovely. “Ian. You’re a hot mess, little dude.” Snatching some tissues from the table, she wiped at his face.

“Yosh!”

That surprised her and her head turned back to Josh, who was standing just inside the kitchen, hands in the back pockets of his jeans, T-shirt pulled tight against his chest. That impossibly black curly hair tumbling over his forehead. She turned away. "Very good, Ian. Yes, that's Josh."

She intended to get a sippy cup of milk and hopefully get him into his bed, but Ian had other plans. He squirmed in her arms and she put him down. He toddled to Josh, who was looking down at him with obvious alarm.

"Yosh!"

"What's he want?"

"For you to pick him up."

"Yeah, no."

"He's going to cry, then."

Sure enough, Ian tilted his head back as he looked up at Josh. And boom. Down on his butt. His face scrunched up but the wail that followed was a normal I-fell-down wail, not a return of the tantrum.

"What do I do now?"

Mickie motioned to the living room. "Take him in there and distract him for a minute so I can get him something to drink."

Despite the terrified look on his face, Josh picked Ian up. He put his hands under the little guy's armpits and carried him that way, with his legs dangling, all the way to the living room. Weird thing was Ian seemed to dig it, kind of. At least the sound of the crying dialed down a bit. He was staring up at Josh like, "hey, this is something new." Mickie could relate to that. She smiled, remembering the first day she'd met Josh and he'd carried Ian the same way. Apparently, he was only comfortable with sleeping kids. As she moved around the kitchen, she could hear Josh talking. Ian had stopped crying. Stepping into the living room, she was surprised to see Josh sitting on the floor in front of Ian, juggling three of his stuffed animals. She was sure if Ian hadn't been so tired, he would be laughing. But the motion seemed to have hypnotized him. Maybe she should learn to juggle.

She sat and handed Ian the sippy cup. He drank it, never taking his eyes off Josh. "That's pretty cool," she said. "Where'd you learn to juggle?"

"Martial arts class. We would juggle bricks."

"Bricks? Like build-a-house bricks?"

"Yep. Great for hand-eye coordination and building grip strength."

"I can't imagine catching bricks like that."

Ian moved to snuggle beside her, sippy cup held in both hands. A very good sign. Josh let the stuffed animals fall. He held up a hand, showing her his palm.

"It'll give you some callouses."

She stared at his hand. It was a man's hand. A workingman's hand. Big, calloused, with long fingers. Josh was so low-key it was easy to overlook how powerfully he was built. The hand was attached to a forearm so muscled it was probably bigger than her bicep. Her eyes traveled up to the worn cotton T-shirt draped loosely over his chest and an almost overwhelming lust swept through her. Her eyes met his and he lowered his hand. There was a brief pop of heat in his eyes before he looked down at the scattered toys. He picked up the bunny and booped Ian on the nose with it.

"Looks like little man is almost down for the count. I'll let you get him settled."

She shook her head to clear it. Just for a moment, she'd forgotten. Forgotten she was a mother. And remembered she was a woman. She couldn't get that calloused palm out of her mind. Or where she wanted it to be.

"Yep. He's done. Thank you for your help."

He stood in one fluid motion. "No problem. Listen. I'm driving down to Charleston today. I'll be back late tomorrow. If you need anything, call me. I can get DeShawn to help you out."

"Okay. Thanks."

She watched him go, which proved to be a mistake because now she wanted to see that tight butt more than she wanted to know what lay under that T-shirt. If she needed anything. She climbed to her feet, hauling Ian up with her. Yeah, she needed something.

She needed to get naked and sweaty. With

Josh. The flare of lust she'd felt still burned deep in her belly. She tried distracting herself with putting Ian to bed. A late nap was going to wreak havoc on his sleep cycle, but there was nothing to be done for that.

The rumble of a motorcycle drew her to the window. Josh paused at the end of the driveway. Again, that lust. His black curls were covered by the helmet, but those forearms were on full display on the handlebars. And she had a great view of his thigh, thick with muscle as he held the bike steady. He pulled out, taking a long curving left turn, bike roaring. What was it about a man on a motorcycle? She let her forehead rest against the windowpane.

Whatever you are planning, just don't. She turned away. Ian was sound asleep. Maybe a cold shower was what she needed.

CHAPTER EIGHT

AS HE ROUNDED the sweeping curve in the road, Josh saw Jules standing at the edge of the lawn waving both hands over her head. He hit the throttle a little, making the bike growl as he approached. Sadie and Wyatt came out of the house and stood on the small front porch as he pulled into the driveway.

"Can I have a ride? Can I? Just around the block? Please, Uncle Josh? Please? Please? Please?"

He glanced over at Wyatt. He was Jules's uncle by blood, but after her mother's death, he'd been appointed her guardian. Recently, he'd signed adoption papers, making her his daughter. Wyatt's head was already moving back and forth.

"I don't think your dad's going to go for that," he said as he pulled off his helmet.

"Absolutely not," Wyatt said.

"I'll hold on tight. And wear a helmet. And Uncle Josh won't go faster than the speed limit."

"No."

Sadie slipped an arm around Wyatt's waist.

"Come on, *Dad*. It's perfectly safe. I've ridden with Josh before."

"No helmet, no ride."

"He's got an extra in the saddlebag."

Jules put her hands on her hips. "Daa-aaad! I am almost ten years old. I am not a baby!"

Josh pressed his lips together to prevent the laughter from escaping. Sadie was doing the same. Wyatt threw his hands in the air and stomped down the porch steps. "Fine. Where's this helmet? Is it even going to fit her?"

Josh unlocked the saddlebag and lifted the extra helmet. "Ta-da!"

After getting the helmet strapped on and getting Jules settled on the back of the bike, Wyatt leveled a finger at Josh. "If I even think I hear you speeding, just drop her off and keep riding, brother."

"Yes, sir," Josh replied briskly. Jules wrapped her arms around his waist as he cranked the engine. He revved it a few times—once just to annoy Wyatt a little and again for the excited squeal from Jules.

"Can we ride by Shiloh's house?" she yelled over the noise.

WYATT WAS SITTING on the porch steps when they returned. Josh helped Jules down and stowed his gear.

"What took so long?"

Jules skipped along the sidewalk, making her long black hair swing wildly. "We stopped at Ms. Charlie and Shiloh's house so they could meet my new uncle."

Wyatt glanced up at Josh with a glint in his eyes. "Oh? And how did that go?"

"I don't even know what to think. She's a character."

Wyatt stood and they went inside. Sadie was at the kitchen table with her laptop and a pile of Cleaning Crew paperwork beside her. She rose to give him a hug. Josh felt the knot of tension that had accompanied him from Columbia ease up a little. Though not related by blood, he considered her to be his big sister. She knew him. She understood him like others could not.

Wyatt's hand came down for a brief squeeze on his shoulder. "Jules and I are going up to Fiery Ron's to get some ribs. What sides you want?"

Josh cleared his throat. "Um. Collards and grits."

"Collards are gross," Jules said.

"Collards are delicious."

"Slimy like snails."

"And you've eaten enough snails to know this?"

"Jules," Sadie said, interrupting the banter. "Go put on a clean shirt before y'all leave."

"Okay, Momma Sadie."

Josh lifted an eyebrow as Jules left the kitchen. "That's new."

Sadie leaned against the counter. "Yeah."

Her voice was soft and Josh looked at her. Really looked at her. Everything seemed soft. Her eyes, her body language. Calm. At peace. He felt his own constant tension more acutely than ever. Sadie had faced her demons, exorcised the pain of a childhood spent in foster care. His jaw clenched as his frustration rose again. He didn't know what to do. So he'd come to the only person he knew would understand.

Sadie reached for his hand. "I know."

"What are we doing, here, Sades? What are we playing at?" he asked in a low, choked voice.

She squeezed his hand and he was able to momentarily forget his fear and confusion. When her eyes darted over his shoulder, he straightened. They weren't alone. He turned his head to see Wyatt and Jules moving past the doorway of the kitchen.

"We're heading out," Wyatt said. "Shouldn't take more than twenty minutes."

After the front door shut behind them, Josh turned to Sadie. "Had this planned, did you?"

"Of course I did." She motioned to the den. "Let's talk."

It was odd, watching Sadie curl up on the

huge sectional couch in the den. It was a family room. Giant sofa. Bookshelves. Big-screen TV mounted on the wall. A place for a family to cozy up together and read or watch TV. A year ago, Sadie would have run in terror from such intimacy. Now she looked completely at home. He was the one who didn't belong anywhere. He sank down in the corner of the sofa opposite Sadie.

"We aren't playing at anything, Josh. This is life. We're living it."

"You're living here now?"

"No. Just hanging out on the weekends. Jules is a good kid. She's doing well dealing with the loss of her mother and all the changes. But change is stressful even if it's good change. Trying to ease into her life a little at a time."

"I guess that makes sense. When did you get so smart?"

"Same place you got so smart. We've seen the wrong way. What are you going to do about your sister?"

"I don't know what to do."

"It's a hard decision."

This is why he'd had to come to here. Sadie understood immediately all the complexities of the situation. She had gone through the same thing, almost. Her half brother had reached out to her and she'd had to decide if she wanted to risk bringing the mother who'd abandoned her back into her life. She'd done it on her own terms. Faced down her mother and was slowly getting to know her half siblings.

"What if she doesn't know, Sades? Huh? What if she doesn't know she was adopted? What if she doesn't know that her biological father was a piece-of-shit monster that murdered our mother and then himself? What if she doesn't know he probably was going to kill us, too, if I hadn't hidden with her?"

Sadie let out a long sigh. "What have you been telling me about Kim ever since I met you? That you wanted to know that she was safe. That she was happy. That the not knowing what happened to her was torturing you. You have that answer now."

He rubbed at the back of his neck, trying to relieve the tension there. "I know."

Sadie let the silence play out. Finally, she stretched out a leg and pushed against his knee with her bare toes. He looked up at her. "Now you want more?"

"Yes. And it's so entirely selfish."

"It isn't selfish, Josh. It's—"

"It is," he said, cutting her off. "Kim is living a normal life. She had parents who loved her. She went to college. She teaches second graders and is planning her wedding. And I want to crash into all that and ruin it with this garbage."

"And what if she does know, Josh? What if she knows all about it and wonders where her big brother is. The big brother who saved her life?"

"What if she doesn't?"

Sadie rolled her eyes and glared at him. The stubborn, bulldog expression on her face was so like the old Sadie that it actually got a smile out of him. "Wallowing doesn't become you, Josh. The question isn't whether or not you want to reach out to her. You do. The question you want answered is will she be receptive or not? Will you be rejected? That's scary. I get it. I never had the courage to reach out."

"But you had the courage to confront your mother."

Sadie flapped a hand at him. "That was rage-driven. Rage is easy. You aren't looking for a confrontation. You're looking for connection. That's some scary shit."

Yeah, that was exactly what it was, and he'd been dealing with it all his life. Running from connections. From commitments. Never daring to expose anyone to the potential monster within him. He'd only let Sadie get close. Because his demons didn't scare her. Nor did they shock her. She'd seen worse.

"You've waited twenty years, Josh," Sadie said

softly. "You don't have to decide right this minute. Give it some time to sink in."

He let his head drop back and stared at the ceiling. He was so tired of thinking about it. Maybe he should forget about it for a while. Put it in a box and shove it way back in the darkest corner of his mind.

Sadie's foot pushed against his knee again. "So, what's the deal with your cute little neighbor who is now your receptionist?"

"Nothing," he said, irritated. Mickie was another problem altogether. A problem he was having more and more trouble ignoring. He certainly didn't want to discuss her with Sadie. "What's the deal with the Momma-Sadie thing?"

He knew that'd get her off his case. She went tense and guarded. It'd been so long since he'd seen her like this and the difference was startling. He wondered if that's how he appeared. Tense. Guarded. Fear and suspicion lurking in his gaze.

"I'm not sure," Sadie said in a low voice. "You know Wyatt adopted Jules, right?"

"Yeah."

"He...well, really *they* want me to adopt Jules, also. After the wedding."

"Really?" The word took about ten seconds to completely leave his mouth. Sadie. A mother.

"Really." Her tone was self-deprecating and she rolled her eyes as she said it.

"I can see it."

She pulled her legs up and turned to face him. "Can you?"

"Yes. Jules adores you. You are crazy about her. I don't know if you realize this, Sades, but you're pretty fierce when you care about someone. Like a mother grizzly. Do you want to do it?"

"I do. And I don't. Wyatt doesn't want her to fall into any kind of limbo if anything ever happened to him. I understand that, but that's a huge commitment. Bigger than getting married, I think. To allow a child to depend on you, that's a lifelong promise. You can't ever go back on that."

"Which is exactly why you will be the best mother for her. You know exactly what you are signing up for. And you're up to the task. And I think you know that or you wouldn't have allowed her to call you Momma in the first place."

A wobbly smile appeared on her lips and she wiped at her eyes. Her expression was soft and relaxed again. "I hate that you know me so well sometimes."

"Too bad."

"Just tell me one thing."

"What's that?"

"Why isn't this true for you?"

He narrowed his eyes, feeling his walls snapping up. "What?"

"You say I'll be a good mother because I'm fierce about those I love. You are, too, Josh. Exactly like me. So why do you think you won't be a good father?"

He got to his feet. "This is not a conversation I'm going to have with you."

"Don't be getting all mad and stomping off, Josh."

"I'm not stomping off," he said. His voice was quiet and tense even to his own ears. Anger throbbed at his temples as his jaw clenched.

"Okay. Running away."

"I'm not running away, either. I've told you before this is not up for discussion. Just because you've miraculously managed to turn yourself into Little Miss Suzy Homemaker and candidate for Mother of the Goddamn Year doesn't mean you can start trying to remake me."

The narrowing of her eyes let him know he'd hit his mark with the insults thrown at her. The hands on her hips and the glare in those dark blue eyes let him know he didn't scare her.

"Knock it off, Josh. You came here asking me for advice. I'm giving it to you. Sorry if you don't like it, but there it is. You're going to have to face your past to know that you aren't your father. You never will be your father..."

He cut coldly across her words. "I already proved I *am* my father."

She took a step toward him and jabbed a finger in his chest. Probably the only person on the planet he'd let get away with that. "No. You. Are. Not."

He should leave. Get on his bike and roar back to Columbia at death-defying speeds. As if he could outrun that particular demon. He could hear Sadie calling his name as he stomped through the house and flung open the front door.

And there was Jules, walking up the sidewalk with a plastic bag dangling from each hand. "Hey, Uncle Josh. We got your slimeball collards!"

"Get back in here, dork," Sadie said from the kitchen door.

Caught. He narrowed his eyes at Sadie. *This isn't over.* Then he smiled at Jules. "They aren't slimy, squirt."

"I'm not a squirt. I'm the tallest girl in my class, for your information."

He reached down and took the bags of food from her. "Well, I stand corrected, tall squirt."

He put the bags on the counter and began opening them. Wyatt and Sadie pulled out plates and Jules got the silverware. It slowly dawned on him what a homey family scene it was. Yet it wasn't a scene. This was real. Sadie had fallen in love and was going to get married. And adopt Jules. And maybe have her own babies. Sadie caught his gaze and smiled. She knew exactly what he was thinking.

They moved to the table and began passing around the barbeque and side dishes, Jules chattering away the whole time about Shiloh's mother, Charlie, asking if Josh was single. Sadie laughed until Josh threw a piece of bread at her.

"Food fight!" Jules yelled as she threw her bread at Josh.

"No!" Sadie and Wyatt said in unison.

"Josh started it."

"Yes, he did. He isn't setting a good example," Sadie said firmly.

Josh and Jules looked at each other and Josh started laughing. He couldn't help it. Sadie? Primly handing out verbal discipline? The old Sadie would have said something like "cut that shit out."

"Don't laugh," Sadie said, smacking Josh on the arm.

"No hitting!" Jules said. She narrowed her eyes and set one hand on a hip, wagging a finger from the opposite hand at the two of them.

"Yeah, Sadie, you aren't setting a very good

example," Josh said. He gave Jules a quick wink and a thumbs-up.

"I'm going to knock all y'all's heads together," Wyatt said.

Josh settled back to eating with a grin. It felt good. Teasing. Bickering. Laughing. He put down the fork and looked around the table. He was part of a family, wasn't he? A real family. The rush of the feeling of belonging only made his loneliness more acute. Forever to be part of a family. Never to have one of his own.

CHAPTER NINE

THE DOORBELL RANG just as Mickie was getting Ian cleaned up after his breakfast. Even though she knew it was Tiana, she peered through the peephole first. Old habits. Except it wasn't just Tiana. Two other women stood on the small porch and sidewalk. Okay…

"Um, hi," she said as she opened the door, raising her eyebrows at Tiana. The other women squealed at the sight of Ian.

"You were right, Tee!"

"He's so cute!"

"Can I hold him?"

Instinctively, she turned to the side, putting herself between the women and Ian, who was riding her hip. "What's going on, Tiana?"

Tiana waved a hand in the air. "Y'all just hush now. You're scaring the baby. Can we come inside because it's hotter than fifty hells out here." She brushed past Mickie and led the women inside.

Mickie watched, unsure exactly what to do. She shut the door behind her. "What's going on?" she asked again.

Tiana fanned herself while flapping the neckline of her shirt. “I don’t remember it being this hot when I was a kid.” She turned her attention to Mickie. “Now, don’t get your panties in a wad, but we have a surprise for you.”

“A surprise?”

Ian lifted his arms toward Tiana and Mickie let her scoop him up. “Yes. A surprise,” Tiana said in a singsong as she lifted Ian in the air. “A big fat surprise for your stubborn-head mommy, my man.”

“Prize!”

She settled Ian on her hip and turned to Mickie. “It’s about the state of your household, Miz Mickie. I couldn’t help but notice that you have no furniture.”

Mickie felt her cheeks go hot. Embarrassment and a not so small slice of shame burned through her. “It’s fine. Temporary. I have furniture. Just not here.”

“See?” Tiana said to the others. “Told you she’d do that. Girl. Stop all that blushing. And stop telling those lies.” She motioned to the women around her. “These are two of my fellow senior nursing students. Elaine is the old hag over there. The redhead is Sally. Without these women, I would have run back home with my tail between my legs after my first week.”

Mickie took a moment to look into the faces of

the other women. She saw shining in their eyes the same compassion she'd seen in the nurses who'd helped her after Ian was born. The same need to help that burned in her. If only she was ever in a position to give that help. "Hi," she said, feeling slow and stupid.

"It was more than just us," Sally said. "We're the moving crew."

"Moving crew?"

Tiana slung an arm around Mickie's shoulders. "I hope you like the eclectic look, my friend."

"I don't know what that means. Or what you mean," Mickie said, but she was beginning to get an idea. Tiana had done something.

"Well," Tiana said, "I was in a meeting with my fellow senior mentoring students and one of them had an incoming freshman who needed help with getting uniforms, so everyone put out the word and within a couple of hours, we had four or five uniforms for her. So I asked if anyone had any spare furniture taking up space."

"We used my daddy's truck there was so much," Sally said with a grin.

"I—I don't know what to say," Mickie stuttered.

"You say thank you," Tiana said, handing Ian back to her.

"Thank you."

For the next hour, Mickie watched in stunned

disbelief as the women carried in an assortment of furniture. A small bistro table with two chairs for the kitchen. Two armchairs. A TV stand. A bed frame. A bookcase. Lamps. Side tables.

"I can help with this," she said as they began to carry in small boxes.

"We got it," Elaine said.

But she couldn't just stand there and watch. With Ian on her hip, she went out and grabbed a shopping bag. She could do *something*. It wasn't just furniture. Several of the school's distinctive garnet-colored nursing uniforms. A stethoscope. Books.

After everything was inside and Tee was directing the others in where to put things, Mickie leaned against the door. A small hand, patting gently at her face. "Momma 'kay?"

She wiped at the tears on her cheeks and hugged Ian tight. "It's okay, baby. Momma's just happy. Happy tears."

She looked up at the women. "Grateful tears."

When a box of children's books appeared, Mickie let Ian loose on them and retreated to the kitchen. The least she could do was fix some drinks and snacks. She set out glasses of iced tea and began brewing another pitcher. The new bistro table was immediately put to good use as she put out bowls of chips and pretzels, some carrot sticks, cherry tomatoes and a bowl of ranch dip. Not too bad for a no-notice party.

"Food!" Tiana cried out when she came in the kitchen.

Before too long, the party had moved to the living room floor, where they sat in a circle.

"I can't thank you enough for this," Mickie said, looking each of them in the eye. "This is the second time nurses have gone out of their way to help me. I promise I won't forget. I will do the same for anyone else I can whenever I can."

And just like the nurses from the hospital, they all seemed embarrassed to be recognized for their help. A hand found hers and squeezed. She looked to Elaine, the older of the women, sitting beside her in the circle.

"I fled my marriage five years ago. I left with my clothes and my books. I slept on the floor of my apartment for almost a year while I built a new life and new home one piece of furniture at a time. I understand."

Tiana leaned forward to dip a carrot in the ranch dressing. "Mickie, the secret about most nurses? We've all been through something. Came out on the other side stronger and more compassionate. And nursing school is not for the weak. No one has that strength alone. We help and depend on each other."

"Amen!" the other women chimed in.

"Thank you. Tiana, I'm serious, please get me the names of everyone who contributed so I can write thank-you notes. And if any of you need anything, please ask."

"Well…what's this I hear about the hot-guy farm next door?" Sally asked.

Mickie almost choked on her tea. Hot-guy farm? She shot a look at Tiana. "It's just a cleaning service."

"Ha! Girl, you're being selfish, just trying to keep that hot-dish menu all to yourself," Tiana teased. She turned to the others. "Seriously. Hot guys constantly coming and going all the time. It's like she's got her own personal Magic Mike show right next door."

Sally went to the front window to peek out the curtains. "When does this show begin?" she asked.

"Not on the weekend. Josh is back in Charleston until tonight and…"

"Oh. Josh? And we know *Josh's* personal schedule how?" Tiana's eyebrows arched so high they disappeared into the curls crossing her forehead.

Mickie felt her blush go nuclear. "He sort of gave me a job."

Tiana put a hand over her heart and shook her head hard, making her curls bounce. "Wait.

Wait a minute. That gorgeous chunk of beef with those blue eyes sort of gave you a job? And you didn't share this with me?"

"It's just temporary. Until school starts. And, um…that's all. He needed someone to answer the phone and make appointments and stuff."

"Stuff?"

Mickie tried to laugh. "Weren't you the one to tell me no men while in nursing school?"

Tried. Because merely thinking about Josh completely derailed any thoughts about no men.

"No men. Best advice ever," Elaine said.

Sally raised her glass in a toast. "To the number-one rule—no men while in school!"

They all clinked glasses. Okay. No men. It made sense. Nursing school was difficult and the pace of classes was insane. Dating would surely interfere. But what if you just wanted a good old-fashioned roll in the hay?

"Momma! Pat! Bunny!" Ian crashed through the party supplies, brandishing a book from the box, and fell into her lap. She barely got her glass out of the way.

"That's all the man you need, right there," Tiana said.

Mickie brought her arms around Ian and hugged him. True. She couldn't let herself get distracted now. Not when her goal was in sight. If not for herself, for Ian. She had to do this for him. It wasn't his fault his mother was a fool. She couldn't be that stupid ever again. Because it wasn't just her now. Everything she did would impact her son.

After Sally and Elaine left, after many hugs and thanks and Ian having gone down for a nap, Mickie caught Tiana's hand. She couldn't continue with her lies. Not after this. "Do you need to head out now?"

"Not really. What's up?"

"I lied to you," she said.

Tiana put the last of the party dishes in the dishwasher and turned, wiping her hands on a towel. "Please tell me you lied about not jumping Josh's bones and now you're going to give me a play-by-play."

"No. About why I'm all alone."

Tiana went very still. "It wasn't your parents?"

"God, no. My parents are awesome. I don't know why I told that lie. It just came out."

"The truth is worse?"

Mickie twisted her hands together. She dropped her eyes to the floor, unable to look at Tiana. She nodded, not trusting her voice.

Tiana held up a finger. "Hold on. I'm thinking this confession needs a wee sip of something."

"I can't drink in the middle of the day!" Mickie said. But even as the words left her mouth, she made a face at the prissy, shocked tone of her voice.

"Come on. All them uppity-ups having white-wine lunches and you're saying we can't talk some hard truth without a sip or two?"

"Mimosas. I've got prosecco and orange juice."

"Deal."

It was harder now. Now that some time had passed between her spontaneous confession and the making of drinks. As they settled down in her new living room chairs, Mickie found herself wishing she'd just kept her big mouth shut.

"Tell me," Tiana said.

"I had to leave. Everything and everyone," she blurted out in a whisper before she lost her nerve.

"Mmm-hmm. Why am I thinking the next words out of your mouth are going to be 'there was this guy'?"

"Because there was. This guy. I was in my first year of college. Away from home for the first time. Naive, insecure, afraid, lonely."

"Oh, I know this story. How bad did it get?"

"Very bad." She dropped her voice so low Tiana had to lean forward to hear. "When I got pregnant, he wanted me to have an abortion. When I said no, he beat me bad enough to put me in the hospital and landed himself in jail for assault and battery."

"Jesus," Tiana whispered.

"I went back home. And somehow, no one knows how, he knew when I'd had the baby. He was out of jail, was supposed to stay away, but he came after me. I was there confidentially so my name wasn't on the door to my room. He went from room to room looking for me. I could hear him bellowing my name."

"Did he find you?"

"No, I took Ian and crawled into the little closet thing but he never got to my room. He pushed a nurse who tried to stop him. Security had to Taser him to get him to stop. The hospital charges were enough to put him in prison for a long time."

"May his worthless ass rot in there. Damn, woman, I thought I was strong. What you went through? And to keep going? That's some serious momma strength."

Mickie wiped at her eyes and Tiana got up to sit on the chair arm and pulled her into a one-armed embrace. "I didn't know I was going to stir up all that. I'm sorry."

"No. I couldn't keep lying to you. I can't keep pretending it didn't happen." Mickie shook her head as she reached for a tissue to wipe her streaming eyes. "It isn't only that. It's what happened next. It's why I'm here."

"There's *more*?" Tiana asked in a horrified tone.

"Not bad stuff. The nurses at the hospital got together and raised money to help me. One of the doctors was married to a lawyer and he got a judge to come to the hospital to change my name before we filed Ian's birth certificate so it would have the new name. Then some of the other units in the hospital found out and the nurses all either gave me baby stuff or donated money. It was enough for me to get far away and start over."

There was silence for a moment. Then, a wave of music as someone drove by, radio far too loud. Just part of life near campus. Mickie smiled, sipped her drink. Tiana leaned forward and looked at her directly.

"That's why you want to be a nurse."

"Partly. If I can help one person the way they helped me, maybe everything I went through will be worth it. And my labor nurse and postpartum nurses were so amazing. I want to do that."

Moving back to her own chair, Tiana shook her head. "Labor? Postpartum? No thank you. I have my limit, and putting my hands up there is definitely past it. Every nurse has her or his

Kryptonite." Mickie smiled at Tiana's completely grossed-out expression.

Mickie nodded, understanding. "But you'll look at someone in the ER with their arm hanging off," she said, a little twist of a smile on her lips.

"That's the beauty of nursing. Something for everyone."

They clinked glasses.

"Plus the money's pretty good for a single mother, huh?" Mickie asked.

"Yeah. Some people don't think so, but let me tell you, my parents never made more than ten, maybe fifteen thousand a year between the two of them. Nursing's going to make me very comfortable. Rich compared to where I used to be."

Mickie sipped the makeshift mimosa and felt the weight of her secret lifting. She'd told the truth and it'd been okay. Tiana didn't look at her any differently. She let out a long slow breath in relief. A tension she didn't know she carried eased in her shoulders. There was an anchor on that relief, though. An anchor by the name of Wyatt Anderson. Private investigator. She'd never even really known they existed outside of movies and TV shows. Yet, not only did he exist, but he'd also gotten through adoption records to find Josh's sister. And if that was possible…

No. You can't think like that. It's done. You have to stop running and start building a life.

"I'm sorry I lied to you."

"Believe me, I understand. It's not an easy thing to overcome, much less tell people about. Something like that... Did you get help? You know, dealing with it?"

Mickie shrugged. "Some. When I started taking college classes and had access to the infirmary, I got some medicine. For the posttraumatic stress stuff."

"Antidepressants?"

"Yes. I'm off them now. Weaned off about a year ago, but I still have Xanax for panic attacks."

"When was your last panic attack?"

"It's been a while."

"That's a lie."

Tiana had her there. The whole private-investigator thing had thrown her for a loop. She sipped her mimosa and sighed. "Okay. Occasionally. Not full-out panic attacks. And I've managed them without medication. Breathing. Meditating. Positive self talk."

"Okay. Thank you for telling me the truth."

"You won't tell anyone?"

"No. But you should know Elaine left her abusive husband. There are more women like you out there than you know. It's not your fault. It's his."

"I know that. But I also know now how abusers choose their victims. There is something in me that he knew he could take advantage of."

Tiana pointed a finger at her. "And the day you know what that is and fix it? That's the day no man will ever mess with you again."

"Yeah," she said. She wasn't sure if she was ready to start probing in that particular wound. "Until then, I think I'll follow your advice and just leave men until after nursing school."

Tiana downed the rest of her mimosa in a gulp. "Truth."

CHAPTER TEN

HE COULD HEAR her voice through the walls. Not clearly enough to make out the words, only the steady, sweet rhythm. By the sound of it, she was giving Ian a bath, and then she must have been reading him a bedtime story, because everything went soft and soothing, a peaceful kind of low drone. He walked into the kitchen, where he couldn't hear it anymore. Where he didn't picture Mickie with her hair pulled up in a ponytail, no makeup yet still beautiful, tending sweetly to her son. He pulled open the fridge and peered in. Grabbing a bottle of water, he twisted off the cap and moved restlessly to the living room. His side of the duplex was silent. Good. He liked silent.

Stretching out on the couch, he sipped the water. Setting the bottle aside, he tried to meditate. Just sit, the way he'd been taught, all those years ago, and try to clear his mind. He started by pulling in a breath, letting it sink way deep down inside him. Amazing how much the simple act of breathing could do. It could, he knew, help him let go of the thoughts vying for his attention. But he couldn't quite let go. He was still feeling the sting of Sadie's words. Still feeling the simmering anger in his gut that he'd hidden from Jules.

Just because Sadie had settled down, was ready to take on motherhood and marriage, now she wanted everyone to join her. He had enough to deal with, thank you very much. Like setting up a business. Like trying to figure out what he was going to do about his sister.

Kimmie. All his life, he'd told himself he only wanted to know if she was safe. Now it wasn't enough. He wanted to talk to her, to know her. He wanted someone to belong to. A real family.

Realizing his teeth were clenched, he relaxed his jaw. Problem was she seemed so normal. And he was so…not. Maybe if he wrote to her adoptive parents? They would know if she knew. Knew about him. About their parents. Rubbing a hand across his eyes, he let out a breath. *Yeah, stupid idea.* They knew Kim's past. And to have her brother show up out of the blue? It would probably scare the hell out of them. Contact Kim and throw a black shadow on her upcoming wedding? He'd be as welcome as a roach on the wedding cake.

He stood, shaking his head as if he could shake loose the thoughts. "I don't have any answers, so shut up," he mumbled out loud. That was the thing about meditation. It was an excellent tool, but it didn't solve everything. Sometimes, the mind was just a mess and you just had to roll with that.

He had intended to go back to the kitchen to find something to eat. Instead, he found himself at Mickie's back door. Hmm. Interesting. He tapped lightly on the glass and some of him—most of him—hoped that she wouldn't hear. But after a moment, he saw a flicker of the blinds and he heard the door being unlocked.

"Hey! You made it back okay," Mickie said. She opened the door wider, inviting him in.

He squinted at her. She looked different. Her hair was up in the ponytail just as he'd imagined. No makeup. Same walking shorts and T-shirt combo she usually wore at home. It was her smile and her eyes that were different. Brighter. Happier. More relaxed.

"How're things going?" he asked. Looked around. There was a dining room set. That was new.

"Great! Better than great. Look." She pointed at the dining room set. "My mentor at school arranged all this." Her fingers closed around his hand and he let himself be pulled into the living room. "Furniture! Like a real person."

He looked around, exquisitely aware that she'd

not let go of his hand. "Your mentor gave you all this?"

"No. A bunch of the senior nursing students got together and donated different things. Isn't that amazing?"

"Yeah. Amazing."

She let go of his hand and moved to the center of the small living room. He flexed his fingers, rubbing the tips across the spot on his palm where her fingers had rested.

"I have not only one, but two actual chairs in which to sit." She gestured at the chairs in a sweeping motion, as if showing off prizes on a game show. She sat with a flourish and crossed her legs at the knee. Another sweeping motion. "A table upon which to rest a beverage."

He laughed. He had to. The transformation was incredible. He thought maybe he was looking at the real Mickie Phillips. Not the scared, worried-out-of-her-mind, stressed-out Mickie of the past few weeks.

She looked up when she heard him laugh. Her eyes went wide and she jumped to her feet, fists on her hips. "But wait. There's more!" She flung her arm out. "A television stand." She pointed with the other hand. "A box of books. Nursing uniforms!"

A bed? The question rose in his mind unbidden as she crossed the few steps between them.

The urge to undo that ponytail and watch her hair fall around her shoulders followed the thought. She stopped in front of him and he looked down into her eyes. Happy. Her presence—the fact that she was almost bouncing off the walls with joy—suddenly made him feel his own black cloud even more strongly. He realized she was waiting for him to say something. *Uh.*

He looked around. "It was really nice of them to do this."

"I know. I love it. This is the second time a group of nurses has..." The words stopped suddenly and he looked back to her. There was a brief flicker of the old Mickie and when she met his gaze, some of her joy was gone. "So, how was your trip?"

He blinked at the rapid shift in topic. "Oh, uh. It was okay."

"Okay?"

"Yeah." She was too close. Maybe that's why he couldn't form a coherent thought. He should go. Home. Away from her.

Her hand was back. Fingers lightly closing on his wrist. "Josh? What's wrong?"

"Huh?" He stepped back and shook his head to clear it. "Nothing. Tired. I should probably get back."

He looked down as she closed her other hand around his wrist. Could she not feel that? The continuous loop of heat circling between them? With a twist of the wrist, he captured her hands and held them loosely.

"Are you sure?"

"Yes, Nurse Mickie," he said, forcing a smile. "I'm fine. Just need about ten hours of sleep."

He dropped her hands reluctantly and made his way toward the back door. She followed him. "Well, then, straight to bed with you. Nurse's orders."

At the door, he turned to her. "Thank you."

She looked surprised. "For what?"

"For caring."

Seriously? Where had that come from? *Go home, Josh. You're making a fool of yourself.*

The worried frown creased her features again. "Hey." She stopped his retreat by grabbing a fistful of his shirt. "What's going on? And don't say nothing. And don't say you're tired."

He stared at her. Her frown disappeared as her eyebrows rose in an I'm-waiting-for-an-answer expression. What was he going to say? That he'd screwed up again? Lost his temper again? That his thoughts were racing around his brain like rats in a barrel and he couldn't make it stop? "It's really nothing, Mickie. I just… The visit didn't go as planned."

She released her grip on his shirt. "What does

that mean? Business-wise? Is it something with the Crew? Anything I can help with?"

He shook his head. "No. Not that. Just personal stuff."

"Oh. Okay. Again, anything I can help with? I'm a pretty good listener."

"No." *Actually, hell no.* She was the last person he'd tell. He rubbed a hand across his mouth as he realized how curt he'd sounded.

"Okay." She reached out and her fingers closed lightly around his biceps and traced down his arm to his hand. "We haven't known each other very long, but I think of you as a friend, Josh. You've helped me so much. I just want you to know that if there's anything I can do to help you, I'm here."

He closed his fingers around hers and slipped his arm around her shoulders, pulling her close so she wouldn't see the sudden flood of emotion he'd felt. She had no idea. If he told her the truth, she would go—should go—running far away. "Thank you," he finally said.

"I mean it." Her words vibrated against his chest. The feel of a warm body against his. The scent of her hair. The touch of her hands as they skimmed around his waist to link together, holding him in place. For a moment, all the confusion and regret and pain faded away. Being with her felt like stepping out of a shrieking wind and into a quiet moment of peace.

"I know," he whispered in her ear. "Thank you."

She leaned back to look up at him. He couldn't meet her gaze. Instead he focused on her lips. Pink. The lower lip fuller than the top. Pretty. He wondered what it would be like to kiss them.

"Josh," she said.

He kissed her. Whatever she was going to say, he didn't want to hear. He just wanted this moment of peacefulness to continue. He felt her hands grab at the back of his shirt, but she didn't move away from the brief touch of their lips. For a moment, he felt her breath against his mouth before her lips met his.

Desire and need flared to an unexpected degree at her hesitant kiss. Tightening his arms around her, he kissed her again. He touched at the corner of her lips with his tongue and she opened immediately for him. A soft, vibrating groan spread through his chest as their tongues met. Her hands moved up his back and through his hair, fingers gripping at his curls, holding him there. He heard her moan…and then a faint wail.

The kiss broke as suddenly as it had begun. Ian's cries grew louder as they stared in stunned disbelief at each other. Mickie raised a trembling hand to her lips.

"I should..."

"Yeah, me, too..."

He stumbled out the back door and hurried the few feet to his side of the duplex. *She has a kid, man. What the hell?*

He stood a moment on his patio, hands on hips, looking up at the half moon, pale and washed-out in the sky, trying to concentrate on the sounds of a summer evening. There was a brief *whoop* of a police siren. Someone down the street was trying to get the lawn mowed before the sun set. Cicadas. Always the cicadas. When the urge to return to Mickie's kitchen left him, he stepped inside his own kitchen.

IAN HAD AWOKEN happy and chatty. Mickie not so much. She'd spent most of the night staring at the ceiling, in alternating throes of horrified embarrassment and astounded lust. Her body's reaction to Josh's kiss and the feel of him against her was something she'd never felt before.

The early morning rush for caffeine and getting Ian to the day care had taken her mind off it for a while. But now as she walked back to the duplex, she felt dread weighing down each step. *What are you going to say? Sorry? It was a mistake? Let's pretend it never happened? Yeah, that's a good one. Let's go with that.*

The duplex came into view and she came to a stop on the sidewalk. *No way.* There was no way she could go in there. It wasn't that he'd pulled her into his arms as if he was seeking comfort. It wasn't that he'd kissed her. It was that *she* had kissed *him*. She should have stepped back. She should have done a dozen things. The one thing she shouldn't have done—grab his hair and pull him back for another kiss. Well, that was exactly what she'd done.

You're pathetic.

A car pulled into the driveway with a kind of slow confidence, newly washed and shining in the sun. When the driver's-side door opened, DeShawn climbed out. He waved at her, a big smile on his face as he recognized her. "You okay over there?"

Yes! Perfect! Hey, there was an idea. She'd walk in with DeShawn and surely Josh wouldn't say anything with another guy there. *Right?*

"Yeah," she called back. "Wait up a second."

DeShawn met her at the front door and held it open for her. Even better, she thought as she crossed the threshold and saw all the guys sitting around the living room. Josh blocked the doorway between the living room and kitchen, leaning casually against the wall, arms crossed.

Damn it. She felt the heat of a blush forming on her cheeks. *Don't look in his eyes. Don't look...*

"Good morning," he said. The words were very carefully neutral. She looked. He turned away the moment her gaze met his. "Okay. Now that everyone is here, let's start this staff meeting."

She slipped past him to the kitchen and he moved into the living room. This was promising. Maybe he wanted to go the pretend-it-didn't-happen route. That would suit her just fine. She would hide out in here and soon they would all leave.

"You, too, Mickie," Josh called from the living room.

She tried for an inconspicuous spot to lean against the wall. But no. When you were the only woman in a room full of Southern men, that wasn't going to happen. Josh sat in a chair borrowed from the dining room table. DeShawn was in the armchair. The other three—two new hires and Aaron from the Charleston office—sat on the couch. Every single stinking one of them leaped up to offer her a seat.

She quickly crossed to the armchair and mumbled a thank-you to DeShawn. At least she wouldn't be in Josh's direct line of sight.

"I don't think so," DeShawn said as the three

others returned to the couch. "Last hired gets the floor."

"Drake," Josh said to the displaced guy. "Just go get another chair."

While they waited, Josh thumbed through a small notebook. A muscle in his cheek jumped and twitched. He was nervous, Mickie realized. It was a bit of a shock. He always seemed so in control. *Except last night.* She dropped her gaze to her hands.

Josh cleared his throat as Drake returned with a chair. "Okay. Well, welcome to the first Columbia branch staff meeting. Drake and Travis, you two are the newest members of the Crew. Welcome aboard. You've both met DeShawn. This is Aaron. He's going to be up a few times a week to help out until we get you two trained and hire another guy."

He turned the page in his notebook.

"And Mickie," DeShawn said.

Josh looked up at her. His gaze met hers and she was happy the guys would think the blush she felt glowing hot on her face was due to being singled out. Especially when DeShawn began clapping out the oh-so-familiar beat of the song "Mickey."

"Hey, Mickie!"

She rolled her eyes. "Like I've not heard that ten billion times before."

"Mickie is going to be with us until she starts school in the fall," Josh said, cutting across the banter. "The plan is to have you guys trained so I can take back over most of the office work until we grow enough to move into a real office and hire a full-time office manager."

"When will that be?" Nate asked.

Mickie relaxed back in the armchair as she watched Josh lead the meeting. As he outlined the plan for growth, both in customer base and employees, she began to realize just what he'd taken on. She had done a Google search. She knew how popular the Cleaning Crew was in Charleston. She knew the reputation it had for excellent service that had nothing to do with the gimmick of sexy guys vacuuming your rugs. And it was his responsibility to re-create that success here in Columbia. No pressure.

Much like herself, he was starting over in a new city. Facing a new challenge. Maybe that's all this was. Just two people sort of in the same boat. Nervous and unsure. He didn't want to let his boss down. So, they needed to just forget about that whole kiss thing. Concentrate on being friends. Yes. That was it. Friends. She crossed her arms and felt her head nodding in agreement with her own thoughts. Because she couldn't be stupid anymore. She had to be smart and focused. Ian was depending on her. Her goal was in sight. Four semesters and she would have financial security for herself and Ian. That had to happen. No matter what she had to give up to get it.

JOSH HAD BEEN happy to escape the duplex. He'd made sure DeShawn and Aaron had everything they needed to start orienting the two new guys. Navigating around a strange city was the most challenging aspect of planning out cleaning schedules. Jobs needed to be close together or follow the shortest path. No running from one side of town to the other. After that, he'd spent the morning and early afternoon meeting with prospective new clients.

And now there was no way to put it off. He had office stuff to do. He was going to have to go back. Face Mickie. Alone. He still had no idea what he was going to say to her. She'd been skittering around like a scared bird this morning.

He leaned his head back and closed his eyes. Why had he kissed her? *Stupid. Stupid. Stupid.* His head bounced off the back of the car seat with each thought. A hug. Yeah, that would have shown her that he was happy for her and the good deed her friends had done. But the kiss. That had been selfish. He'd used her to calm the cacophony in his mind.

And she kissed you.

A long sigh slipped from his lips. *Yeah. Why'd she done that?* He knew his reasons. He didn't know hers. *God. What if she was interested? In a daddy-for-her-baby kind of way?* The sigh turned into a groan. He started the engine. Only way to deal with this was head-on. Nip it in the bud. Sorry. Mistake. Never happen again. Simple.

She was on the phone when he let himself in. Good. Gave him a minute. He hesitated just inside the front door. He could just make a break for his office in the second bedroom. Ignore the entire situation. That sounded like a great plan. Taking a deep breath, he shook his head. No. Delaying was going to make it worse. He walked to the kitchen.

Mickie's gaze flickered up at him for a millisecond before returning to whatever she was writing on a notepad. A faint pink stained her cheeks, but her voice did not waver as she continued the phone conversation. Another chance to go hide in his office. It took a good bit of willpower to remain in the kitchen until she ended the call and reluctantly looked up at him.

"Hi," she said.

"Hey."

And it just hung there between them. All the words he should be saying. The gulf growing and expanding as each second was audibly clicked off by that coffee-cup-shaped clock the previous tenant had left.

She squared her shoulders and clutched her hands together on the table top. "Listen, I'm sorry about last night."

He felt his jaw drop. Of the dozens of things he'd imagined she might say, an apology had never made the list.

"No," he finally said. "No. That was me. I'm just— I just— I don't know."

"I do."

Again, he stared at her, flabbergasted. She tucked a wayward strand of hair behind her ear and met his gaze squarely. Only the deepening of the pink on her cheeks indicated she wasn't as calm and cool as she seemed.

"What?"

"Last night. Look, Josh. This is what it is. We're both in a strange, new city. We're both facing a new, scary challenge. You're trying to start up a new business. I'm about to start a very difficult college program. I don't know about you, but I'm terrified. I have so much riding on succeeding and graduating from nursing school."

His shoulders relaxed as relief coursed through him at her words. *Sure. Okay. This would work.* "Yeah, that's true."

She stood and crossed the kitchen to him, arms crossed tightly against her chest. The pink of her blush was gone. "So we had a moment of weakness. It's okay."

"Moment of weakness," he mumbled back. Because even as his head was nodding, he could smell her. Smell the shampoo or whatever it was that she used. His moment of weakness was coming back pretty strong.

"Yep. So. We know that. I'd like to think we can be friends, Josh. Help each other out. Support each other while we adjust to our new lives here. We just can't..."

Can't what? Let this atomic-level heat get in the way of being buddies? "Yeah, you're right. We've both got enough going on without, uh, complicating things."

"Exactly. Great! I knew you'd understand."

"Of course." He glanced at the clock. "I'm going to be in for the rest of the day if you want to cut out early. Get some errands done or something before you have to get Ian from day care."

"Really? That would be nice. I'm trying to get all my study notes organized. Do some refreshing before starting school."

"Yeah, go on. See you tomorrow."

He stood rooted in place as she collected her things and left out the back door. He could still smell her. Muttering several curses under his breath, he found the bottle of Lysol. A few spritzes of that took care of the problem. He had work to do.

He was beginning to understand why Sadie would retreat to her office whenever she was under stress. Plowing through paperwork kept the mind from wandering to places it shouldn't be going. Mostly. The kiss wasn't what was nagging at him, though. No, it was her neat packaging of the entire mess into the mistake box. He should be relieved. He should be grateful she'd found a way to let them both off the hook and continue to be friends. And he was.

And you want to do it again.

He slumped back in the chair. His phone vibrated on the desk and he scooped it up, eager for the distraction. Wyatt's name on the caller ID completely squelched any thoughts of Mickie.

"Hey, man, what's up?"

"I'm getting ready to email you copies of the police reports," Wyatt said. "I just wanted to give you a heads-up."

"Okay. Thanks." His lips had gone numb. Actually all of him had gone numb.

"There's some information in there you might find helpful, but I gotta tell you, Josh, it's not a pleasant read. Take your time. Don't look at them until you are completely sure."

"Okay."

"You all right?"

Josh shook his head, trying to break through the sudden murk of feelings. He cleared his throat and ran a hand through his hair. "Yes. Well. Sort of. Thanks for the heads-up. I think I'll need some time to work up to reading it."

"Good. Sadie said she's coming up there on Friday to meet the new guys. She can stay the weekend if you want to have her there."

That wrenched a small smile out of him. Sadie. She'd saved him all those years ago. She'd seen through all of his sullenness, anger, bitterness and bad choices—just nodded and said, "Me, too." And with those two words, he'd been able to create an entire new reality for himself. A new life. A new Josh. And reading those police reports was going to rip a hole through to his old life.

"I'll let her know."

"Sure thing. Josh, call us, either of us, if you need us."

He ended the call and clicked through on the laptop to his email inbox. Yep. There it was. Subject line: Police report attached. He let the cursor hover over it for a moment before sliding it up and shutting down the computer. He leaned back in the chair, rubbing his hands across his face. Because Sadie wasn't the first person who had saved him.

Oh, sweet Jesus, save us all.

Those were the words his mother would yell out. It wasn't a prayer or a plea for divine intervention. No. It was his signal. When he heard those words, he would slip out of bed or out of the room, wherever he happened to be when the monster came. His job was to get his baby sister and protect her. Leave the trailer or hide. When it was all over, she would call for him to come out. Except the last time.

It was late. He remembered coming out of a deep sleep to the sounds of crashing furniture. When the warning was sounded, he got out of bed and, hugging the wall, made his way to Kimmie's room. She was getting big and it was hard for him to lift her out of the crib. Especially when she was sleepy and cranky. He hushed her, but was sure her soft whining wasn't louder than the screaming coming from the living room.

But there was something new. A loud cracking noise that silenced everything else. He remembered the primal terror that had filled him. He hadn't known what it was, but he knew it was very, very bad. He carried Kimmie to the closet and tucked them as tightly into the corner as he could. Shielding her body with his, he reached up and yanked down clothes to cover them. And waited. The eerie silence continued. Had they left? What was that noise?

Footsteps let him know that, no, they weren't

alone. The monster was still there. Light flooded the room as the monster flipped the switch. He expected the monster to call out for him. Tell him to "get his ass out here right now." But that never happened. His arms tightened around Kimmie and he pressed his cheek against hers. *Please don't cry. Please don't cry.*

After what seemed forever, the footsteps moved away, back toward the living room. He relaxed a little. The monster would fall asleep and his mother would tell them to come out. The second loud cracking noise made him jump. The jerking woke Kimmie and she began to whine. He shushed her again, waiting for the signal to come.

But it never came. He waited. Soon the complete silence inside the trailer was broken by sounds he did know. Police sirens. Knocks on the door. Shouted orders of police officers. Now there were more footsteps in the trailer, accompanied by crackling radios. He didn't know what to do. Police were the good guys. But his mother hadn't told him to come out yet. Outside the trailer, he heard the lady who lived next door say, "There are two kids in there."

A few minutes later, the closet door opened and a hand pulled back the cover of clothes. "Oh, little man, little man," a warm, rich voice said. "Who you got there? Your baby sister?"

Josh pushed away from the desk and stood. His shaking hands clenched the top of the chair as he took several slow, deep breaths to try to slow his racing heart. He'd shut that night away in the furthest, darkest corner of his mind and left it there. The sudden outpouring of memory overwhelmed him. The sense of suffocation under the pile of clothes, the sweet smell of Kimmie's hair, it all came back. The ice-cold terror. All of it closed in on him.

Finally, as if in answer to his silent wish for guidance, the warmth of that cop's voice entered his mind again. The tender hands that lifted him and Kimmie from the closet. It was like a splash of cold water, waking him up from the dream, the nightmare, the cold place he'd already begun to let seep into him. Everything had been wrong and now, all of a sudden, there was kindness, and he didn't even know why.

He slammed the chair against the desk. Heart pounding, he spun around, looking for something, anything, to hit, to destroy. *The bastard. Murderous cowardly son of a bitch.* The sound of the front door opening was the only reason he didn't punch a hole through the wall. *Get yourself together.*

"Hey, Josh, you back there, man?"

Calm washed over him at the sound of DeShawn's voice. A surface-deep calm, but enough of a facade that he could act normally. Just as he'd done most of his life. Act. He left the office. "You all done for the day?"

"Yep. Unless you've got something for me to do?"

"No. Wait. Yeah. I let Mickie go a little early. Can you hang out for a while? I really want to get to the gym before the after-work crowd shows up."

DeShawn flopped down on the couch. "Not a problem. Go get some lifting in. You're starting to look flabby. Been meaning to say something."

"Right, dude. You might want to work that core while you're lazing around on my couch. Looking like a busted can of biscuits over there."

DeShawn pointed a middle finger at him and Josh laughed as he grabbed his gym bag and headed out the door. The familiar feeling of the back-and-forth trash talk calmed him enough that he no longer wanted to put a fist through Sheetrock, but he still couldn't wait to pull on some gloves and go a few dozen rounds with the punching bag.

He'd known digging around in this was going to stir up old feelings. He hadn't realized how strong and fresh those feelings were going to be. *Talk to Sadie.* Problem was, once he got Sadie involved, she wouldn't let him quit. She'd want him to see it through to the end. And he wasn't sure he had the strength to do it. He'd spent years disciplining himself. Yoga. Meditation. Martial arts. Learning to calm his mind and control his body. But when the dark things came slipping out of the corners of his mind, he was still as helpless as the five-year-old boy he'd been. And helplessness made him furious. And the monster lived in the fury.

Can you face this and not release the monster? He didn't know. It seemed like his only choice was to continue living this half life or risk destroying everything and losing everyone.

CHAPTER ELEVEN

THE STACK OF index cards was six inches high. Mickie knew this because she'd measured it. The stack represented every class she'd taken, every test she'd taken, all the accumulated biology, chemistry, human anatomy, physiology, psychology knowledge she'd crammed into her brain over the past two years of taking prerequisite classes for nursing school.

And she couldn't remember a thing. And she was going to completely fail. And she'd end up as a waitress at the Waffle House on night shift, start smoking and live in a trailer park her whole life. She smacked her hands over her face with a groan.

"What's all this?"

"My doom," she said, dramatically collapsing forward and pretending to pound her head on the table.

"Sounds serious. Am I going to need a new secretary or is this doom still to come?"

Mickie straightened and huffed out a sigh as Josh crossed the kitchen to perch on the edge of the table. His voice was warm with humor but the small smile lurking at the corners of his mouth didn't match the look in his eyes. Maybe it was because he was still weirded out by the kiss.

He reached out and took a card off the top of the stack. "Diastolic pressure?"

"The minimum arterial pressure when the, uh… During the relaxation and dilatation of the ventricles… When they are filling with blood?"

"You're asking me?" He flipped over the card and read the answer. "Yep. Perfect. I think your doom isn't quite as close as you think."

"I hope not. Tiana is bringing me some study guides she used for her first year. Apparently, I need to be prepared to hit the ground running from day one and it doesn't stop until I graduate."

"Huh. I think you'll be fine." He picked up another card. "Nature versus nurture?"

"Easy to answer. Difficult to know. But it's the question of whether your genetic makeup or the environment you were raised in has more influence on the kind of person you become."

She smiled up at him. Somehow it was easier to come up with the answers when another person was asking her. Her smile faded at the look on Josh's face. Any trace of humor or teasing was gone. He flipped over the card and stared at the answer on the back. A frown creased his forehead as he replaced the card on the stack.

"Josh? You okay?"

"Me? Yeah. Great. Listen, I gotta get going. Not much happening today, so hopefully you can get some studying in. DeShawn is coming by later to interview a couple of guys, that's about it."

He was gone before she could ask anything more. Because the question on the card had triggered something in him. She clapped her hands over her face. *Of course. He was in foster care, you dork. Maybe you could have worded that a little better.* She secured the cards with a giant rubber band and shoved them back in her backpack. Grabbing a clipboard, she tried to quiet the stings of guilt by doing the most boring of her duties: counting inventory.

By noon, she had all the office duties completed. As she ate her lunch of a bologna sandwich and potato chips, she propped her feet up on a half-open file cabinet drawer and flipped through the study cards. Glomerular filtration in nephrons. *Got it.* Blood types. Red blood cells, white blood cells. *Easy cheesy.* Immune response. B cells. T cells. *Yep, yep and yep.* Peripheral somatosensation. *What the what?* She flipped over the card. *Oh, yeah. Sure.*

The front door opened. She glanced at the

clock. "Hey, DeShawn," she called out. "Your interviews aren't here yet. But do you know what the hell the Krebs cycle is?"

"It's the main metabolic pathway in aerobic organisms and the number-one cause of complete mental breakdown in nursing students."

Mickie spun around in the chair. "Tee!"

Tiana crossed the room to drop a box on the table. It landed with an ominously loud thud. "Look at you, Miss Cutie on Duty! All kicked back and relaxing with a stack of anatomy cards like a good little paranoid nursing student." She looked over her shoulder and turned back to Mickie. "Where's all the hot dudes?"

Mickie laughed and stood to begin pawing through the box. "All out working."

Tiana smacked at Mickie's hand. "Hold up. Don't be messing up my system. Each file represents a class. In each, there is the class syllabus along with my own study guide and notes. They are color-coded by semester. First semester is the red files. Second semester is the blue files."

"Now who's the paranoid nursing student?"

"Yeah, well, I'll let you in on a secret. The paranoid, overprepared types are the ones who make it. You can't half-ass or fake anything. And this is just the class work. Clinicals are a whole other experience. Nothing can prepare you for that."

"Yeah, I'm most afraid of that. Like they really are going to let me take care of sick people? Me? What if I kill someone?"

"You won't. I hope. It's a balancing act. You want to be positive, eager to learn and help the nurse, but you don't want to get in the way. You will have one patient, the nurse may have up to five."

"I just hope none of them yell at me and make me cry."

Tiana laughed. "That may happen. I've been lucky. The whole nurses-eating-their-young thing isn't really as prevalent, I think. I've not had any bad experiences in clinicals with nurses. Most have been very helpful and wanted to show me and teach me. The worst was they seemed too busy to really let me try to do things."

The front door opened again and a voice sang out, "Hey, Mickie!"

Mickie rolled her eyes. "Not funny anymore, DeShawn."

"Oh, Mickie..." DeShawn's teasing words stuttered to a halt as he entered the kitchen. His gaze drifted over Tiana. "Hello."

"Eyes up here, man maid."

Mickie smothered a giggle at Tiana's no-

nonsense tone. Because she was ogling DeShawn just as much as he was eyeing her.

A slow, sexy grin spread across DeShawn's lips. Mickie's eyebrows rose. Hot. He stepped forward and offered a hand. "DeShawn Adams."

"Tiana Nelson."

"Tiana is my support person for nursing school, DeShawn. She's starting her last semester. And DeShawn is just helping us out for a while, Tee. He graduated with a degree in engineering and is going to join the US Army Corps of Engineers."

Why she was babbling her brains out, she didn't know. Probably because the two of them were just standing there, staring at each other. *Awkward.*

Tiana pulled her hand from DeShawn's grip with a frown. She turned to Mickie. "Girl, I gotta go. Let me know if you need anything else. I've got the books, but you know how they change them every year. Show me the list before you buy any."

"Don't run off on my account," DeShawn teased.

Tiana shot him her best withering stare. "Get a hold of yourself, man. I ain't doing nothing on account of *you.*"

DeShawn laughed as she left. "I think she likes me. Don't you?"

Mickie tried out her nurse scowl. "I think you're insane."

"I think you're cute when you try to look mean."

"I think you should go get ready to do your interviews."

He gave her a quick, snappy salute. "Yes, ma'am. By the way, you got Nurse Ratched's number?"

She gave him her own one-finger salute. "I think she's got *your* number, DeShawn. Besides, she's told me herself she doesn't have time for men."

"I don't have time, either, to tell the truth. I'll be back in the office waiting on the interviews."

Mickie watched as he left the room. No time. Wrong time. Sounded a lot like her situation with Josh.

MICKIE MANAGED TO keep her hands off the box of study material until after she'd gotten Ian to bed. When she was sure he was good and asleep, she splashed some wine into a cup. *Wineglasses.* Nestling down in the comfiest of the donated armchairs, she propped her feet on the coffee table. *One day I'll have real wineglasses.*

One day. What a nice place this was going to be. With its matching furniture, dish sets and wineglasses. Beds with mattresses. Cars that didn't break down. Yep, one day was going to be awesome.

A small smile played on her lips and she let herself dream. Something she tried to avoid. No sense building up hopes that might be dashed. But she could see it. A little house. She didn't need anything fancy. A cute little cottage in a nice school district. Maybe a park nearby where Ian and his puppy could play. Maybe a Labrador. They were supposed to be good dogs for kids.

She glanced down at the box with a sigh. All that stood between her and one day was in that box. That box, classes, tests. Days spent in the hospital actually providing care for patients. After all that, she would have to pass the big NCLEX test to get her license. And the cherry on top of this mountain was she'd have to pass entry testing at almost any hospital she applied for a job at. She put down the wine.

One day might be closer now than ever, but the obstacles were higher than ever. And she was going to have to climb every single last one of them. The no-men-while-in-school idea was only half-serious. The last two years were going to take all the energy, time and focus she could muster. Taking care of Ian was the only other thing that was going to be possible.

"Well, then. Let's get started," she said out loud. The bigger the head start she could get, the less chance of falling behind. First up—pharmacology. *What the hell is this?* It looked like gibberish. She flipped through the syllabus, her heart pounding, hands shaking. Tiana's notes were neat and orderly and she still didn't understand a single word on the pages. She fumbled for her phone.

"I can't do this."

"Put the pharmacology down, Mickie."

"Tee..."

"Why'd you go straight to the worst of it? Mickie, put it down. Go look at the pathophysiology. You'll actually recognize words there."

"I..."

"I'm going to say one thing and then I'm hanging up on you. This is what you will be taught. You don't have to know all this before you start. I gave those to you to help you while you are in school. Do not use them to freak yourself out or I will come over there and take it all away. Got it?"

"Okay."

Mickie dropped the phone in her lap and put the pharmacology notes away. Pathophysiology. *Because that sounds so much better.* Rolling her eyes, she pulled out the file. *Okay. See. This isn't so bad.* Nodding, she ran a finger along the class outline. Basically it was everything that could go wrong with the human body. Sort of the flip side of all the anatomy and physiology she'd learned. That was all. The phone buzzed in her lap and she snatched it up, thinking it was Tiana calling back.

Unknown number. She hesitated for a moment. *Never answer unknowns.* But it was local. Might be the school or the day care or one of the other nurses she'd met. She set down the phone. That's what voice mail was for.

CHAPTER TWELVE

"WHAT ARE YOU being so fidgety about?"

Josh stopped wiping down the kitchen counter and looked over at Mickie. "I'm not fidgeting. I'm cleaning."

"Dude. I'm the mother of a toddler. I know what fidgeting looks like."

He stashed the cleaning supplies away with a sigh. He *was* fidgeting. Sadie was on the way to meet the new hires. He hadn't realized how much her approval meant to him until now. How much he depended on her. Owed her. He hadn't spoken to her since their argument. He'd left Charleston without resolving it with her and he knew she was going to want to finish that conversation.

"I'm just getting the place cleaned up before Sadie gets here."

"What's she like?"

The question caught him off guard. *What was Sadie like? The new one or the old one?* "She's tough, but fair. Doesn't take bullshit or excuses."

"Are you worried we won't be up to her standards?"

Josh leaned against the counter, arms crossed against his chest, and looked at Mickie. A small worry line appeared on her forehead. "No. Not you guys. Me. Sadie and I have a, I don't know… a complicated relationship."

Mickie's worried look transformed to one of curiosity. "Complicated?"

"Yeah. Oh. No! Not like that. God, no. She was raised in foster care, too. We consider ourselves brother and sister. But she's also my boss. And I don't want to let her down."

Mickie crossed the kitchen to him and put her warm hands on his shoulders. He couldn't breathe when she was so close to him. When those ice-blue eyes looked directly into his. "You won't. Didn't you say the business was growing faster than you anticipated? That's good, right?"

"Yeah."

"Just *yeah*?" Her hands dropped from his shoulders. "Don't tell me you're one of those *über*competitive men who has to be better than everyone else."

That made him laugh. A short, bitter laugh. "No, Mickie, the only person I compete with is myself."

"Boss is here," DeShawn called from the living room.

Showtime. Josh pushed himself away from the counter and went out to meet Sadie.

The gathered Crew members were in stunned awe. Josh smiled as he took in their faces as Sadie captivated the room. She made them feel as if they'd won the lottery, not gotten a job as a maid. They were the few, the elite, the Crew.

"All right," Sadie said after giving her pep talk. "I'll let y'all get back to work. Josh? Let's take a look at the books."

Like a fool, he had dared to believe for a moment Sadie was going to keep the visit purely business. But the moment the office door closed on them, she plopped down in his chair, toed open a desk drawer and propped up her feet.

"So, Wyatt told me he sent you the police files. Have you looked at them yet?"

He sat. "Some."

"What do you think you're going to find there, Josh? You know what happened."

Anger bubbled up but he pushed it back down. "I don't know. I'm just grabbing at straws, Sadie. I don't know what I should do."

"What do you want to do?"

Great question. One that became murkier every day. "I want to not have to deal with this.

I want to have had a different life. But I can't. This is my life. This is who I am. Kim escaped it. I didn't. I want to not be selfish. I don't want to want to know her."

Sadie stared at him steadily. "You did escape it, Josh."

"No. I didn't. It's there. It's always there."

"What? Anger? Anger is normal, Josh. Everyone gets angry."

"Not everyone punches a hole through it two inches from the face of the woman you said you loved."

Sadie's face went stony and her eyes closed down to slits. His heart was pounding and he had to concentrate to slow the ragged breathing. Consciously unclench his fists and jaw. Sadie looked away with a deep sigh of her own.

"It happened, Sades," he said in a low voice. "I can't pretend it didn't. I am my father's son. Nurture and nature."

She looked back at him. "What the hell does that mean?"

"Nature is in your genes. Nurture is the environment you grew up in. My father was a violent, wife- and kid-beating monster. I lived in that environment the first five years of my life."

"Oh, so that automatically makes you a wife-beating monster?"

"I've already abused one woman. I won't abuse another."

"Josh. You were eighteen. Tossed out on the street. Just trying to survive. Ruby had her own issues. Both of you were young and angry. Neither of you had any coping skills. That you didn't hit her only proved that you aren't your father."

"Still. It was there. It's still there."

Sadie threw up her hands. "I can't even talk to you when you're like this."

"Like what? Telling the truth?"

"Playing the martyr." Her voice raised in a parody of woe. "I'm so mean! I must never allow anyone to love me! I'll stay alone and lonely all my life!"

"I'm going to go talk to the cop. The one who found Kimmie and me that night."

That cut through her dramatics. "Why?"

He shrugged. "I don't know. I just feel like I should do it. Just like how you felt you needed to face your mother. I have no one to face, Sadie. You forced your mother to confess her wrongs. Maybe the cop knows something. I don't know."

"Okay. I'm sorry. I get needing answers, Josh. You know I understand that. But I've known you a long time and I've watched you heal and grow into a good man. I want you to see that in yourself, too. It can't make the other stuff go away, but you can't ignore that you've created an entirely new, better life."

"I do. It's just still there. Like some dark spot that I can feel inside me still. I want it to go away."

Sadie dropped her feet and rolled the chair closer to him. She took his hands in hers and looked into his eyes. "It will, Josh," she said in a rough whisper. "It will. And I'll be here for you no matter what it takes. You're my baby brother and I love you. That will never change."

FINDING RETIRED NORTH CHARLESTON police officer Nathaniel Gathers required Wyatt's aid, and his address had been easily procured. Finding the actual house was a different story. A number on a back country road. Mailboxes were few and far between, and Josh slowed the Harley at each one. The landscape was an unrelenting repetition of farmland, woodland, farmland, woodland. Occasional dirt roads broke off, heading to the farmhouses presumably. His GPS dinged off a warning as he rounded a curve. He brought the motorcycle to a halt. There at the edge of another dirt road was a mailbox, neatly painted bright white with stark black numbers. The same numbers he was looking for.

His heart began a hard pulse in his chest as his fingers clenched on the handlebars. *Do you really want to do this? Just ride up there, knock on his door? What if he doesn't even remember? What could he say that would make any difference?*

He sat for a long minute or two staring at the road. It was so isolated out here and not a single car passed him as he summoned his courage. *Nothing to lose. If he doesn't remember, no harm, no foul. But maybe he knows something that will help. Maybe.*

He turned up the dirt drive careful to stay out of the ruts, going along at about ten miles per hour. The road was well maintained and whatever the crop was that was growing in the field beside it was green and he could hear the cicadas even over the rumble of the engine. At the end of the road was a small, neat brick house with a long, wide front porch. As he puttered to a stop, an older black man stepped out on the porch.

The man shaded his eyes with his left hand, his right hand riding lightly on his hip. Josh turned off the engine and slowly removed his helmet. The guy was a retired cop living in the middle of nowhere. For all he knew, the strange white guy who rode up unannounced on a Harley probably had a gun stuffed in his waistband.

"Officer Gathers?" he asked as he swung off the motorcycle.

"Used to be," the man answered, coming down

the porch steps. He let his left hand drop and he squinted at Josh. "I know you?"

"Sort of."

"Did I arrest you?"

"No, sir."

The man stepped even closer. He tilted his head and squinted harder. "I do know you."

"From a long time ago."

Josh searched the man's face. Nothing about it seemed familiar. But the voice. That deep, mellow voice, rich with a country Southern accent. As he watched, the man's face changed. Something dawned in his expression and he held both his hands out to Josh.

"Little man," he whispered. He walked closer and put his hands on Josh's shoulders, looking up into Josh's face with dark brown eyes full of sadness. "Little man. You've been on my heart all these years."

The echo of those words—*little man*—hit him hard in the gut. Gathers pulled him into an embrace and Josh did something he'd never done since that horrible night. He cried. This man remembered him. Thought about him. He had meant something to this man. Meant enough to be remembered.

After a bit, Josh pulled back, wiping at his face with his arm. "I'm sorry. I didn't think..."

"Aw, ain't nothing. That was a night that left a

mark on all of us. Come on in the house. Clean yourself up a bit. I've got some good sweet tea. We can rock on the porch and talk."

AS JOSH SPLASHED his face with cold water, he couldn't quite look at himself in the mirror. The rush of emotion had shocked him. He remembered Sadie saying she'd felt invisible until she'd faced her mother. He hadn't understood it until just now. Someone knew about him. He'd been real to this man.

"Guess you're wondering about your family. What happened that night. How old are you now? Twenty-five? Twenty-six?" Mr. Gathers asked as they settled on the porch.

"Twenty-eight."

A long mournful whistle fled from Mr. Gathers's lips. "Time. It sure does pass."

"Yes, sir. It sure does."

"Tell me what you've been up to, little man."

Josh filled him in. The foster homes. The trouble fitting in. Finding Sadie. Building a new life. And now, finding his sister.

"Your momma and daddy were well known to the police."

"I figured that."

"Yeah. Your daddy tried. He'd get sober. Stay sober a few months and slip up again. Your mother was trying to get away."

"She was?" He'd never even considered the possibility.

"Yep. If I recall correctly, the time he hit her before that night, she took the information on how to get in touch with the women's shelter. You may not know this, but trying to leave an abusive man is the one thing most likely to get a woman killed."

Josh stared at Mr. Gathers. His face and hands felt oddly numb. "You think she told him she was leaving and that's why he…"

"I couldn't answer that," Mr. Gathers said with a slow roll of his shoulders. "The shelter doesn't encourage announcing it or using it as a threat to try to get the man to straighten up. If I had to guess, I think he found out about it somehow and that's what set him off."

"You think she was really leaving?"

"I talked to the director of the shelter as part of the investigation. But, yeah, she'd called and talked to them. She was planning to bring y'all there. She'd told the director you were both getting too old to watch what your daddy was doing."

"She did it for us."

The words slipped out softly. This was something completely new. Like a flare shot up into the darkness. His mother had tried to help them. Tried to save them. She had cared about them.

Cared about how they were living. Trying to save them was probably what had gotten her killed. But she'd saved Kim. Kim had gotten out before she could remember what had happened. Before she could be abused. Adopted. Loved. *And me, what did I get?* Ten families in thirteen years. Moved from house to house, school to school. Constant chaos. *But you were safe. No one beat you. You didn't witness beatings.*

"You in touch with your sister?"

"No. They separated us that night. I talked to my last social worker about it and she looked into it. She said it was because the emergency foster home available didn't take under-four-year-olds so she had to go to another county. We were never reunited. She got adopted. I've found her now but haven't approached her."

Mr. Gathers nodded. "Why not?"

"I don't know what to do. I want to know her. But she's about to get married and I don't want to just show up and ruin everything."

"Is that why you're here, son? To ask what you should do?"

"No. No, sir. I don't know why I'm here. I just needed to talk to someone who knew my parents, knew what happened. Try to get some sort of grasp on it."

"Did anything I say help?"

"Yes. It did. Immensely, actually. Just knowing my mother was trying to get us out of there… I don't know. I can see her differently now."

"I'm glad you came. I've thought of you all these years. My late wife and I talked about trying to get you, but before we could finish qualifying to be foster parents, she got the cancer."

Josh briefly touched the man's hand. "I'm so sorry for your loss."

Mr. Gathers nodded. "Thank you. It was a blow. We sure did want to get you. But after she was gone, I wasn't in any shape to take on a young boy."

"You wanted me, though. Why?"

"You just looked like a boy who needed a good momma and daddy. There was something good in you, Josh. I saw it that night. The way you protected your sister. Do you remember leaving the house?"

Josh shook his head. His memory went from Officer Gathers lifting him to his feet and picking up Kim, to sitting in a stranger's kitchen the next morning while a police officer asked him questions.

"I had to lead you out. Past the…past the bodies. You insisted I give your sister back to you. So I let you carry her. I thought it might help distract you, so you wouldn't see anything."

"I don't remember seeing anything."

Mr. Gathers shrugged. "I saw your eyes cut in that direction, but I was right beside you so maybe I blocked your view. But you turned your sister's face away. You made sure she didn't see. How's a five-year-old boy gonna know do to that unless he's got a mighty wide streak of loving kindness inside him?"

Josh sat back and sipped some tea to wash down the lump in his throat. He either hadn't seen anything or it was so repressed that his brain wasn't going to give him access to the memory. He'd known for some time that the reason he was moved around so much when he was younger was due to his anger. He'd acted out. *But, jeez, what kid wouldn't?* "I had a lot of trouble adjusting to foster care," he said. "I always thought I never got adopted because I was a bad kid."

Mr. Gathers laid a warm, strong hand on Josh's forearm. "Josh. Angry doesn't mean bad. And you had plenty to be angry about. But that little five-year-old boy was strong and brave and loved his sister and was taking care of her the best he could. That's a good heart. And you can't be bad if your heart is good."

"I don't know about that," Josh said with a laugh.

"I do. I saw a lot in thirty years. It comes down to heart. You got a good one or a bad one.

Now, good hearts can do little bad things and bad hearts can do little good things, but at the core, you either care about others or you only care about yourself. I think you know which side you fall on, son."

Josh smiled. "I'm still figuring that out, but I do know what side you fall on, Mr. Gathers. Thank you."

"Let me give you my number. Call me if you have any more questions."

They exchanged numbers and Josh stood to leave, reaching out to shake the man's hand.

"Anything else I can answer for you?" Mr. Gathers asked.

"Do you know where they are buried?"

The question took Josh by surprise. It'd just rolled out unbidden. He'd never even wondered about it before. But it seemed right now that it had been asked. It felt like the next step to take.

HE'D BARELY REACHED the end of Mr. Gathers's driveway when his phone rang. Sadie. Josh knew better than to not answer. He just wasn't sure if he wanted to talk to her yet. He shut off the engine.

"How'd it go?" she asked the second he answered.

He pulled the helmet off and ran a hand through his hair. "Okay. Good."

"Okay. Good. Wow. As well as all that, huh?"

"He remembered me."

"I'd guess so. A crime that like would stay with a person."

"No, Sadie. He remembered *me*. Stared at me for a minute and recognized me. Called me 'little man' just like he did the night he found us."

His throat burned and he put a hand across his eyes.

"Really? That's amazing."

He took a deep, calming breath. "I keep thinking about how you said facing your mother made you not feel invisible anymore. I don't know. Something about knowing that someone is somehow out there who remembered us and cared about us."

Sadie's breath was the only sound for a long moment. "I'm glad, Josh. Really. So glad for you. The smallest things can be so important."

"There's more."

"Are you ready to talk about it? I called because I wanted to know you were okay. That you didn't need me. I understand if you need time to digest it all. You know I did."

"I'm okay. It was a good thing. It was a lot and I'm still trying to process it all."

"I understand. Facing my mother caused me to have to reevaluate a lot of things I believed about myself."

"Can you do something for me?"

“I’ll do anything for you.”

“He told me where they are buried. It’s in North Charleston. Can you meet me there?”

“Now?”

“I’m way out near Sumter. It’ll take me an hour or so to get there.”

“Give me the address. I’ll be waiting for you.”

CHAPTER THIRTEEN

SADIE WAS SITTING on the hood of her SUV, waiting for him as he puttered up the paved road that circled the cemetery. The land itself was flat and treeless. A few small azalea bushes bloomed by the road. Small gravestones marked most of the sites. A few had larger headstones. He parked the motorcycle and pulled off his helmet. Sadie slid off her car and approached him. After pulling him into a tight hug, she pushed back and looked in his eyes.

"I talked to the groundskeeper. I know where they are."

The words sent a chill down him. He had no idea why he was here.

Sadie's arm slipped around his waist. "You ready to do this? You need some time?" she asked.

"Will I ever be ready?"

"I wanted to run away right up until the moment I saw my mother. Then I was too terrified to run."

"You didn't look scared. You looked pretty fierce to me."

"That was after I got mad." She gave him a squeeze. "You need a minute?"

He shook his head and moved to open the saddlebag on the bike. He'd stopped at the Bi-Lo just up the road for a small bouquet of flowers. Sadie looked from the flowers to his face. She didn't say anything but the question was there.

"She was trying to leave. She was trying to get us out."

Sadie nodded. "Whenever you're ready."

He looked out over the large cemetery. "Is this like where they bury the poor people? What's it called? Pauper's graveyard?"

"I don't know. They were buried at the county's expense, so I'm supposing there was no family, or no family who wanted to claim them."

He dropped his arm around her shoulders and pulled her close. "You were a busy little bee while you were waiting."

"Didn't have anything else to do."

He smiled. She always made it seem like nothing. She went and asked the hard questions so he wouldn't have to. She'd smoothed this path the best she could. "Are they together?"

"Next to each other but a separate plaque for each."

His jaw clenched. That made him angry. She'd

been trying to get away from the monster. Now she was spending eternity next to him? Didn't seem right.

"Okay. I'm ready."

He purposely didn't look. He watched the ground in front of him as Sadie led him through the silent cemetery. No, not quiet. The buzz of cicadas could be heard from the swatch of trees that separated the property from the strip mall next door. Cars could be heard whizzing along the highway.

Sadie's hand appeared in his line of vision. "Your mother is on the left there."

As if she knew. He shifted his eyes to the plain white marker and stepped closer. Martha Baxter Sanders. Had he ever known her name? He didn't think so. Born 1971. Died 1993. He looked over at Sadie. "Damn, she was…" He did the math. "Seventeen when I was born. Twenty-two when this happened. Shit, Sadie."

He sank down to his knees and placed the flowers against the slab. Sadie hunkered down beside him and put an arm around him. He shifted to sit cross-legged before the grave, unable to take his eyes off those dates. Twenty-two. She was nothing but a baby herself. He saw Sadie sitting beside him out of the corner of his eye. He was still trying to process this. In his mind, he'd seen his parents as grown-ups. Old enough to know better. But she wasn't. She'd been just a kid.

Sadie's hand found his. "So young."

An emotion welled up, weighing down his shoulders and clogging his throat. It took him a moment. *Pity. She barely had a life*. "I didn't know she was so young."

He was older now than his mother had been when she died. He thought back to himself at twenty-two. He'd found Sadie by then and had his life back on track. He'd only applied for the job so he'd have enough contacts to satisfy the unemployment people and get another check. Instead, he'd gotten a chance at life. A life his mother never got a chance at. Sadie stretched her legs out in front of her.

The movement caught his attention and his eyes fell on the other grave marker. The numb shock began to wear off as a slow-moving anger filled him. He moved his gaze to read the words there. Gerald Sanders. Born 1965. Died 1993. He stared at it, letting the anger fill him. He climbed to his feet and walked a few paces away, turning his back and stuffing his hands in his back pockets. *Goddamn him.* He had been old enough to know better. *Same age you are now.*

He turned back and walked up to the edge of his father's grave marker. Sadie rose to her feet and tried to take his hand. He pulled away, perhaps more roughly than he intended. “How?” he said, his voice thick with fury. “How does a man put a gun in the face of a woman, another human, and pull the trigger? Kill the mother of his children?”

“Josh,” Sadie whispered.

Too late. His foot rose and slammed down on the marker. “You piece of shit!” He kicked at the marble, trying to dislodge it. He wanted it out of the ground, away from his mother. “Fucking coward. What were you going to do? Kill us all? Shoot a two-year-old baby? You were nothing but an evil monster!”

With one last kick at the unmoving stone, he collapsed to his knees, breath raging in his lungs. He grabbed at the grass surrounding the marker and ripped it out—roots, dirt clumps and all—then threw it on top of the marker.

“You don’t deserve to be remembered. You don’t deserve to have your name here.”

He sat back and covered his face with his hands. Tears clogged his throat but he refused to cry. Sadie sat back beside him, saying nothing, just letting him feel her warmth. Groping blindly for her hand, he felt the rage shift as her hand closed around his.

“I want to move her,” he said.

“We can make that happen.”

“He doesn’t deserve to have her here. She

doesn't deserve to be stuck here beside him. I want her moved to a different cemetery."

Sadie squeezed his hand. "We will. Anywhere you want, Josh."

The subsiding of his rage left him feeling hollow. He spent a long moment just staring at the ground between the two markers. He could feel his heart beating and hear the sound of his lungs pushing air in and out. Everything else felt numb.

"I understand what you meant now," he said quietly.

"About?"

"It not making you feel any better."

"Right away. It didn't make me feel better right away, Josh. It took some time for me to work through it all. But it did help."

"How do I feel better about this, Sadie? How?"

"I don't know, Josh. I'm sorry. All I know is that once I confronted my mother and knew the truth about her and my father, it made me feel worse. The truth was worse than what I'd imagined all those years. Once I'd faced it, sorted it through, I don't know how to explain it exactly, but there wasn't any more unknown. I knew the truth. So I only had that one truth to deal with, not a million what-ifs. Does that make any sense?"

"I'll take your word for it."

She slipped an arm around his waist and leaned against him. “Let me call Wyatt to come get your bike. Come home with me. I don’t want you driving back to Columbia like this.”

His first impulse was to say no. To go back to Columbia, throw himself back into work and the distracting temptation of Mickie. Forget all about this. But a feeling of nostalgia washed over him. Maybe he should spend some time with Sadie.

“I don’t want Jules to know about this.”

“I’m staying at my place. Come on. It’ll be good for you. I’ll cook spaghetti. You love my spaghetti.”

He sighed. “Okay. But I can drive the bike back to your place. I’m okay.”

IT HAD BEEN a good decision. He’d seen a few of the Crew guys. Tossed a ball around in the backyard with Sadie’s dog, Jack. Now he and Sadie sat side by side on her couch, feet up, shoveling pasta into their faces. It felt so much like all those long nights he and Sadie would stay up late, trading foster-care stories, laughing and helping each other heal.

“So, that’s something, right, Josh? That your mother was trying to leave?”

“Sades, I don’t know. When Mr. Gathers told me she’d said Kimmie and I were getting too old to be around that, I felt… I felt like…”

His words tapered off, his throat tight, his heart pounding against his chest at the enormity of it all. He hadn't allowed himself to take his thoughts this far yet. The end of that thought was foreign territory. It was a place he'd never been and he had no idea how he should act or be.

"What did you feel, Josh?" Sadie whispered.

He couldn't answer.

"That she loved you?"

The words were spoken softly, tenderly and with a depth of understanding that went straight through him. And because it was Sadie. Because he knew she understood. Because she was safe, he let himself have it.

"Yes." His voice broke on the word. Wiping his hand across his eyes, he rubbed away the burning wetness there. His mother had loved him. And his sister. Tried to help them. "Sorry."

"Don't be sorry. This is pretty heavy stuff."

"That's not even all."

"What do you mean?"

He let out a long breath. "Mr. Gathers. He kept track of us for a while. He knew Kim had been adopted but I hadn't. So he and his wife wanted to take me. They were going through the process of becoming foster parents when she was diagnosed with ovarian cancer."

"Jesus, Josh."

A rueful smile crossed his lips at her tone.

Once again, Sadie instantly comprehended the entirety of the situation. "Yeah. All these years I thought no one would adopt me because I was a bad kid."

"I hate cancer."

He set down the plate and paced around the small living room. He felt better. Still completely overwhelmed and not quite sure who he really was anymore, but better. "Thanks for telling me to stay. I'm okay. I just need to, I don't know… something."

"You just need to rearrange your entire set of beliefs about your past and yourself. I understand. Been there, got the T-shirt, baby brother."

"Love you, Sades."

"Love you, Joshie. Are you finished with your plate?"

"No."

"Jack's eating it."

CHAPTER FOURTEEN

THERE WAS SOMETHING WRONG. Not like a little wrong. Big wrong. Mickie eyed Josh every time he came through her little office space in the kitchen. He kept his eyes averted when he spoke to her, even did it with the guys. When required to speak, he used the fewest words possible. He seemed flat. It couldn't be the visit from the big boss. That seemed to have gone well. Sadie had been very complimentary with everyone. She'd said the business was doing better than they had projected.

So it had to be something else. Something personal. And she wasn't sure if she should get into his personal business. Since that kiss, she'd been trying to keep it as impersonal and businesslike as possible. But he'd been out of town overnight again. Something was going on. She shook her head. She had a long, hard row to hoe the next two years and she couldn't allow herself to be distracted.

The usual Monday morning calls were enough to distract her for most of the morning. Seemed like people heard about the Crew over the weekend and made it their first order of business on Monday morning to get in touch. As she ate lunch at her desk, she focused on her latest obsession: making new index cards from the study notes Tee had given her. If she could get a head start on the work, maybe she could keep ahead or at least keep up.

The front door opened and she leaned to see who it was. DeShawn strolled into the kitchen and helped himself to one of her potato chips.

"Thief," she said, shooing his hand away before he stole a second. "Hands off the Pringles."

"Sharing is caring," he said, snatching another from the neat stack.

Mickie leaned back in her chair, crossed her arms over her stomach and gave DeShawn a speculative look. "How long have you known Josh?"

DeShawn opened the fridge and rummaged inside, taking out lunch meat and cheese. "Um. Probably about three and a half years." He opened and closed a few cabinets until he found the bread. "Why?"

Mickie shrugged. "He just seemed not quite right this morning. Did you notice?"

"Yeah."

Mickie waited for more, letting the silence spin out as DeShawn made his sandwich. "And?"

"And what?" DeShawn pulled the chair out from the end of the table and sat. "Josh has some issues. Sometimes he gets a little down. He'll be normal tomorrow."

"He went away over the weekend, but he didn't say where."

"He likes to take the motorcycle out. Probably went up to the mountains."

"I don't think that's it."

"Look, Mickie," DeShawn said, his voice serious. "Just let it be, okay. Whatever it is, Josh will deal with it in his own way." He had that way about him, that way of making everything seem okay. It was one of the best things about him. He wasn't just a great-looking guy, he had an air of decency, of kindness. She hoped something good was coming his way. He deserved that.

She looked down at the index cards and picked up her pen. "Okay."

But she didn't think it was okay. Issues. Like growing-up-in-foster-care issues? Did it have to do with finding his sister? Had he reached out to her and been rejected? Is that why he was so down?

"You're still thinking about it. I can see it on your face."

"Go away, DeShawn. I heard you."

"Your nurse friend coming by anytime soon?"

"Bye, DeShawn."

She'd started with the pharmacology notes because that class seemed to require the most memorization. Classes of drugs. Systems. Effects. Side effects. Method of action. Contraindications.

She heard a thump and rumble of something from outside, wondered if it might be the sky breaking up into thunder, but that was ridiculous. Blue skies all around. Her never-too-far-away nerves stirred to life at the unexpected sound before she remembered it was trash day, when the big ugly truck grabbed the apartment-complex Dumpsters and flipped them upside down. It was over soon enough, the sound receding as the truck sped off to its next stop.

She tapped her pencil on the table and tried to make herself focus on her books again.

By that afternoon, her head was spinning and her hand hurt from writing. Tossing down the pen, she massaged her achy right hand. It astonished her how much she'd done.

Not long after, the door opened. This time it was Josh. He looked tired, low, like the day had beat down on him. Should she say something? None of the signals she was picking up from him invited conversation, but, just the same…

"Hey," she said as he walked to the hall, each footfall slow and steady. "You all done for the day?"

He stopped in the hall but he didn't come in the kitchen. "Yeah," he said. He didn't really look at her, just sort of glanced in her direction. "You can go on now, if you want. I can man the phones for the next hour."

With that, he turned and went down the hall, closing his office door behind him. Mickie stared at the empty doorway. *Go talk to him. No, leave it be like DeShawn said.* She slowly packed up the index cards and study guide. *Go home, get some chores done before picking Ian up at day care.* Yep, that's what she should do. She nodded and briskly stuffed the study materials into her purse and stood. But something was going on. Josh wasn't angry. He wasn't sick. He wasn't tired. He was upset. Sad. Hurting. Something. She had to at least try.

Her light tap on the closed door was met with a heavy sigh and an irritated sounding "Yeah?"

She opened the door and peeked in. Josh sat at the small desk, back to the door. He didn't turn around. "Josh? Are you okay?"

She thought she saw his body stiffen at the question but he shook his head. "Yeah, I'm fine. Go on home."

"Are you sure? You seem…"

He spun around in the chair to face her. "Mickie. Go home. Study your index cards and stop trying to turn me into one of your patients."

She flinched at the words. The tone of them. It wasn't angry or annoyed. It was…resigned. "Oh. Okay. Sorry."

Cheeks burning, she hurried out the back door. *You deserved that. DeShawn told you to leave it alone. Forget about it.* She stepped into her kitchen and glanced at the clock. Just a little before four. That gave her an hour to get the floors mopped and rugs vacuumed and bathroom cleaned up before having to pick up Ian. Gave her something else to think about. *What's it matter to you anyway? He's just your temporary boss. Just two more months. Let him be moody. You can't cure the whole world.*

Before she could get started, there was a tap on her sliding glass door. Josh. Gah. That man made her feel so stupid. She stared at him for a moment.

"Come on, Mickie, open the door," he said. "I'm sorry."

She crossed the room and slid the door open a couple of inches. "Apology accepted."

She started to shut the door but he wrapped his hand around the edge. "What?" she asked.

"May I come in?"

She let go of the door. "Suit yourself." Going back to the sink, she continued filling a bucket with Pinesol and hot water.

"Look," he said. He stopped for a moment,

hands at his sides, looking utterly defeated. That was a sentiment Mickie could understand, and then some. “I appreciate you worrying about me. But you’ve got enough of your own worries, Mickie.”

She turned off the water and lifted the bucket from the sink. The sharp pine scent went right up in her nose, burning her nostrils, and she turned away from it. “I can’t help it. That’s what I do, I worry about people.” She set the bucket on the floor and plunged the mop into the foamy water, then gave it a good swirl to mix it thoroughly.

“That’s why you’ll be a good nurse, I guess.”

She wrapped both hands around the mop handle. “What’s wrong, Josh? Where did you go? Did you try to meet with your sister?”

A rueful smile crossed his lips. “No. I decided I’m not going to reach out to her.”

Mickie studied him carefully. He’d shoved his hands deep into his pockets. His head was bowed and he stared at his feet. A look of resignation. “Why?” she asked softly.

His head come back up and his eyes met hers. “Because she doesn’t deserve it. She has a great, normal life. She’s happy. I don’t want to ruin it.”

A thousand rebuttals rose in her mind, but she kept her mouth shut. There was nothing she knew about Josh that would ruin his sister’s life. A long-lost brother who runs a successful business? A genuinely nice guy? How could he ruin anything?

"I don't understand, Josh. How?"

He turned away and paced around the small kitchen. "I went to talk to someone who knew our parents this weekend. It wasn't a nice story. It's best if she just never knows."

She caught his arm as he passed. "Josh. I'm sorry. I don't completely understand, so if you think not contacting her is the best thing, I won't argue with you. I just want you to know that if I were in her shoes, I'd be happy to find you."

She let go of the mop. It tapped against the kitchen countertop, near the sink, and nearly slid off to the side, but she made a slight correction and it balanced. She walked over to Josh and brought her arms around his shoulders, standing up on tiptoe to reach him. She hugged him because she couldn't stand the look of pain in his eyes. He stood there like an oak tree in the wind: his core was hard, stiff, unyielding. But she could see the slight movement around his edges. Something slight, she had to look for it, but it was like a rustle of leaves just before a big rush of wind hit hard enough to sway a branch.

That's when something in him broke loose and he relaxed against her. His arms encircled her as he pulled her closer and brought his mouth down on hers. There was no hesitation in this kiss. She met his lips with a deep need, plunging her hands into his hair. His hands skimmed up her back, pulling her ponytail loose. In two steps, he had her pressed against the counter, his hands in her hair and his mouth hot on hers.

Yes. Yes. Forget the housework. Forget being a mommy. Forget about school and money and...

Josh's hands cupped either side of her face as he pulled back. She put her hands over his. "Don't stop."

"We can't do this."

"Why not?"

She pressed her hips against him, letting him know she knew just how ready he was. She was rewarded with a low groan. Sliding her body against his as she rose up on tiptoe, she pressed her lips to his. He gave in to the kiss and his hand, strong and calloused, traced down her back to slip beneath her shirt. She wanted to be naked, needed to be naked against him. She was ravenous.

Then he was gone. She slumped back against the counter, her heart beating at an alarming pace, and brought a hand to her lips. He was leaning against the kitchen table, his chest heaving with his own loss of breath.

"This is wrong, Mickie," he said. "I'm your boss. Even if temporary. You've got a kid and school and I can't make any commitments. Especially if there's a kid involved."

"I'm not looking for a baby daddy, if that's what you think."

"Okay. But still. He doesn't know it's temporary."

It was on the tip of her tongue to tell him she just wanted some no-strings-attached, good old-fashioned sex, but there was no way she could say that out loud. She felt her cheeks burn. She'd thrown herself at him. Practically climbed him like a tree. She couldn't even look at him. She turned her attention to the bucket and mop. *Mop the floors. Go pick up Ian. Make dinner. Put him to bed. Study. Try to sleep.*

Josh's hands gently touched her shoulders. She stiffened. "I'm sorry," he said.

She shook her head without turning around. "No. It was me. It won't happen again."

"Maybe it was both of us."

"Okay," she said, flustered, frustrated, near to done with this. She looked back at the mop in the bucket, leaning neatly in place where she'd left it, and waved a hand in that direction as if pointing out the obvious. "I have to mop this floor now." She looked down at the bucket, wondered if she'd have to refill it with hot water. Had it gone cold?

Leave. Leave now. Because I'm going to cry or scream or both.

He stepped away. "Okay. I'll see you tomorrow?"

"You still want me to work for you?"

He stopped, looked at her like he wasn't understanding her words. He held his hands out, palms up, like "what, seriously?"

"Of course I do," he said. "Mickie. It's okay. So we have this—this…attraction. It doesn't mean we have to act on it."

She nodded. Brought the mop down on the floor with a wet splash. A pool of sudsy water ran out from underneath it. "Okay." She began to move the mop in wide arcs across the floor, not looking up again until she heard the glass door slide shut. Pulling in a long, slow breath, she stared up at the ceiling. *Well, that was a complete disaster. Because tomorrow isn't going to be awkward. Not at all.*

JESUS, JOSH. YOU almost lost control. He went back to his own kitchen. His heart was still slamming against his ribs and he could still feel the soft silk of her skin. For an instant, he'd lost control. He'd almost used her to stop the pain, to stop the confusion, to hush the constant storm that raged in his mind. *That can never happen again.*

Returning to the back room that served as his office, he powered up the laptop and focused on his to-do list. Paperwork. Emails. Reviewing applications. Eventually, though, there was nothing else to do and his thoughts turned back to Kimmie.

A few clicks and her picture appeared on screen. Light brown hair. Curly, like his. Blue eyes. Lighter than his. The light in her eyes matched the smile on her face. A pretty young woman in a quiet, unassuming way. He tried to think back as far as he could. The night in the closet was where his memory began. But there were flashes. Spoon-feeding her in a high chair. Her crying after falling and bumping her head. Brief, random, like looking at a faded photograph.

She'd had everything that he hadn't. Parents. A home. Love. Stability. Education. He didn't resent her for having those things. He was glad for it. But. *But what about me?*

He shut down the computer and stood. He wanted to meet her. He wanted to have a sister. A family. Even if he'd resigned himself to the fact that he'd never have a family of his own, he still wanted to belong to one. A real family. He loved Sadie like a sister but Kimmie was real. Kimmie was blood. He could be an uncle. That'd be cool.

That'd be...completely selfish. He left the

room, grabbed his gym bag and motorcycle keys. He could feel the anger simmering in his gut. It wasn't fair. *Life isn't fair, asshole. Best you can do is limit the damage and prevent further casualties.*

Mickie and Ian were turning up the sidewalk as he puttered the bike down the driveway. She waved and he waved back. Like that. She was exactly what he needed to stay away from. For her own good. And the kid's.

MICKIE FELT STUPID and awkward waving at Josh. Acting as if they hadn't almost had sex on her kitchen floor an hour ago. But okay. If he could pretend it never happened, so could she. Fine. Perfect. She pushed the stroller up the sidewalk. As she approached the door, she noticed the doormat was flipped over.

"That's weird." She stood there a moment, frozen, trying to read the situation. She reached down, put a hand on a corner of it. For a second, just this little flicker of a second, a chill ran through her. She turned it back over, quickly, not getting it quite square with the door, not caring, and she glanced over her shoulder. Nothing, no one. Her hand trembling, she slipped the key into the lock, missing on the first stab before getting it into the keyhole. For one terrifying moment, she thought it wouldn't work, that the lock had been changed or this was somehow the wrong key, or that a hand would drop on her shoulder—*Stop it.* She turned the key, everything worked as it should, and she pushed the stroller inside. A light tingle of fear traced along her skin as she locked the door as quickly as possible. She left the stroller and the grocery bags hanging from it and picked up Ian.

"Hungee," he announced.

"Okay, baby," she soothed in a low voice. "We'll get dinner in a minute."

After a quick search of the house, she felt silly. There'd been a note on the door last week that the duplex owners were going to have the buildings power-washed. The workers probably moved the doormat. *You've got to stop with the paranoia.*

She got Ian fed and bathed and down for the night and returned to the pharmacology notes. Her phone vibrated on the table. Tiana. "Hey, what's up?"

"Nothing. Just wanted to let you know one of the girls in my class is losing her roommate. She has a two-year-old little boy and a three-bedroom apartment a bit closer to campus. Her old roommate had a kid and the kids shared a room, so there's already all the furniture and stuff there."

"Oooh. That sounds promising. How much would my share of the rent be?"

Yes. Rooming with another single mom. Living in the same house as a nursing student a year ahead who could help her. Ian having a playmate. No Josh next door tempting her.

"I don't know," Tiana said. "I'll give her your number and have her call you."

"No. No. Don't do that. Give me her name and number and I'll call her."

There was a long pause on Tiana's end. "Girl, you can't keep living like that."

"I know. It's getting better. I just still need to do it this way."

"All right. Got a pen?"

"Yes. And ten trillion index cards. Tell me pharmacology isn't as bad as it looks."

"My momma didn't raise a liar," Tiana said before giving Mickie the contact information.

"We still on for the zoo on Saturday?"

"Definitely. My mom is bringing my baby girl for a visit. So we'll make a day of it."

CHAPTER FIFTEEN

"GIRAFFES! GIRAFFES! I wanna feed the giraffes, Mommy!"

Mickie grinned at Tiana's little girl, Lillian. She was tugging at Tee's hand, urging her to walk faster. "Lilly. The giraffe feeding doesn't even start for another thirty minutes."

"But I wanna be first!"

Both Mickie and Tiana's mother, Viv, burst into laughter at the bulldog expression on Lilly's face. Tee glared back at them with the same look. "You two got something to say?"

"Not a word, baby girl," Viv replied.

Mickie continued to grin as she pushed Ian's stroller along the shaded walk. It was early enough that the summer heat wasn't too oppressive. If you didn't think about it too much. They'd definitely have to grab some refreshments after a while, though, when the sun really started in on them. She watched Tee and Lilly. Their clasped hands swung back and forth between them. Like best friends. The smile faded away as a lump rose in her throat. A warm hand gently squeezed her wrist.

She needed this. Smiles. Family. Laughter. It had been a long, awkward week. With both she and Josh trying to pretend that smoking hot kiss hadn't happened. She couldn't even look him in the eyes without wanting to do it again. And not stop this time.

"You'll be okay, little momma," Viv said. "Just like my Tiana. You got what it takes. Grit, guts and brains."

"I hope so."

A happy shriek let them know they'd reached the giraffe enclosure. Mickie found a spot on a bench in the shade. She and Viv sat down as Tee took Lilly to get in line for the giraffe feeding.

"I'll tell you this," Viv said as Mickie freed Ian from the stroller. "There comes a time when it all looks too hard. Tiana almost quit college because the schools back home were so bad she didn't know she was so far behind. That's where the grit comes in. You just have to stay with it."

"I'm working on it. Every time it gets hard, I just picture this guy."

She scooped up Ian and hugged him, much to his squirmy disapproval. She put him down and gave him a sippy cup of water. "Want to see the giraffes, Ian?"

He pulled the cup from his mouth. "Graffs?"

Viv stood. "I'll take him if you don't mind. Been too long since I had such a little one. What you say, little man? Want to meet a giraffe?"

Mickie slumped back on the bench as she watched Viv settle Ian on an ample hip. As she walked away, a wave of homesickness washed over Mickie. She missed her mother. Ian should have his grandmother. None of this was fair. Or right. She pulled her phone out of her purse and looked at it. Why couldn't she just call her mother? Was there really a danger? Or was it the fear he'd filled her with? What if he'd found some new victim and she never even crossed his mind? Was she ruining Ian's life for nothing more than old ghosts?

"That is not a happy face." Tee plopped down on the bench next to her.

"Where are the kids?"

"Mom's got them. She's happy as a hog in mud. Ran a day care out of the house most of her life. Still does. What's got you all down?"

Mickie shook her head. "I want to jump Josh's bones."

"Hot-dude-next-door Josh?"

"Is that wrong?"

"What? Wanting to jump his bones? Or shall we say 'bone'?" Tee made air quotes and Mickie frowned at her as she felt her face go hot. "Or just wanting to jump anyone's bones?"

"I wouldn't jump just anyone's bones."

Tee leaned back, stretching her arms out along the back of the bench. "It's not wrong. I considered that chunk-of-man DeShawn for a minute or two."

"But everyone keeps telling me no men while in school! You even said it."

"A girl's got needs, you know. It's just a fact. You just got to not complicate things."

"I can't believe we're even having this conversation. I thought you would tell me no men."

"Is that what you want? Me to tell you?"

"No. Yes. No. I don't know. I've never wanted to just have sex for the sake of having sex before."

"It's not wrong. You think it is because that's what we've been told all our lives. Good girls don't. Well, let me tell you, good girls do indeed. Trick is finding a good guy who knows the rules."

"The rules?"

Tee lifted fingers as she ticked them off. "Consent. Respect. Discretion. And to be good at it."

Mickie laughed. *Oh, Josh would probably meet that last one*. But could she do it? Just have sex? Go separate ways? That was the real question. Would she fall into a relationship she didn't want to be in? Give up on her goals and dreams? Because that was her track record.

"Look, Mickie," Tee said gently. "I can't imagine how scary it would be for you to let yourself trust a man to that degree. To be vulnerable. Don't do it if you have any doubts."

"It's not that."

"What is it?"

"Well, my man-choosing skills are pretty unreliable."

Tee straightened from her slouch and turned to face Mickie. "Let me tell you something. The problem with us? Is the same reason we want to be nurses. We like to help people. To fix people. And that isn't the job. That is *us.* And every one of us has had our own version of your story. Most way less traumatic, but we pick a guy who needs us, who needs help. And thing is, most guys like that are like that for a reason. There isn't any fixing them. Because they don't want to be fixed."

"So how do I tell? How do I know?"

"I don't know. Trust your gut."

"Well, it ain't my gut that has my attention right now."

Tiana's laugh turned several heads in their direction. "Does Josh know you're thinking about his bones?"

"Well..."

"*Well*, by that lovely shade of pink popping up on those cheeks of yours..."

"We sorta kissed."

"Sorta? Like your lips accidentally bumped into each other?"

"Yeah. I was showing him all the stuff you guys got for me and I was happy so I hugged him and it kinda turned into a kiss."

"Chemistry?"

"And then some."

"So one kiss. Is he interested?"

"Two. Twice. It happened twice."

"Whoa, whoa. Slow down. When was this second kiss?"

"I was poking in his personal business. He told me to stop trying to turn him into one of my patients. It hurt my feelings."

"So he just kissed you instead of saying 'I'm sorry'?"

"The kiss was after the sorry."

"Tongue?"

"Let's just say, if he hadn't stopped, the sex thing would have been a done deal."

"He stopped?"

"Yeah. We've both got too much going on for a relationship. And he definitely does not want to be a baby daddy."

Tiana let out a frustrated growl. "Why do they automatically assume that's what we want? Like I don't want to have a romantic relationship?"

Mickie shook her head. She put a hand on Tiana's shoulder, tilted her head a bit, tried a smile.

"No. I don't think it was like that. It was more like he didn't want Ian to get attached to him if he wasn't going to be a part of Ian's life."

"Oh," she said. She smiled back, nodded as if considering, weighing the possibility of it in her mind for a moment before responding. "Wow. Well. I don't know what to say about that. Like he was thinking about what was best for Ian? Mickie, I think you found a real man! Like a grown-up adult man!"

Mickie laughed. "Yeah, well. Doesn't help me with my problem."

"You got two solutions—tell him you want to just do the deed, or buy a good vibrator and use your imagination."

"Oh. My. God." Mickie clapped her hands over her face. She could feel the rush of red run from the middle of her chest, to her neck, and up onto her cheeks. She put her hands on her thighs, smoothed herself out. A crooked little smile formed on her lips and she looked up at Tiana, almost shyly. "I cannot believe you just said that."

"Welcome to being my friend. You'll get used to it. Here comes Mom and the kiddos. Bet Lilly wants to go feed the birds now."

MICKIE SEEMED FINE when she walked through the back door. Maybe a little pink around the cheeks, but her "good morning" sounded perfectly normal. Good. Because he didn't have time to clean up the mess he'd made with her last Monday. Not right now. He had another mess.

"Hey. We're going to have to rearrange some things today. Drake was in a car wreck this morning..."

"Oh, no! Is he okay?"

"Yeah. He's at the emergency department. Some asshole ran a stop sign and T-boned him. He's fine, but has some cuts and bruises. I'm going to go check on him, get him home. After he's settled, I'll meet up with DeShawn to help him with his schedule today."

"Okay. I'll reschedule your interviews for today. When do you want me to make them for?" She flipped through the calendar on the table. "Tomorrow afternoon looks okay."

"Perfect." He scooped up his keys. "This isn't a heavy day for DeShawn, so hopefully, I'll be back early afternoon. If anything comes up, let me know."

"Okay. Call me and let me know how Drake is."

"Will do."

Part of him was glad to get away. He'd lost control last week. He didn't like to do that. At all. Ever. But Mickie made him do things. Want things. *Feel* things. He shook his head.

Just focus on what is in front of you, Josh. Get Drake home. Get the work done. Focus.

Traffic was so bad that Drake and been seen and released by the time Josh hurried through the doors of the emergency department. "You okay? What'd the doctors say?"

Drake turned his head. There was a line of stitches across his left cheek. "This is the worst of it for now. Doc said to expect some bruising to show up tomorrow."

"Great. I mean, not great, but great that you weren't hurt worse. Come on, let's get you home."

"Thanks. On the good side, chicks dig scars, right?"

"That's what I hear."

Physical scars, maybe. They didn't dig a heart and soul so scarred and damaged they didn't even work right.

By the time he caught up with DeShawn, he was at his second house. He was happy to throw himself into work. Get Mickie off his mind. Not that he was happy Drake's car was totaled, but it was obvious he couldn't trust himself around her.

"Thanks for showing up, dude," DeShawn said, miming looking at an imaginary watch.

"Ah, screw you," Josh replied, grabbing the upstairs supplies bucket.

"Drake okay?"

"Yeah, a couple of stitches. Gonna be sore tomorrow."

It felt good to be back on the job. It was simple work yet the quality the Cleaning Crew was famous for took focus and concentration on the smallest details. It was almost a form of meditation. He didn't realize how much he missed it. He and DeShawn worked together well. They should. DeShawn was the second guy Sadie had hired, the first he'd trained. They fell back into that routine easily.

"How're you doing?" he asked over lunch. The grandmother who had raised DeShawn had passed away that summer. "With your family?"

DeShawn let out a long sigh. "It's a mess, man. I just had to step away. My mom showed back up, still drinking. She wanted to sell Mama G's house. Drink the money. After that, all the other relatives started wanting a piece."

"I'm sorry."

"Nothing to be done about it. I said my goodbyes. Made my peace. Left them to fight it out. Mama G saved my life. Put me on the right track. I don't need anything else from her."

"Family is weird."

DeShawn laughed. "That's the truth, man. Look at us. I'm running away from my messed-up family. You want to find your family."

"Do you think there are families out there that are just normal? Happy?"

"I hope so. I'd like to be part of one someday."

"You going to do that? Find a woman? Get married? Kids, mortgage, the whole thing?"

DeShawn shrugged. "Yeah, man. I hope so."

Josh sat back. DeShawn had had a rough go of it. Both his parents were alcoholics. His grandmother took him out of their home and raised him. But there had been skirmishes along the way. The parents often used the threat of taking DeShawn back to get money for alcohol.

"How, man, how do you know you can do it?"

DeShawn's dark eyes met his. "I don't. I just know what I don't want it to be like. I'll just do the opposite of what my parents did."

Josh focused on finishing his burger. *Just do the opposite. Like it was that easy.* But he'd tried that once. Once was enough to prove he couldn't ever do it again. That moment when he'd lost control, when Ruby just wouldn't stop and he was trying to leave, trying to get away from her. *Walk away when you get angry*, he'd told himself. Just walk away. But he'd tried and she'd grabbed his arm and was trying to pull him back. And something in him snapped. He'd put his fist through the drywall two inches from her face.

And that wasn't even the worst of it. The worst

was as the look in her eyes changed from fury to fear, he'd liked it. It had made him feel powerful. The rage had burned away his pain and it had felt good. Until she sank down to the floor, crying. That was when it hit him. He was his father. He was the monster now. And the revulsion and shame he felt was overwhelming. Never would he put himself in that position again. Nor any woman. He thought about Ian. And never a child.

"You ready, man?"

DeShawn's words cut through the memories. He threw his half-eaten hamburger on the tray. "Yeah. Let's go."

CHAPTER SIXTEEN

IT HAD TAKEN Mickie only half the morning to get all the Cleaning Crew work done. Now she was just manning the phones. She studied her note cards between phone calls as she waited for Josh to come back. She'd hoped to have this conversation first thing this morning, but Drake's accident had put that on hold.

Finally, just after two, Josh and DeShawn showed up. "Hey, guys," she called out.

Josh smiled as they walked in the kitchen. "You study an awful lot for someone who isn't even in school yet."

"I want to get ahead. There is so much to learn."

"Isn't that why you go to class? To be taught?"

DeShawn grabbed a bottle of water from the fridge. "Leave her alone, Josh. I was the same way." He leaned against the counter and glugged half the bottle. "I was terrified I was going to fail right up to the moment they handed me my diploma."

Mickie pointed at DeShawn. "Yes! That! That

right there is what I'm talking about. I can't fail. I can't. Ian's future depends on it."

Josh held his hands up in surrender. "Okay. I give. Mad respect to both of you for doing what I never even considered possible for me."

"Anything is possible, Josh," Mickie said. "You just have to want it bad enough. Sometimes you have to take a step or two. Sometimes you have to scale a damn wall."

DeShawn snorted out a laugh. "Sometimes you scale a damn wall that's booby-trapped with explosives after swimming a polluted moat filled with alligators." He crossed the floor and fist-bumped Mickie. "I'm outta here. Got a date with some free weights tonight."

"Yeah, let me know if you finally reach your lifetime goal of benching over twenty pounds," Josh said, earning himself a one-finger salute from DeShawn.

Mickie smiled at the banter. She was an only child. Working here was like having big brothers. "Josh," she said as the front door closed. "I wanted to talk to you."

He turned from the fridge, where he was getting his own bottle of water. He didn't quite blush, but his complexion darkened just a little. "About the last week? Mickie, I'm sorry about that."

She felt her own face go hot. Unfortunately,

she didn't have the complexion to hide it and was sure she was glowing like Rudolph's nose. "No. Not that." She looked down at her study cards. Now the conversation she'd had with Tee replayed in her mind and her face went hotter.

Josh pulled out the chair across from her and sat down. "Sorry. What did you need to talk about?"

She took a breath, shook her head to clear it. "How much longer do you need me to work here for you?"

The water bottle froze halfway to his mouth and he lowered it slowly back to the table. "You thinking about quitting?"

"Well, no. Not now. I found another place to live. It's a bit cheaper and closer to school. I'll be sharing with another nursing student and she's got a little boy close to Ian's age. And the day care where Ian goes is looking for some temporary help because one of their employees is going to be out of work for two months to have some kind of surgery."

"So you won't be right next door anymore?"

The question threw her off. Of all the things he could have asked about, why that? "Um, no. What's that have to do with it?"

"Nothing. Brain freeze. If that's going to be a better situation for you, Mickie, do it. We'll manage here. Now that I have DeShawn until the end of September, we'll be fine."

"Well, I don't know if it'll be better, just maybe more convenient."

"How so?"

She shuffled the study cards between her hands. "I don't know, Josh. I just don't know what to do."

His hand closed over hers, stilling her restless movements. "About what?"

"I don't really want to move in with Diane. I feel like I'm doing it for selfish reasons."

"Such as?"

She looked up at him. Let herself look into those dark blue eyes. Let herself feel the heat of his fingers on the back of her hand. He had a way of calming her when her thoughts and fears and anxieties ran amok. "I like living on my own. I like the independence. Feeling like I am in control of my life."

"Understandable."

"And I feel like my wanting to move in with her is selfish because I really only want to because she's a year ahead of me in school and could help me."

His eyebrows lifted and he leaned back in the chair and crossed his arms across his chest, distracting her with those biceps. "Maybe she wants to help you."

Mickie felt her mouth drop open. “Oh.”

“Never considered that, did you?”

“No.”

“Remember the day we met? You were moving in all by yourself? I had to practically beg you to let me help you.”

She smiled at the memory. “I know.”

“Let people help you, Micks. If it’s going to be good for you and Ian to move in there, then do it. It’s like what you said just a few minutes ago about studying because you couldn’t fail for Ian’s sake. You don’t have to do everything all by yourself all the time.”

She sat, frozen, unable to move or breathe against the overwhelming rush of emotion that swept over her. She blinked and twin tears ran down her cheeks. “That’s the problem,” she said in a rough whisper. “Yes, I do.”

Because she was still letting him control her. Still terrified to let people into her life. Because what if? What if he showed up and hurt someone? What if he showed up and turned them against her? What if he showed up and exposed her shame? What if? She’d tried everything. Changed her name. Moved out of state. Moved again. And again. Cut herself off from all her friends and only maintained minimal, anonymous contact with her parents. None of it had helped stem the fear.

She was clinging to the hope of a nursing degree. To have financial stability. To be able to afford a nice, safe place with alarms and a big, barky dog. Then she'd feel safe. But deep down, she knew it was all a lie. Nothing was going to make her feel safe. Never again. Not until she found some way of exorcising him from her mind.

"Hey." Josh's voice pulled her out of her thoughts. He leaned forward across the table, both her hands in his now. "Hey. What's really going on, Mickie?"

"I'm sorry. It's just. You know. It's hard for me to take help."

"But why?"

She forced her lips into a smile and tried to make it reach her eyes. "Because I help people. They don't help me. Duh. A nurse."

He didn't look away or let go of her hands. "No. That's not it. You're lying."

"No, I'm not."

"Yes, you are."

Now she was angry. "Let go of me."

He dropped her hands immediately and sat back. "I'm sorry. I was prying."

She shook her head. "I don't know why I'm like this, Josh. I just am."

His eyes let her know he still thought she was

lying. But he just nodded. "Okay. I'm sorry I upset you."

"You didn't. I upset myself."

"We'll miss you if you leave."

That got a real smile out of her. "Will you?"

"Yeah, the guys all adore you. You're like our little sister."

"Not what I meant."

His eyes met hers and the heat flared for a long, sweet moment. Her stomach fluttered with excitement and her heartbeat jumped a few notches. She'd never done this before. Engaged a man like this.

"You know the answer to that," he said, his voice husky.

"Yes?"

"Yes. Mickie. I thought we weren't going to do this."

Her resolved failed. She could feel her face getting hotter and hotter. She dropped her gaze to the table. "Yeah. I know. I'm sorry."

Neither of them said anything for what seemed like forever. Finally Josh stood and sighed deeply. "We tell each other we're sorry way too much."

As he left the room, she covered her face with her hands. *You are such a dork. What were you trying to do? Seduce him? You?* She'd never be able to face him again. She snorted out a laugh. *Yeah, this is like the third time you've left yourself in this position.*

JOSH STAYED LOCKED behind his office door until he was sure Mickie had left for the day. She didn't know how close he'd come to showing her just how much he'd miss her right there on the kitchen table. *She was leaving.* He was going to miss her, he realized. He liked her. She made him laugh. And she seemed to understand him in a way no other woman, besides Sadie, had. Shutting down the laptop, he shook his head. *No. Just no. We aren't even going down that road.* Grabbing his gym bag and motorcycle keys, he headed out to the gym. There was a yoga class starting in thirty minutes. Some meditation and a nice workout would fix all this.

Damn it. After a grueling one-hour level-three class, he should be blissing out in Shavasana. Instead of drifting into that amazing moment when his mind went completely silent, everything, everyone, every thought gone, she was there. Random flashes. The swing of her hair in that ponytail. The little crease between her eyebrows when she frowned. Those damn study cards. The way she'd acted like a game-show model showing off the secondhand furniture. The amazing sound of her laughter.

He gave up on the blissful nothingness he

was seeking and simply lay there on the yoga mat, staring at the ceiling. It was an interesting ceiling. Done in the same light oak planking as the floor. *Okay, so you like her. She's a friend. Okay, she's a friend you'd like to haul off to bed. Doesn't mean anything. You're allowed to miss a friend when they move away, right?*

The instructor began to quietly pull the class out of the deep relaxation of the pose and end the class. Josh usually stayed longer, until the rest of the class had left the room. This night, however, he got up immediately. At least he had a great workout. His arms still trembled a bit when he gripped the handlebars of the bike. He cranked the engine and slipped on the helmet. *Now what?*

The class must have done some good because now he was thinking a bit more clearly. He'd told Mickie that it would be fine if she had to take the other job, but really, he did still need her. Drake's accident had proven just how few resources he had for an emergency situation. Even with Mickie there to move appointments and get paperwork done, he was still behind. If he'd had to do everything by himself, nope, it would have been a disaster. He needed at least three fully trained crews and DeShawn training more before he could stay in the office all the time. He was going to have to convince her to stay.

He waited until later. When he was sure she'd gotten Ian to bed. The vertical blinds covering the back sliding door were closed, so he couldn't tell if she was in the kitchen or not. But the light was on so he tapped gently on the door. No answer. He knocked harder. After a moment, there was a tiny flutter in the blinds.

"It's just me," he said.

The blinds pulled open and she toed a board out of the sliding door's track. She slid the door open as she propped a baseball bat in the corner next to the door. That was very new.

"What's up with the new home security system?"

She rolled her eyes. "I'm a woman. Living alone. With a baby."

"Yeah. Guess I didn't think of it like that."

"What's up?"

"Nothing."

She waited, patiently looking up at him.

"Oh. Yeah. What if I gave you a raise?"

"A raise?"

"I really could still use your help, Mickie. If you decide to move in with that other woman, if I gave you a raise, would you consider staying with me until school starts instead of taking that other job?"

The vertical frown line appeared. God, it was

so adorable. “Come in,” she said, turning away. “Can you open this?”

He crossed the kitchen to the counter, where she handed him a bottle of wine with a flimsy opener sticking out of the cork. He pulled the cork loose with a loud pop. “At your service,” he said, presenting the bottle to her with a flourish.

“Thank you,” she said as she poured some wine into a coffee cup. “First bottle of wine I get in a year that isn’t screw-top and I can’t even open it. Want some?”

“No. I don’t drink.”

“Not at all?”

“Nope.”

“Personal choice or problem?”

He shrugged. “A risk I don’t want to take.”

“I can respect that. More for me.”

“You planning on getting toasted?”

“I’m a mother. I can never get toasted. Come on.”

He followed her into the living room. She plopped down in one of the armchairs and motioned at the other. “Have a seat.”

He sat down, studying her carefully. If he hadn’t known better, he’d swear she’d already had a glass or two. There was a looseness about her. In the fluid movement of her body and the ease in her words. “Are you even old enough to buy wine?” he joked.

She shot him a murderous glare. “Here. Make yourself useful.”

He took the handful of study cards she handed him. “What am I going to do with these?”

“Test me. Please. I’m going insane. The answers are all running together and my brain is Jell-O.”

“Maybe you should take a break.”

“And do what? I’ve already cleaned the house. I’m caught up on laundry. I don’t have cable. About all I have left is sleeping or studying.”

She twisted in the chair, curling her legs under her and facing him. She held the coffee cup of wine in both her hands. “I can’t sleep anymore.”

“Probably because you’re stressing yourself out with all this study-card stuff.”

“No, actually, the studying makes it better.”

“Makes what better?”

A flicker of a shadow crossed her features. Her eyes looked weary and sad as she looked away from him. Her lips pressed together before she blew out a sigh. “Nothing. It’s just me. Please, Josh. Pretty please with sugar on top. Quiz me.”

The change in her mood was so abrupt that it took him a moment to catch up with it. He hesitated, wanting to pursue that dark mood. She reminded him of Sadie. How the dark moments would creep up on her and how efficiently she’d learned to push them away. Instead he looked down at the cards in his hand.

"Lymphocyte."

"Easy peasy. It's a type of leukocyte. Responsible for immune reactions. There are two types—B cells and T cells."

Josh flipped the card over. "Yep. You got it. Next—Suboxone. Is that how it's pronounced?"

"Yes. Suboxone is a schedule-three drug. Generic name is buprenorphine and it's used to treat opiate addiction."

"Correct. Cranial nerves."

"Oh, shoot. Um. Hold on."

Josh smiled at her. She'd scrunched down in a tight ball in her chair, her chin resting on her knees, arms wrapped around her legs with the coffee cup clenched in her hands. She squished up her face. "On old Olympus towering top a Finn and German viewed some hops."

"Excuse me?"

"Shh! Olfactory, optic, oculomotor…towering top a…trochlear, trigeminal, abducens…Finn and German…facial, auditory, glossopharyngeal, um…viewed some hops…vagus, spinal accessory and hypoglossal. Right? Right?"

Josh looked up from where he was following on the back of the card. "Exactly, Micks. Why're you worried about this? You got it down."

"Because I can control this. I'm staring at

nursing school like this huge unknown. It's famous for weeding out the weak and those who don't belong. I don't know how I'll do in the program. So instead of freaking myself out about that, I study."

"Makes sense. But I think you're going to do just fine in school."

"Oh? And why do you think this?"

He held up the cards. "First of all, you're amazingly smart. I can't even pronounce most of this stuff and you know all about it. Second, you are incredibly compassionate. I've seen it. I've seen that caretaker aspect of your personality come out just a naturally as you breathe. Third, you are one of the most obstinately stubborn people I've ever met. If you want to be a nurse, you are going to do it."

She loosened from her scrunch. "I am not stubborn. Nor obstinate."

He shook his head. "Hey, I see you're pushing a baby back and forth in ninety-nine-degree weather moving bags and boxes on a stroller. Can I help you? *No.*"

"I did let you help me."

"Eventually."

There was a lull as they looked into each other's eyes. Josh felt his heart rate kick up a notch. She had her hair twisted up in a bun, held in place by crisscrossing pencils. The walking shorts had been replaced by bright blue yoga pants and a white tank top with a picture of Betty Boop on the front. Her cheeks went pink but she didn't look away.

"I lied," she whispered. Her cheeks went from pink to red.

He kept eye contact. "About what?"

"Why I can't sleep."

Her breath was coming faster and he could see the cup shaking in her trembling hands. "Oh?" *Oh? Get your ass out of this chair and kiss her. That's what she wants.* He knew it because he could feel it. "Micks..."

"Are you going to make me say it, Josh?"

She uncurled from the chair and set down the cup. She stood and he sprang to his feet, unsure exactly what she had in mind. "No. I think I know what you're saying. I'm just not convinced it's a good idea."

She stepped closer. The mad blush spreading across her cheeks and chest made him believe she'd never been this bold before. "Why not?"

"Why not? A billion reasons, Micks. I'm your boss."

"Only for a few more weeks."

"I'm not in the market for a relationship right now."

She took another step, pressing a hand against his runaway heartbeat. He meant to step back, but instead, pressed his hand over hers.

"I'm not looking for a relationship, either."

His fingers tightened around her hand. "What are you looking for?"

As light as a feather, her free hand traced up his arm, caressing the curve of his biceps before moving to his chest. "I think you know, Josh. I think you want it, too."

He caught her hand and clasped both of hers between his. "To be one-hundred-percent clear here. You want to just have sex?"

"One night. Just once. We have this attraction, Josh. Don't lie, I know you feel it. Why can't we just…do it?"

She blushed again and he laughed. "Do it?"

She pulled her hands out from between his and clapped them over her face. "I am so bad at this."

"No, you aren't."

"Yes, I am. I was getting the wine open. I was going to change into something way sexier than this and call you and make something up. We were going to have a glass of wine and talk and at some point you'd lean over and kiss me and…"

"That was the plan, huh?"

She dropped her hands but didn't look up at him. "Yeah. Dumb, huh?"

He put his hands on her shoulders. "Mickie."

She looked up at him and he kissed her. A sweet, tender brief kiss. *His* plan was to give her this chaste kiss, tell her she was making a tempting offer, but he just couldn't. But she slid her hands up under his shirt, across his stomach and up to his chest. The heat of her hands on his skin was nearly unbearable. His hands lifted and pulled the pencils from her hair, sending the waves of silk tumbling over his hands.

His mouth found hers again. This time hot and hard and full of want. Her body pressed against his, tiny and hot, soft and yielding. She turned her head, trailing kisses across his cheek to his ear. "I have protection," she whispered.

As he lifted her into his arms, she wrapped her legs around his waist and kissed him again. *Protection. Yeah. Good.* But what was going to protect his heart? Because this girl was making him want more than her body.

MICKIE ROLLED OVER on her back and tried to quiet her breathing. She listened, worried Ian might have woken up because she'd been, well, rather loud. Since this was a one-time deal, she'd made the most of it. And Josh had been…well, perfection. She turned back on her side and looked down on him. Yeah, perfection.

Hands tucked behind his head, he was laid out like a buffet just for her. The muscles of his abdomen jumped as she lightly traced a finger around the outlines of his six-pack. "You are so beautiful," she said.

"Men aren't beautiful."

"But you are. Look at you." She ran her hand up his abdomen, across the thick thatch of hair across his chest, over a muscled shoulder. A jagged scar broke the smoothness of his skin at the top of his bicep. "How'd you get this?"

"Bar fight."

"No, you didn't!"

"Yes, I did. I was eighteen. Playing pool in a bar. Some guys started a fight. Turned into a bit of a brawl."

"What was it? Like a knife? Broken beer bottle?"

"No. I got pushed against the cue rack. Caught it on a metal bracket."

"Hmmph. I'd make up something more exciting if I were you."

"What about you?"

"What about me?"

He rolled to his side, facing her. His hand slipped around her waist and up her side. His fingertip filled the round scar. "You have two of these. One on each side. Chest tube scars would be my guess."

She froze. She'd trained herself not to see the scars. So well she hadn't even thought about them. "Car accident. Long time ago."

"Must have been a very bad accident."

"Broke a bunch of ribs, collapsed a lung. I don't like to talk about it."

She sat up and he caught her lightly by the elbow. "Where do you think you're going?"

"To check on Ian and get some water."

"Hurry back. I'm not quite done with you yet."

Heat flooded her. "Well," she said, "I'm not all that thirsty." If once was all she was going to get, she was going to make it last as long as possible.

CHAPTER SEVENTEEN

JOSH CAME AWAKE INSTANTLY, feeling something was not right. He opened his eyes and had a moment of complete disorientation until the memories of last night hit him. *Mickie.* It was her makeshift bed on the floor but he was alone in it now. The light filtering through the window felt like early morning. He sat up, rubbing at his face. *Just once*, she'd said. *Just once*, he'd agreed. They'd both taken everything they needed from each other during the night. *And you want more.*

The clink of dishes caught his attention. He could hear Mickie's voice, sweet and sunny. *Damn.* The kid. He was out there. Awake. *Great, Josh. What are you going to do? Go walking out there in front of the kid?* He eyed the window. Laughed. No, he couldn't slip out on her like that. But he didn't want Ian to see him. *Kid's too young to understand.* He got up and began to retrieve his scattered clothes. If they were in the kitchen, he could slip out the front door. He dressed and cautiously opened the bedroom door.

"Hold on, baby man. Let me get your book."

Mickie appeared in the hallway. "Hey," he whispered. "I didn't want..."

She slipped her arms around his neck and went up on tiptoes to kiss his cheek. "Thank you. Last night was the most amazing time of my life. Sneak out the front door."

He squeezed her in a brief, tight hug. "Better than amazing."

Back in his own house, he hesitated before getting in the shower. He could still smell her on him. Could still feel the silk of her hair and the heat of her skin on his fingertips. *Get it together, man. It was a one-night stand. That's all she wanted. And you gave her a great one. Don't be thinking anything else.* He jerked back the shower curtain and got in, scrubbing vigorously as if that would help remove her from his mind.

A couple hours of paperwork was usually enough to take his mind off anything. Not today. He leaned back in the desk chair and stared up at the ceiling. Mickie had somehow gotten under his skin. In the ten years since that night he'd left Ruby, he had never once had any problem drawing that line. What he'd done with Mickie last night, he'd done before. Mutually agreed-upon, no-strings-attached sex. Sometimes a single night, sometimes a weekend. But he'd always walked away with not a twinge of feeling other than respect and gratitude.

But Mickie. The memory of her—scrunched up in the chair, coffee mug full of wine, two pencils holding her hair in a tight bun—rose in his mind. He couldn't figure her out. She seemed so together and strong. But at times, she'd let the wall down and he could see how alone and frightened she was. But still, she kept going. Refused help. Was determined to make it on her own despite her fears. It was okay to respect that. It was not okay to want to fix that.

He shut down his laptop and leaned back in the chair. *You can't even fix yourself. How're you going to fix her problems?* The feeling still haunted him. Waking up with the sunlight flooding the room, hearing the sound of her voice as she moved around the kitchen making breakfast. It sounded like a home. *Family.* He jerked up out of the chair and ran a hand through his hair. Heart hammering, he shook his head. No. He had to get out of here. Right now.

Minutes later, he cranked up the motorcycle, heading out to check on the progress of the new guys and to see new clients.

MICKIE HEARD JOSH leaving and a small frown creased her forehead at the sound of the motorcycle speeding away. Too fast. *He always wears a helmet.* "Yeah, like a helmet is going to help when you hit a car going ninety miles an hour," she said out loud.

"Go?"

"No, baby. We're not going anywhere. Your mommy is going crazy."

"Kazy?"

"Yep."

While Ian finished his breakfast, she cleaned up the kitchen. Memories of the night before kept surfacing. Dear Lord, she'd seduced a man. Josh. She'd seduced Josh. A smile crossed her lips. And damn if it hadn't been worth it. Maybe. Just maybe they could renegotiate on that just once deal. No. She shook her head. No more. *You got want you wanted. Leave it at that. He doesn't want anything more and neither do you.*

There was a note taped to her front door. She stopped and stared. Her initial spasm of fear dissipated when she recognized Josh's handwriting.

> Mickie: I've got the phone. Going to do some field work today.
> Take the day off.
> Josh.

Her face burned as she crumpled the note in her fist. He didn't even want to look at her. Stuffing the note in her purse, she felt the stirrings of something that was suspiciously close to relief. Maybe she should have listened to him. The sex had been better than she'd ever expected. But now they were going to be all awkward and weird. She let out a sigh.

"Maybe we should go, Ian. Want to go to the playground?"

This was better. Out in the fresh air, pushing Ian in his stroller down a shady street to the park. Not a thought of Josh in her... *Yeah, right.* She pulled her phone out.

"Hey, Tee. What's up?"

"Me. Now. What are you calling me this early for?"

"It's after nine."

"I worked a night shift last night. Girl, I need to sleep."

"Sorry. I needed someone to talk to. Besides Ian. His conversational skills aren't the best."

"Something wrong?"

"No."

"Okay. I'm going back to sleep now. Bye."

The call ended. Mickie sighed. Maybe there would be some other moms at the park and one of them would be chatty. Because she seriously needed a distraction. When the phone rang, she tapped it.

"That was really rude, Tee."

Silence. She looked at the number. Icy fear shot through her limbs. Unknown. She ended the call. Crap. *Never answer an unknown call.* All thoughts of Josh and his talents were immediately extinguished as the paranoia crept back. She glanced over her shoulder. Nothing but a shady street. She slowed her steps. Maybe they should just go back home. Forget the park today. She felt exposed and helpless.

"Swing!" Ian called out. His little hands waved in the air.

She squared her shoulders. "I see the swings, baby."

They were going to the park. She was going to push Ian in the swings and let him play. She was not going to be afraid. She was not going to hide behind locked doors and closed curtains. The phone rang again and she flinched. Unknown number. The same one that had just called. She sent it to voice mail.

"Swing!" Ian's voice contained a bit of a whine this time.

"Okay, baby man. We're going."

Heart hammering, legs wobbly, she pushed on to the park.

SHE HADN'T KNOWN she was waiting until she heard the sound of Josh's motorcycle pull up the driveway and a knot of tension between her shoulders loosened. It was late and Ian had long gone to bed. She looked down at the card in her hands. NSAID. *Nonsteroidal anti-inflammatory drugs.* She flipped over the card. Heard the thump as Josh shut the door of the storage unit behind the duplex. Statins. A class of cholesterol lowering drugs that inhibit the enzyme… *What the heck is it? HM something something-tase.* She looked at the back. HMG-CoA reductase. *Yeah, right. How'd you forget that one?*

Her phone buzzed on the table. *Stop it. Stop jumping every time it rings.* The name flashing on her screen chased the fears away. Josh. Why was he calling from right next door?

"Hey," she answered. "What's up?"

"Nothing. Just wanted to check on you."

"Check on me? Why?"

"Because I sort of ran out on you this morning."

"Oh! Oh. No. I'm fine. You didn't run out. I thought it would be better, I mean…less complicated if Ian didn't…"

"Yeah, yeah. That's what I thought, too."

"I thought when you left that note that you didn't even want to talk to me anymore."

There was a long pause. "Damn, Micks, I'm sorry. That wasn't it. I was just trying to get my head straight. You make me think things."

"What kind of things?"

"Things I can't have."

She scrunched up in a tight ball in the chair, pressing the phone close to her ear. She wanted to pursue his meaning, but he had that sad, defeated tone of voice that she'd pried into once before and got barked at for her troubles. She didn't want to make him mad right now. She wanted… Him. Again. "Thank you for last night. It was pretty marvelous."

"It wasn't bad, was it?"

She laughed, happy to hear the snark in his voice. Much better than that sadness. "Smart-ass. You know how good it was."

"So what are you doing now?"

"Studying."

"Of course you are. How stupid of me to ask."

"Why?" Her heart began to pound as the word fluttered out. Was he thinking what she was thinking? The sensations of the previous night washed over her. His hands and mouth… "Did you want to come over?"

"Yes, I want to. No, I don't think I should."

"Oh."

"Do you want me to?"

"Yes, I want you to. No, I don't think we should."

He laughed and she smiled at the warmth of it. "So we'll stick to our original one-time deal?"

"We should."

"Yeah. We should."

"O-r-r-r," she said, drawing the word out. "You could help me study."

"Well. That would be a completely acceptable reason to come over. To help you study."

"Yes. Admirable, in fact. Such a great friend."

"What will we be studying?"

"Anatomy."

The word was barely out of her mouth when there was a tap at her front door. "Is that you?"

"Put your phone down and open the door."

She opened the door and he stepped through, smelling of leather and man. He pulled her into his arms and pushed the door shut behind him.

"Lock it," she said quickly.

He reached back and flipped the lock without breaking eye contact. "Better?"

"The chain?"

He slid the chain into place and turned her in his arms so she was pressed against the door. He put his forehead against hers and looked down into her eyes. "I'm not going to kiss you until you tell me why you made me do that."

She looked up at him. "I'm not going to tell you until you tell me why you're here."

"Anatomy lessons. Your turn."

"No. I mean why you changed your mind about just once."

He stepped back, his hands still warm on her shoulders. "You changed your mind, too."

"You changed your mind first."

"Do you want me to leave?"

He lifted a hand and traced his fingers along the curve of her cheek and across her lips. Her breath hitched in and out of her lungs. "No," she whispered.

"Tell me why."

"Habit."

"No kiss."

Oh? No kiss? Who was he kidding? "Fine. No kiss." She lifted the hem of his shirt and drew a finger along the ridge dividing his abdominal muscles. The muscles twitched beneath her light touch. "We'll begin the lesson here." She traced her finger around one of the six-pack of muscles there. "This is the tendinous intersection."

He went perfectly still, his eyes fixed on hers. "Cheater," he whispered.

She smiled as she pulled at the hem of his shirt. "Off. Can't continue the lesson with this in the way." He flung the shirt off in one fluid motion. She slipped her fingers around his waist to his spine. "External obliques. Latissimus dorsi."

Her fingers dropped to the button of his jeans and he pulled her to him with a groan. "You win," he whispered and brought his lips down on hers.

"OKAY. THAT WAS even better than last night. How is that even possible?"

"The anatomy lesson you gave me. It was very inspiring."

Mickie laughed and clamped a hand over her mouth. "Shhh. Don't make me laugh so loud."

Josh rolled to his side. "Laughing isn't the only thing you were being loud about."

Covering her face with her hands, Mickie groaned. Lifting her hands away, she looked over at his face.

He traced a finger along the curve of her cheek. "Why do you look sad all of a sudden?"

"I'm not. Not really. Just a little."

"Why?"

She shrugged and sat up, reaching out for her scattered clothes. They'd never quite made it out of the living room. "Because. You're a nice guy. And you are fantastic in bed."

"Well, we haven't actually been in a bed yet."

She threw his shirt at him. "You know what I mean. It's just a little sad that we met each other at the absolute wrongest time of our lives."

Josh froze in the middle of reaching for his jeans. *You let it go on too long.* "We both have a lot of things going on in our lives," he said carefully.

"Please," Mickie said as she pulled her yoga pants back on. "Stop staring at me like I dropped the *L* word on you or something. I know what this is. I can think you're an awesome guy and be sad when I have to move on without expecting some kind of long-term commitment."

Relief flooded him. He didn't want to hurt Mickie. The very idea of hurting her brave little heart made him flinch. "Are you going to be moving on soon, then?"

She looked up at him. "Now you're the one sounding sad."

"Yeah. I'll miss you guys a little."

"A little. Gosh. Thanks."

"Okay. A lot."

"Aww. You're so sweet." Standing, she pulled on her T-shirt. "Want something to drink? Water? I've got some sweet tea."

"Water'd be good."

He busied himself gathering his own scattered clothes while she was in the kitchen. This had been a mistake. He needed to stop. It wasn't her. It was him. He was having thoughts and feelings he shouldn't be having. He needed to back off. Keep his distance. Because it wasn't her inching toward the *L* word. It was him. He rubbed a hand across his lips. *No. That's not it. You're just all mixed up about the graves and Kim.*

Her phone buzzed as she came back into the room. She looked down at it and froze. Her gaze shifted from the phone to Josh. "Answer that for me."

"Why?"

"Please?"

He raised his eyebrows but grabbed the phone. "Hello?" His eyes never left hers. "Hello? Anyone there?" He ended the call. "No one there. What's going on, Micks?"

Folding her arms across her chest, she shook her head. "I don't know. I keep getting calls from unknowns but they never leave a message."

Josh stood. "Same number?"

"No. Different numbers."

"Weird."

She dropped her hands. "Yeah. Weird."

He put his hands on her shoulders. She'd looked terrified when the phone rang. "What's wrong?"

She shook her head and handed him a glass of water. She curled up in the armchair. "Nothing," she mumbled but her eyes were focused on the floor.

"Mickie..."

She smiled up at him. "It's okay, Josh. Really. Multiple unknown numbers are odd. I don't like odd."

"Probably a telemarketer or something."

"Okay. Yeah. Probably nothing."

"Want me to stay and really help you study?"

"No. Go home. It's getting late. I'll see you in the morning."

CHAPTER EIGHTEEN

MICKIE WAS GRATEFUL for the morning chaos of the Crew coming in to get the day started. It gave her something to concentrate on other than Josh. Because she had to stop thinking about Josh. That was done and over with. She'd gotten a couple bonus orgasms and that was all well and good but that was it. They had to quit playing this just-sex game. Or at least she did. Because her feelings were trying to sneak over that line she'd drawn.

After everyone had left and she was alone, she was better able to focus. Check email, answer the ones she could, leave others for Josh. Answer calls, schedule appointments. Check the online applicants, send promising candidates to Josh. Once she had all the tasks done, she pulled out the stack of study cards. This truly was an easy job. Essentially, Josh was paying her to sit here all day and answer phones.

See, there was another point. He was such a nice guy. She shook her head. *Nope. No. You have a plan. Stick to the plan, Mickie. Stick to the plan.* She pulled a card off the top of the pile. "Side effects of Zoloft," she said. "Um. Ugh. Insomnia. Dizziness. Decreased sex drive."

Flipping over the card, she made an exasperated noise. Three out of ten. "Gotta do better, girl, you've got to do better."

An hour later, she put down the cards. "That's it," she announced to the empty room. "I'm going to fail. I'm never going to graduate. I'm entirely too stupid for this. I'll never be a nurse."

She propped her chin in her hands. This wouldn't be so bad. She'd just be Josh's secretary for the rest of her life. She could do this. She'd be poor and never actually do anything like buy a car or a house. But that'd be okay. She made a face. Nope. She had to get away from Josh. It was more than the scorching-hot sex and the fact that he was a nice guy. He was a wounded soul. And she knew enough to understand that wounded souls were a huge personality trigger for caregiver types. Nurses loved their wounded ones. But the wounded ones didn't love back.

"Ah," she said, disgusted with herself. "Stop wallowing. It's lunchtime."

Her phone vibrated on the desk as she stood. Unknown. She stared at it, barely able to breathe, frozen on the spot. *Don't let it freak you out*, Josh had said. But it was freaking her out. Because if…

She stepped back from the desk. *No. Do not even let your thoughts go there.* But they went there anyway. He'd found her. Found them. He was toying with her now. Biding his time. Waiting for the right moment to…

"Stop it," she said loudly, her voice echoing in the small kitchen. Her thoughts quieted, but the adrenaline flooding her body did not. Hands shaking, heart pounding, she sank back in the chair. *Okay. So what if it's true? You need a plan. You need something better than running away again.*

That guy! She stood. That private investigator guy who helped Josh find his sister. What was his name? Wyatt? Maybe she could call him. Ask him if it was possible. She took a few hesitant steps toward the hall. She couldn't ask Josh. He'd want to know why. Maybe he had a phone number in his office.

She hesitated at the door. It was open but it seemed like snooping. *Do it for Ian, Mickie. You can't be a good mother living in fear and running all the time.* She stepped through the door and looked around. Josh had two desks set up. One was his work desk. The other was where job applicants took the personality tests. She'd been in this room a dozen times. Why was her heart pounding? *Because you are snooping.* If she could just remember Wyatt's last name, she could Google him.

The top of Josh's desk was a mess of papers and stacks of envelopes. Pulling back the chair, she sat down. His email would probably be the best place, but she didn't have a password for that and she most certainly was not going to attempt it. Do people even keep real address books anymore?

She moved some of the papers so she could see the desk calendar below. That was no help. On the day Wyatt had come, there was merely a *W* written. Slowly, she pulled open the center drawer.

"What are you doing?"

She froze at the sound of Josh's voice. Guilt and shame sloshed in her gut. She felt her cheeks burn. She pushed the drawer shut and turned around.

He stood just inside the door, hands on his hips, a frown creasing his forehead. She lurched to her feet. "I… I'm sorry. I was looking for… something."

He leaned against the doorway, crossing his arms against his chest. "So what's up with the guilty look?"

"I was…" Her words trailed off. She was going to have to tell him. She needed to know. She had to talk to Wyatt. She tried to meet Josh's eyes. "I was looking for a phone number for that private investigator guy you know."

"Wyatt? Really? Why do you need to talk to him?"

She dropped her gaze to the floor and pressed her lips together. "I just do."

Josh crossed the room in a few long strides. He put his hands on her shoulders. "Mickie. Look at me."

She lifted her head, feeling tears stinging at her eyes. Tears of shame. She couldn't bear to look into his eyes. Couldn't bear to watch what emotion she might see there.

"Is this about the unknown phone calls?"

Not trusting her voice, she nodded. Her throat felt tight and she twisted slightly away from Josh's hands. "Yes," she said and cleared her throat.

"What's going on?"

"I lied to you."

"About what?"

She looked at him then. He looked puzzled, not angry. "About the scars. The chest tube scars."

"I don't get what you're saying. They aren't chest tube scars?"

She perched at the edge of the desk, her arms wrapped around herself as tight as she could. To keep the trembling under some control. "Yes.

They are. But I didn't get them in a car accident. I was beaten. Kicked until my ribs broke."

The look of stunned horror on his face was a familiar one to her. Anyone who heard her story had the same look. "Who did that to you, Mickie?" His voice was a ragged whisper.

She turned her head away, unable to answer.

"Ian's father?"

She forced herself to nod.

"Jesus Christ, Micks."

"He was…controlling. I was young and stupid. When I got pregnant, he wanted me to get an abortion. I didn't want to."

This was where she would see the pulling away of empathy. Where she would see the judgment. Sometimes faint, sometimes outright and damning, but it was always there. It was somehow partly her fault for being with such a man. She kept her eyes on the floor because she didn't want to see that judgment in Josh's eyes. That, she couldn't bear.

He said nothing but she could feel the warmth of him as he came closer. His hand tenderly slipped across her shoulders, pulling her lightly against her side. "Do you think he's found you? Is that what this is?"

The words. Those words. Said out loud like that. The fear she never really let herself feel. Blindly, she turned to Josh, letting him fold her in his arms. Crying against his broad chest, she tried to explain. She tried to tell him that she didn't know. She just felt like something wasn't right. Like the brush of a spiderweb against the skin, something was there.

Josh said nothing. He just held on to her, rocking her from side to side. When she started to get herself under control, he loosened his hold. She felt his lips press against her forehead. "We'll call Wyatt. We'll get to the bottom of this. Okay?"

She nodded and wiped at her face. "I'm sorry."

"Why?"

The genuine confusion in his voice made her look up. *Why? Because she was pathetic. Dragging her drama around like a chain. Dumping her dirty past in his lap.* "I didn't want to get you involved in any of this."

"Hey," he said. His voice was stern. "Look here. You are one of us. You are part of the Crew. The Crew is family. We are here for each other."

"Don't tell the others."

"I won't. I'll call Wyatt and tell him what you need. You can give him all the details."

JOSH SENT MICKIE home early. Glad to have her out of his sight. If he'd ever thought he could have a relationship, she was walking, living proof of why he couldn't. She'd survived one monster. A monster so horrible, he tried to kill her for carrying his child. She didn't need another.

No. He'd never risk her, or any woman, to suffer that. And Ian. He was only a baby. He didn't deserve… He twisted away from his thoughts with a physical jerk. *Okay. We have a problem. Let's fix it.* He could do that. What he couldn't do was continue this fantasy he'd been nurturing. The one where he wasn't the monster. A bitter laugh ripped at his throat. *Dream on.*

He wanted to wait until after hours, when Wyatt would be done with his work at the insurance company, but the visions that were haunting him, of Mickie being viciously beaten and kicked, played over and over and over in his mind. He had to know she was safe.

"Hey, man. What's up?" Wyatt answered the call with a warmth and ease that felt jarring against the turmoil of Josh's emotions.

"I need help."

"Talk to me."

The instant transformation wasn't lost on Josh, even in his desperation. Some of the weight lifted. He had people who were there for him. At a moment's notice. Sadie. DeShawn. Now Wyatt.

He filled in Wyatt on the story Mickie had told him. "I don't know. It's probably nothing, but she's scared. It's a gut thing. She's feeling it. I felt it."

"Gut things are usually right," Wyatt told him. "I can clear some time and come up tomorrow to talk to her."

"I don't know if that's necessary. I don't want to put you out. Maybe a phone call?"

"No. I don't have a lot of experience as a PI with domestic violence, but I had enough as a cop. If she feels something is wrong, we need to check it out."

"Only if it won't cause a problem. I'll pay your normal rate. Whatever."

There was a long pause. Josh felt his face go hot as the implication of his words sunk in.

"You have some interest in this, Josh? Other than helping a temporary, part-time employee out?"

"No," he lied. "She's a Crew member. We protect our own."

"If you say so. How's the security there?"

"Nonexistent. I know she recently started using a bar on the back door. Double locks on front. And she has a baseball bat now."

"Started? Now? Are these new things?"

Josh thought back. Were they new? "I noticed them right away the other night, but I hadn't noticed before, so I'd say yes."

"Think she'd use the bat?"

Josh paused, thinking. "Yeah," he said after a while. "For the kid."

"Okay. I'll come up tomorrow afternoon. I don't like that she's adding security to the place. Something is worrying her. But I'm going to have to get all the gory details from her. Names, dates—everything. Is she ready?"

"I think so. I think she's been running for a long time and wants to stop."

After finishing the call with Wyatt, he called Mickie. She was on the street—he could tell by the traffic sounds. Pushing Ian in the stroller. Along a busy street. He shook his head. He couldn't buy in to her paranoia.

"Wyatt is coming to talk to you tomorrow," he said. "Are you going to be okay until he gets here?"

"Yeah. I feel kind of silly now. All of you are going out of your way for what's probably nothing."

"Don't. Even Wyatt agreed gut feelings need to be looked into."

"Okay. I appreciate this, Josh. I really do."

"It's nothing."

"No. It's pretty much everything."

She ended the call, leaving him staring at the phone. Everything. What was that supposed to mean? And why had he been contemplating asking her if she wanted to stay over at his place tonight? She and Ian could have his bed. He'd sleep on the couch.

Before he could chase that thought too far down the rabbit hole, the phone rang. Sadie. *Great. Thanks, Wyatt.*

"Wyatt tell you already?"

"Hello, Josh. How are you? Yes, he told me, you dork. However temporary, she's one of my Crew. How credible do you think this is?"

"I believe her story. Whether or not all these calls she's been getting are related, I have no idea."

"Do you think we ought to have someone stay with her tonight? DeShawn or one of your guys?"

"No. I'm right next door. Nothing's really happened except some phone calls."

"Okay. So, what's the deal here?"

"Deal?"

"With you and your cute next-door neighbor? She gets a few weird phone calls and you're up on your white horse?"

Josh scowled at the phone. "I think you are imagining things. Take off those rose-colored glasses you've been wearing."

"Cut the crap, Josh. Wyatt told me how worried you sounded about her. He might not know how out of character that is for you, but I do. You care about her. And her kid."

"She's a nice person. She's in a bad spot. I can help. That doesn't mean anything. I liked you better before you fell in love and got all Hallmark Channel."

"Screw you, Josh."

"There's the Sadie I know."

"Yeah, and this Sadie also knows you love nothing more than trying to change the subject when it starts hitting too close to home. Insult away. You like her."

"Doesn't matter. None of that matters, Sadie. And I'm really not in the mood to get into with you right now, okay?"

"Okay. Fine. What have you decided about Kim?"

"I'm hanging up on you now."

He jabbed at the end-call button. Problem with Sadie was she knew how to go straight to his sore spots. And she was always right. That's what really pissed him off. Because he did care about Mickie. And the kid. But none of that mattered. He was the problem here. Especially with Mickie, who'd already suffered at the hands of a monster. The fear in her eyes was identical to the fear he'd seen in Ruby's.

This is the choice you've made. That monster is inside you, man. You can never take the risk.

"I FEEL STUPID about this. I'm sorry I got everyone worried. It's probably nothing."

Mickie rubbed the palms of her hands against her thighs. Wyatt shifted in the chair and glanced over at Josh. "Can you give us some privacy, Josh?"

Mickie felt Josh's gaze move over her and bowed her head. *This was so embarrassing.*

"Sure," Josh said, standing. He took a few steps toward the door. Stopped. His fingers closed gently on Mickie's shoulder. "Be honest with him, Mickie. Tell him everything. You can't keep living like this."

Unshed tears clogged her throat and she managed a nod. After Josh closed the office door behind him, Wyatt leaned forward and plucked Mickie's hand from its nervous rubbing. "I want you to know, this is completely confidential. I won't tell Josh or Sadie or anyone anything without your permission, okay?"

"I know. Thank you. It's just… I don't know. He should still be in prison. He was sentenced to ten years. It's barely been two. He couldn't be out already, could he?"

Wyatt let go of her hand with a shrug. "Who knows these days? Let me check it out for you. At least we'll know what we're dealing with."

Yeah, that was the problem. She wasn't sure if she wanted to know. Part of her wanted to keep believing in the system. That she was safe for ten years. That the authorities would remember to notify her parents when he was released. But they'd let him out early once before. With no warning to her or her parents.

"Start at the beginning," Wyatt said quietly.

The beginning? In the beginning she was a stupid, sheltered, lonely only child who'd tried to be a grown-up by moving to the big city for college. Who'd met an older man who was charming and handsome and loved her completely.

"My real name isn't Michael Phillips. I changed it. Picked a male name to add one more layer of protection."

"Smart. You a Stones fan, I take it?"

She smiled at that. People rarely got the reference. "That was for my dad. He is a huge Mick Jagger fan."

Wyatt picked up a notepad and pen. "Tell me."

"My real name is Samantha Erickson. So I guess all the police reports and stuff will have that name."

For some reason, once that truth was out, the rest was easy. She told the story feeling somewhat detached, as if it had happened to someone else. The initial descent into the controlling, abusive behavior. The isolation from friends and family. The first brutal attack. The move home, pregnant and alone. The attack at the hospital.

All the names. All the dates. She watched, numb, as Wyatt scribbled it all down.

"And then I ran as far away as possible," she said. "And have been running ever since."

Wyatt's green eyes met hers and a weak smile trembled at the corners of her mouth. Sadie was a lucky lady. "You tired of running?"

She slumped in the chair. "Yeah."

Tucking the notepad into his laptop case, Wyatt nodded. "We'll help you. I'll check all this out and get back to you as soon as possible. Meanwhile, I want you to let Josh know if you don't feel safe. Promise? No more not wanting to 'bother' people?"

"I promise."

AFTER WYATT LEFT, Josh shut the front door and turned to Mickie. He gently cupped his hand against her cheek and turned her face up to look into her eyes. "You okay?"

She made a face. "Yes. No. I don't know. I'm all jumbled up right now."

Jumbled up. Yeah. "I know the feeling."

"What are you jumbled up about?"

You. Me. Kimmie. The past. The future. The now. He let his hand drop away from the warmth of her cheek. "First thing we're going to do is keep this front door locked while you are on duty alone here. I'll tell the guys. They can come around to the back so you can see who you are letting in."

Crossing her arms against her chest, she frowned up at him. "Don't be making a fuss about this, Josh. Really."

"Too bad. Don't worry, I'll tell them there was a burglary in the neighborhood so we're tightening up a little. Second thing—is Ian's day care safe? Do they know?"

That got him a smile. "Day cares have pretty strict rules. Only person besides me who can take Ian out is Tiana. I made her my emergency backup person. The doors are locked and you have to show ID to be buzzed in."

The relief that flooded him was unexpected. "Okay. Yeah, that's good."

"Josh."

Her voice was sweet and tender and stirred some long forgotten feeling within him. Going up on tiptoes, she slid her arms over his shoulders and around his neck, pulling him close and tight.

"Thank you for worrying about us," she whispered in his ear.

As he slipped his hands around her waist and up her rib cage to enfold her in his arms, he was acutely aware of how tiny she was. *How had she survived a grown man beating her?* He lowered his head to press his cheek against hers and breathed in the scent of her hair. The corners of his mouth twitched up in a smile. He could have stayed here, in her arms, doing nothing but smelling her hair and feeling her heart beat against his chest, forever. In her arms, all the noise in his head went away. A peacefulness that usually took a long yoga class and meditation came instantly when he was with her.

He stepped back suddenly. *No.* Catching her by the shoulders, he steadied her from the wobble his sudden move caused. "We can't keep doing this, Mickie."

Looking down at the floor, she took a deep breath and nodded. "You're right," she said, looking back up at him. "This is not the time, or the place. I care about you Josh, I really do. But I need to concentrate on Ian and school. You have your issue with your sister to deal with. We both need to get our lives straight before we think about…"

Her words trailed off and her cheeks went pink. The cold logic of her words, the way she held herself tall and straight, arms folded against her stomach, contrasted with the pink on her cheeks. *She cared about him? Shit.* It was one thing for him to start having feelings and get hurt, he was used to that. The idea of hurting her made his skin crawl.

Mirroring her stance, he crossed his arms

CHAPTER NINETEEN

THERE WAS HARDLY any stress that a good two hours in a gym couldn't cure. Arms and legs still shaky, his abdomen burning with every move, Josh felt clearer as he rode home. The best thing with Mickie was to let it go. Leave her alone. Stop playing this game they'd been playing. Because she was beginning to think it was real.

The lights were off in her side of the duplex when he walked around to his front door after stowing the bike. Good. He wouldn't hear her voice through the walls. After throwing a frozen burrito in the microwave, he grabbed a bag of corn chips and a bottle of water. Deciding to dine formally tonight, he put the chips in a bowl and dumped the burrito on a plate. He tucked the water under his arm and carried his feast to the living room, where he flopped down on the couch and clicked on Netflix. He needed a movie. Something thin on plot and thick with explosions and noise. The opening credits hadn't even finished rolling when his phone vibrated on the coffee table. He snagged it with his fingertips, wincing at the burn in his triceps, and looked at the number. A frown creased his forehead. This was unexpected. He paused the movie.

"Mr. Gathers. Is everything okay?"

"Oh, sure. I was checking in on you. Making sure you're okay after our talk. That was a lot for you to take in at once."

"Yes, sir. I'm okay. Still trying to process it all and figure things out."

"Did you go see your parents?"

He hesitated. He'd been trying not to think about that. He had contacted the cemetery management and was beginning the process of hacking away at twenty years of red tape and legal mumbo-jumbo to get permission to move his mother's remains to another spot. And a proper headstone. His father could stay where he was. Alone and forgotten. But his mother had tried. She'd been even younger than Mickie. With two kids. She'd tried. And deserved some honor and respect for that.

"Yes, I did."

"Ah. I was going to offer to go with you in case you hadn't. I was worried about it after you left. Worried you'd go straight there and it would be too much."

Josh stood, ignoring his protesting sore muscles. Pacing to the kitchen and back, he pressed a hand against the wetness that was forming in his eyes. He felt…strange. An odd unfamiliar sense of warmth welling up inside him took his breath away for a moment.

"Son? You okay?"

It was that word *son* spoken in that voice. That voice sounding like everything good and strong in this world brought the emotion to life. Grateful. He was grateful for this man, who cared for him in spite of the years. In spite of the distance. In spite of merely being the cop who answered the call that night. *You've been on my heart all these years*. Mr. Gathers' words came back to him.

"Yes, sir. I'm okay. I'm just…" A small laugh escaped him. "I'm… Thank you for caring about me."

"Ah, shoot. That ain't no hardship. I'm real sorry I didn't follow up on you all those years ago."

"You had your wife to care for," Josh said. "It helped a lot that you even remembered me. I don't know how to explain it, but that someone from before knows me, it makes me feel…"

His words trailed off. How did it make him feel?

"Validated?"

"Close. A friend from foster care, she went with me to the graves, she said when she confronted her mother, she realized she'd felt invisible all her life and to have the mother who abandoned her *see* her, made her feel visible."

"That makes sense. Sounds like you have a good friend there, Josh."

"Yeah. We sort of adopted each other. She's my sister and I'm her brother. We've come a long way together."

"Good. Good. I had another reason for calling. A little more selfish. I was wondering if you could come out here some weekend. Your visit got me thinking and there are some other things I'd like to talk to you about, but I don't want to do it on the phone. This is kind of a sit-on-the-porch-in-a-rocking-chair talk."

"Oh, okay. Sure. That would be great. What's best for you?"

After they'd decided on a date and time, Josh slumped down on the couch. He turned the movie back on, but couldn't keep his mind on it. What else could Mr. Gathers have to tell him? He smiled. Most likely nothing. He was a retired cop living alone out in the middle of nowhere. Probably wanted company. And that was fine with him. He felt he'd found, not a friend, but maybe someone to be to him what Abuelito had been to Sadie. A grandfather figure.

He grabbed the phone to call Sadie, but frowned at the time. It was getting late. He didn't know if she was at home or staying at Wyatt's. He put the phone down. Returning to the kitchen to rewarm his cold burrito, he found himself listening for any sounds from Mickie's half of the duplex. Silence. His fingers drummed on the countertop and he realized his heart felt light in his chest. Even though his muscles were still screaming, he felt pumped full of restless energy. He wanted to tell someone. Anyone. He'd found a link to his past. A good link.

You're excited. You want it to be Saturday so you can go visit him. The realization made him laugh out loud. That's what it was. He grabbed the burrito out of the microwave and returned to the living room. *Is this how kids felt before they went to camp or Disney or whatever it was that normal parents did with their kids?*

"Dude," he said out loud. "You've lost your mind."

Still, he was smiling as he turned the movie back on.

MICKIE STOOD LEANING into the refrigerator, one hand holding the door open, the other gripping the freezer door handle. She stared at the contents. *What did I come in here for? Food. Yeah, you need to eat something.* Her stomach disagreed. Her stomach was a tight ball of sloshing anxiety. What had she done? Why had she involved Wyatt in this? Did she really want to know the answers?

She grabbed one of Ian's string cheese packs and shut the door. Biting into the cheese, she made a face as she walked down the hall. *What the hell am I feeding him?* Ian lay sleeping on his pallet of blankets. *Soon, baby man. I'll get you a real bed soon.* Finishing the cheese as she went back to the living room, she plopped in the chair and picked up her phone.

"What's up, chickie-poo?" Tiana answered.

"I'm scared." The words came out unbidden. It wasn't what she had planned to say. To make it worse, she started to cry.

"I'll be there in fifteen minutes," Tiana said.

"You don't have to..."

"Shush. Are you scared like I should tell you to take the baby and go to the hot guy from next door? Or is this some existential scared?"

"I don't know what existential even means, Tee. But it's my head. I've got a bad head."

"Well, in that case, I'll be there in twenty minutes with a nice bottle of wine."

It was thirty minutes. Mickie knew because she peeked out the curtains at every sweep of headlights. But as soon as Tiana's car swept up the driveway and Mickie saw her climb out of the car, she felt the fear begin to dissipate.

She wasn't alone. That thought brought tears to her eyes.

"Tell me what's going on, boo," Tiana said as they settled at the dining room table with glasses of a very nice Chardonnay.

"I don't even know where to begin."

"Begin at the beginning."

"It's him."

"That guy? Isn't he in prison?"

"Maybe. Maybe not. But he's here." She tapped her temple. "He's here all the time. And I let it get to me. I was getting all these unknown calls. And I started jumping at shadows and feeling scared all the time. So I…did something."

Tiana leaned forward and covered Mickie's hand with her own. Her dark eyes looked deeply and directly into Mickie's. "What did you do?"

"Josh knows a private investigator." The words came out in a whisper. "He agreed to help me. I told him everything. He's going to check on… things."

"Okay. That's good. At least you'll know, right?"

Mickie took a sip of wine. "I hope it'll work like that. I hope Wyatt will come back and say he's still in prison. But I feel I may have asked a question I don't really want the answer to."

"Because what if he's out?"

Mickie went still and pressed her lips together.

A creeping, crawling feeling spread from her gut to her arms and she rubbed her hands along the length of her thighs. *Because yeah, what if he's out?* "He got ten years," she said in a hoarse whisper. "It's only been two."

Tiana lifted her shoulders in a shrug. "I don't know, girl. I don't know how that would even happen."

"Yeah. I'm probably freaking myself out for nothing."

"When's the last time you ate? Real food?"

"This morning?"

Standing, Tiana squeezed Mickie's shoulder. "Sit right there, momma. I'll make you some food." She began rummaging through the fridge and cabinets. "Sounds like you are having some PTSD flashbacks about this."

Mickie snorted out a laugh. "Ya think?"

"I'm serious. Something kicked all this up. More than a few phone calls from unknown numbers. What else have you been up to?"

"Nothing."

Frying pan in hand, Tiana turned and sent a don't-lie-to-me look at Mickie. "You slept with that slab of beef next door, didn't you?"

Feeling her face go hot, Mickie sipped more wine. "Yeah, but that's not..."

"Oh, I think that's exactly it. You had you

some good—I hope—times. He's the first man you been with since?"

"Yeah."

"That's what's going on, Mickie. It's old ghost stuff. It's hard to trust again after something like that."

Mickie shook her head. "I trust Josh. He's a nice guy, for real."

"That's what you thought about the last one, too. At some point."

Mickie stared as Tiana turned back to the stove. Her blood felt like ice in her veins. Her hands, they wouldn't stop shaking. She clasped them together. *Oh, my God. She's right. Because you let this go further than just sex. You let him into your heart. That treacherous, stupid heart of yours.*

"You want some cheese on this omelet?"

"No."

After she ate, under Tiana's watchful eye, every last bite of the food, she did feel better. "Am I ever going to know? Am I never going to be happy and fall in love and all that?"

"Probably. There has to be things that when you look back, you can see were signs. You know what those are, you know how to spot them, right?"

"I don't like to look back. In fact, I actively do not look back."

"Understood. But maybe you should."

Mickie jumped up and began washing the dishes. "I don't want to talk about this anymore."

There was a moment of silence. "Okay. So how was the sex?"

A real laugh made its way out of Mickie, surprising her. "Pretty damn fantastic."

"That's always a plus."

This was one of the things Mickie was beginning to love about Tiana. She knew exactly when to stop pushing. And when some good, juicy girl talk was needed.

JOSH SHUT HIMSELF up in his office the next morning so he wouldn't have to face Mickie. He had to stop messing around with her. The sooner school started and she quit, the better. He ran the litany through his head again. She'd already been hurt. She had a kid. *Stay away from her.* A sharp rap on the door jolted him out of his thoughts. DeShawn opened the door and strolled in.

"I didn't say come in," Josh said.

"I didn't ask. Trying to be polite. In case you had your finger up your nose or something."

"What's up?"

"Got a call from my recruiter yesterday," DeShawn said.

A jolt of panic hit Josh hard and fast. If the

army was making DeShawn leave now, crap, everything would fall apart. He forced himself to be calm. They'd work it out. They always worked it out. "What? They got a good look at you and decided you couldn't lift a rifle?"

DeShawn flexed an impressive bicep and kissed it. He smirked at Josh. "You wish with them noodle arms of yours. Nah, there's some paperwork. Some physical stuff. I think I need some shots, I dunno. But they want me to go down there next week to get it taken care of. They won't let me do it here for whatever bureaucratic bullshit reason."

Trying to hide his relief, Josh nodded. "Better get used to dealing with that. You're going to be marching to it for the next twenty years. Not a problem. Go get it done. Quicker they take you, the quicker I'm rid of your chicken-leg self."

The phone rang as DeShawn got to his feet. "Get that. Later."

Josh grabbed the phone. "Yo, boss, what's up?"

"Checking in."

"On?"

"Wyatt's little pro bono freelance for that cute little next-door neighbor of yours. You and all the stuff you're dealing with."

"I don't even know what she asked Wyatt to look into. She wanted it confidential."

There was a long silence on the phone. He began to wonder if he'd gotten Wyatt in trouble. Finally, Sadie let out a breath. "Is she okay?"

"I guess."

"You guess? You don't know? She's an employee, Josh. We take care of our own. There is something going on with her."

"How do you know that?"

"I don't know. She's got this look about her. Like if a car backfired, she'd jump a mile in the air."

"Her ex beat her. Very badly. She was in the hospital."

He hadn't meant to say that. Or maybe he did. Maybe he wanted Sadie to leave him alone with her snarky little comments about him and Mickie. There was an even longer silence this time.

"Piece of shit."

"Yeah, so let's stop trying to match her up with another one, okay?"

"You know what? I'm not even going to talk to you. You aren't even rational about it."

"What's to be rational about? I almost punched a woman in the face. And I liked it. I liked watching her afraid. You think I want to risk anyone else's safety?"

"I'm only going to say one thing to you—take

a good, long, honest look at where you were then and where you are now."

"I'm still me..." he began before he realized Sadie had ended the call. Why did she refuse to understand this? He powered down the laptop and scooped up his phone. *Get to work, Josh. Work was simple.* Work didn't leave him with a pounding head. Work didn't make him want things he couldn't have.

"Hey, Josh?"

He stopped with his back to the kitchen doorway and closed his eyes. Mickie. He couldn't deal with her right now. Couldn't look into those blue eyes. He let his shoulders slump as he turned. "Yeah?"

"Can you sign these papers before you head out? I can get them to the post office later."

"Sure." He crossed the floor and took the pen and papers from her hand. He glanced through them quickly as he signed. Government stuff.

"You okay?"

"Yeah. Headache. I took some Motrin. It'll pass."

"Chug a little caffeine with it. That'll help the medicine kick in quicker."

He looked up at her. He hadn't meant to. She was smiling at him. A happy smile that crinkled the corners of her eyes. He tossed the pen on the table. "Was that on one of your index cards, Nurse Mickie?"

"As a matter of fact, it was not. I already knew that one."

She crossed her arms and gave him a smug look. He felt his mood lighten and his own smile begin. *No. You can't keep letting yourself feel this.* "I gotta run. Busy day. Keep that front door locked. The guys know to come around to the back."

He got the hell out of there. She made him feel things. Want things. Things he had no right to have. Sadie's words echoed as he drove to his first appointment. He knew what she meant. The thing with Ruby was a long time ago. He'd been young and stupid. Ruby wasn't a poster child, either. They'd both been just out of foster care. She'd come out with a drug addiction and a suitcase full of attitude. He'd had a matching suitcase but luckily not the addiction.

He shook his head against the thought. It didn't matter. That was what Sadie didn't understand. It didn't matter that he actually hadn't hit her. The only thing that mattered was that he'd realized that the monster lived inside him. The only thing he could do was never put another woman in harm's way. Especially not a woman like Mickie.

She'd met her monster. And survived.

Whatever this was between them, it couldn't be. If he had to be the one to end it forever, so be it. A small hurt now was better than the betrayal of her trust later. Pulling into the driveway of his first appointment, he put the car in Park and pressed his forehead against the steering wheel. *Damn headache.* He lifted his head and rotated it from side to side, trying to stretch out the tension. *Stop thinking about her. That's your problem. You're letting her get under your skin. End it.*

MICKIE LEFT WORK a few minutes early. DeShawn and Drake had returned for the day so she took advantage of the opportunity to get to the post office before picking up Ian. Traffic was getting hectic as she negotiated Ian and his stroller across busy Devine Street, but once across, it was a pleasant walk along shady sidewalks.

As she rounded a corner, a child's wading pool caught her eye. It was at the end of a driveway, with other household items piled around it. Garbage? She stopped and toed the pool. It looked okay. She glanced around, and seeing no one, turned the pool over to inspect the bottom. No cracks or holes that she could see.

"Whatcha think, Ian? Want a swimming pool?"

"Poo?"

"Pool-l-l." She rolled the l-sound.

"Poolalalala?"

She laughed and lifted the plastic pool. "Let's give it a shot, yes?"

"Yes!"

After getting dinner fixed and Ian fed, they went out on the back porch, where she'd stashed the pool. She moved it onto the grass and Ian climbed in and sat down. Glancing around, she noticed a hose connected to the water spigot on Josh's side of the duplex.

"Come on, Ian, get out for a minute so Mommy can fill it up."

"Up?"

It was good. No leaks. Took forever to fill and Ian was about a minute from full meltdown when she stripped off his shirt and shoes and lifted him in. She sat down in the grass and laughed as he squealed and stomped around in the pool. Leaning back on her palms, she smiled. This was such an exciting age. He was learning new things, soaking up everything like a sponge.

"Water!" he shouted at her as he smacked the water with his hands.

"Yep. You are splashing the water." Mickie glanced over as Josh walked around the little brick divider between their patios. He stopped at the pool and reached in, smacking the water with his own hand, making Ian squeal with happy laughter.

"Spash Yosh!"

Josh splashed at the water again. He turned to Mickie with a grin that about melted her heart to goop. She sat forward as Ian lost his footing and splashed down on his butt.

"Uh-oh!" she called out in a singsong voice.

"Uh-oh," Ian echoed. He held his arms above the water and looked down at himself. Cautiously, he lowered his hands and patted at the water. "Fun!"

Josh sat down beside Mickie. "Lots of fun," he said to Ian. He shoulder-bumped Mickie. "Where'd this come from?"

The heat she felt exploding within her had nothing to do with her slight shame at stealing junk from a trash pile. "Found it thrown out. It's perfectly good. And free."

"Free's good."

They sat in silence for a while, watching Ian. He got up on his hands and knees and was experimenting with putting his face in the water.

"When does school start for you?"

"A month."

"And yet here you are, sitting out in the sun, not an index card in sight."

"Are you teasing me?"

"Not at all. Making an observation."

"That has to wait until little man there is in bed. I can't get anything done with him around."

Josh made a hmm-ing sound and nodded. Leaning back on her hands, Mickie stretched her legs out and let herself take in the moment. The summer sun was lower in the sky but the heat of the day remained. The cicadas were shrilling in the thin line of trees at the back of the lawn. Somewhere a lawn was being mowed. It felt so peaceful and normal. A late summer afternoon in the suburbs. The only thing missing was a grill full of burgers. She smiled, picturing Josh at the grill.

She shook her head. *Stop dreaming. Stop pretending. You've got a long row to hoe. Focus on that. School. Ian. Nothing else.* The charm of the moment dissipated under the weight of reality. She rose to her knees and duck-walked to the pool. "Up, little man. You're hands are probably pruned."

"Puuned?"

She lifted him out as Josh laughed. Ian's diaper, now soaked with water, surrounded him like a giant bubble. "Wrinkled." She set him down and turned his palms over to show him. "Come on, little man. Let's get cleaned up and we'll have story time."

Josh's hand appeared in front of her and she took it, allowing him to help her to her feet. She looked into his eyes and felt that warm wave again. More than lust. A painful twinge tore at her throat. He was such a nice guy. More than that, he was a good man. A friend. She was going to miss the everyday interaction once school started.

He let go of her hand, but not before she saw the same warmth mirrored in his eyes. He smiled and stepped back. “I’ll let you tend to business.”

“Bye, Yosh!” Ian yelled. Because that was his default volume setting.

Josh leaned down. “Later, dude.” He held out his hand, palm up, and Ian smacked his palm down hard against it.

“Ater doo!”

Mickie laughed. “Where’d you learn that?” she asked Ian.

“It comes with the Y chromosome,” Josh said. He straightened and caught her by the elbow. “You guys be safe. I’m a phone call away, okay?”

Whatever warmth she’d felt was frozen beneath those words. *Right. Never forget.* Until she heard from Wyatt, everything was temporary.

JOSH WENT BACK to his side of the duplex. He’d left his dinner uneaten on the plate when he’d heard Ian playing in the pool. Why? He didn’t know. He put the plate in the microwave. *Yeah, you do. Because it feels good to be with her.* He sat back down and pushed the food around on the plate.

Stop lying. He'd gone out there to tell her. To end it once and for all. Tell her they had to stop playing this game. There was no future. But he hadn't been able to do it. Didn't want to be the cause of any more pain in her life. *Going to have to edge her out, man. Be cool. Stop getting drawn in.*

A heavy blanket of sadness settled over him. *It felt like having a family.* His biological family had been ripped away from him in one violent night. Sadie had provided him with a second family, a family of choice, but now she and Charleston and the guys seemed so far away. Now the fates were dangling promises of family before him. Kim. Mickie and Ian.

A grin crossed his lips as he remembered the saturated diaper. It looked like something out of a cartoon. What would it be like? To have a woman like Mickie? And a kid? Be the dad his father wasn't? Reach out to Kim? She was getting married. Maybe she'd have kids and he could have some and they would be cousins. Lots of cousins so if anything happened they wouldn't be alone in this world.

"Stop depressing yourself," he said out loud. Giving up on eating, he pushed the remains of his dinner into the garbage can. *Wish in one hand, spit in the other. See which one fills up first.* Who had told him that?

He had to stop thinking like this. Stop believing he was normal and could have any kind of normal life. He had Sadie. He could play cool uncle to Jules. But he would never have a family of his own. He forced himself to remember the look in Ruby's eyes. The anger that went to fear with a blink. And how it had made him feel. Powerful. In control. He had the monster within him and he needed to never forget that. He couldn't do anything about the past, but he sure could make sure it didn't continue.

He scooped up his phone and dialed. "Hey, DeShawn, you up for a little pool tonight?"

Because he had to get out of here. Had to get away from the temptation next door. Because soon, she'd be putting Ian to bed and he'd hear her voice. Sometimes she sang, sometimes she read books to him. And he'd sit on the other side of the wall and listen. And wish for things he couldn't have.

Yeah. That was a plan. Get out for the weekend. Head up to the mountains. Ride the Tail of the Dragon up in Tennessee. Put as much distance between himself and Mickie as he could.

CHAPTER TWENTY

MICKIE WAS HAVING THOUGHTS. Bad thoughts. She was glad Josh was out of the office today because she needed to get her head straight. Friday evening, when he joined them for the impromptu pool party, it had all seemed so clear. They had something. Not just she and Josh, but with Ian, too. But then he'd left for the entire weekend without a word. Just roared out on his bike at dawn on Saturday.

Whatever little idea was brewing in the back of her head needed to be squashed. And fast. She finished up the day's paperwork. Returned a few phone calls. Scheduled a couple of new customers. It didn't seem fair. If she'd met Josh after she was finished with school, maybe?

She blew out an aggravated sigh. *Stop it.*

Pulling out her study stack, she picked up the top card. Antipsychotics. She snorted out a laugh. Maybe she needed some.

"A class of medication used to manage psychosis. Schizophrenia and bipolar disorder in particular." She turned over the card and read the back. "Yes!"

She was getting more of the pharmacology questions right than wrong now. Maybe she should move on to pathophysiology.

It only took a minute to run next door and scoop up Tiana's notes and a fresh stack of index cards. She paused as she returned. Had she not closed the sliding door all the way? It was open about a half inch. Icy fear traced down her arms to settle in her gut. She peered into the kitchen. No one was there. She shook her head, trying to shake loose the fear. *You were in a hurry. You probably didn't shut it all the way. Stop letting him have room in your head.* Still, it took everything she had to open the door and step inside. "Hello?" she called out. There was no answer. A quick check of the rooms revealed no intruder. *Get yourself together, woman.*

Soon, the rush of fear was forgotten in the orderly discipline of index-card making. She loved study cards. The simplicity of them. The flexibility. Want to study one particular subject? Pull those cards. Want to keep general knowledge fresh? Use all of them. She opened the file with Tiana's neatly written notes.

Pathophysiology. The disordered physiological processes associated with disease or injury. *This should be easy. The reverse of everything you learned in physiology.* She rolled her eyes with a quiet laugh at herself.

She began. Pathophysiology of the circulatory system. Of the lungs. Of the musculoskeletal system. Of the skin. The brain. Two hours later, she sat back, rubbing at her sore hand. It was going to take her until school started to finish making the study cards. *Should have started sooner. Shouldn't have let yourself get bogged down in pharmacology.*

A knock on the glass door sent the pen she was reaching for skidding off the table. Heart pounding, she turned to see DeShawn and Drake at the door.

"Sorry. Didn't mean to scare you," DeShawn said as she opened the door for them. "Came back for some lunch and a supply run."

"It's okay. I didn't notice you walk up."

DeShawn looked at the table. "More index cards?"

"I've got a lot to learn," she said, leaning down to pick up her pen before returning to her seat.

Drake crossed the kitchen to open the fridge. "Pretty sure they don't expect you to know it all before you start. That's sort of what you're paying for—them to teach you."

"Don't be picking on my Mickie," DeShawn said, draping an arm around her shoulders. "I did the same thing before I started the engineering classes. Was afraid if I fell behind, I'd never catch up."

"Exactly!" Mickie said. "See? I'm not insane. I'm just..."

"Insane," Drake said as he carried sandwich fixings to the counter.

"Who's insane?" Josh asked as he came in the back door.

Drake pointed a mayonnaise-covered knife at Mickie. "That one."

Josh's eyes met hers before moving to the index cards on the desk.

"Yeah, those. Does seem a little compulsive." He smiled at her.

She turned away from those dark blue eyes and began straightening the cards. "It's a tad OCD, but well within normal limits. I like to be prepared. That's not insane. It's prudent."

"Thinking ahead," DeShawn added.

"See? DeShawn agrees with me."

"Yeah, but he's crazy, too," Josh said.

"Go away. All of you."

Josh went away to his office. DeShawn and Drake, however, remained in the kitchen, taunting her. She teased them back, grateful for the distraction. Because Josh was back there. Sitting there. Alone. The bad thoughts were back.

"You aren't going to fail," DeShawn said. "I'll put money on it."

Mickie crossed her arms on the table and leaned forward. “And what makes you so sure about that?”

“You don’t have any other option but to pass. Am I right?”

Her teasing smile faltered on her lips. He was right. The weight of it pressed down on her. But she’d shouldered heavier loads than this. This was only the longest distance she’d have to walk with the weight. “One hundred percent right,” she said, turning her attention back to the notes and the index cards.

The moment they left, her concentration went to hell. No amount of pathophysiology would get Josh off her mind. They were alone. This was the perfect time. She only needed to work up the nerve to say what she wanted to say. Well, the nerve and exactly what it was she wanted to say. Because she didn’t know what she wanted. She only knew what she didn’t want. She stood.

And sat back down. Her fingers played over the fresh stack of index cards. *Angioplasty. Something about fixing a blood vessel.* Yeah, she was going to have to get busy on this subject. She looked up at the hall doorway. *Come on. Go do it. You’ll find the words. Or are you going to take the coward’s way out?* She stood.

"COME ON IN," Josh called out after a tentative knock on the door. Mickie opened it and sort of slunk into the room. She stood against the wall right inside the room, her hands clenched together. "What's the matter?"

She cleared her throat. "Nothing."

He spun around in his chair to face her. "Something's wrong. Ian?"

"No."

"Did Wyatt have news for you?"

She crossed the room quickly and sat in the other chair, facing him. "No. Nothing like that. Josh, I—I wanted to…talk to you."

A bad feeling came over him. His stomach seemed to fall away to his feet while icy cold fingers gripped his heart. *No. Don't let this be that.* He glanced at his phone, willing it to ring. Anything to derail whatever was about to come out of her mouth.

"Mickie…"

"Listen to me, Josh. We've got something here. Don't we? I know I feel it and I think you do, also."

"Mickie."

Her cheeks went bright red but she stammered on. "I mean, I know neither of us is in a place where we are ready…but that doesn't mean we have to let this go, does it?"

He had to stop this. Before she fell further down this rabbit hole and dragged him down with her. Barely able to look into her eyes, he reached out and took her hands. "Mickie, we can't continue this. I can't continue this. It's best if we walk away friends."

"Why? Don't tell me you don't feel it. Don't tell me you don't care about me. Or Ian. I know how I feel about you."

He lowered his head and stared at the floor. Why didn't she stab him in the heart? Because she was right. He did care. He did want to be a part of her life. But he couldn't. And she had to understand that.

"Mickie," he said softly. "You can't. I'm not who you think I am."

She pulled her hands away and sank back in the chair. "What do you mean?"

He looked up at her, knowing his pain meant nothing. Saving her was what was important. "My father beat my mother almost every day. When I was five, he murdered her, then killed himself."

The confusion in her eyes began to shift to something else. Concern. Sympathy. He shook his head. "No. When I was nineteen, I learned I have that same monster in me, Mickie. During an argument, I slammed my fist through a wall two inches from the face of a woman I said

I loved. I can't ever risk hurting another person. The best thing for you would be to take that job at the day care and move in with that woman. Get as far away from me as possible."

He forced himself to watch her eyes as the warm sympathy melted away to be replaced with fear. *You did that to her, Josh. You put that fear there.* She stared back at him for a moment before standing and walking out. He slumped back in the chair, sick to his stomach and burning with shame. *It's for her own good. She had to know the truth.*

MICKIE BARELY MADE it to the sink in her kitchen before everything she'd eaten in the last week came up from her horrified stomach. Grabbing a handful of paper towels, she ran water over them and sank to the floor. *Dear God. You did it again. Threw yourself at another man you should have run away from. What is wrong with you?*

She wiped at her face. Every part of her was shaking. *Stupid. Stupid. Stupid.* She should have known it was too good to be true. Nice guy next door. Helping her move. Giving her a job. Jumping her bones. She wrapped her arms around her drawn-up legs and rested her forehead on her knees. Even now, she was looking for excuses.

Looking for reasons why it wasn't true. When he'd come right out and told her.

"Believe him." Rising to her feet, she cleaned up her mess. *Back to the original plan. Find another job. Find another place to live.* Hopefully the apartment offer would still be good. *Get away from Josh and his blue eyes and wounded soul that turns off your common sense. No more thinking with your heart.*

She glanced at the clock. Plenty of time for a nice long shower before she had to pick up Ian from day care. Wash this day away. Where she could pretend she wasn't crying. Where her sobs wouldn't be heard.

Again. You're hiding and crying in the bathroom again. She turned off the water, disgusted with herself. This was different. *Stop beating yourself up. Old you would have argued, would have tried to convince him that what was in the past was the past. Old you would have continued to pursue him. This is new you.*

She toweled dry and, wrapping the towel around her wet hair, moved into the bedroom to dress. A quick glance at her phone showed a missed call. She tapped the screen to make sure it wasn't from the day care. It wasn't. Cold fear made her shiver. Wyatt Anderson. She dressed quickly and contemplated the call. Good news? Bad news? Did she even want to know?

She squared her shoulders carried the phone to the living room. Might as well get it over with now. Before she had to pretend everything was okay in front of Ian.

"It's a bad-news, good-news, bad-news, good-news situation," Wyatt told her when she got him on the phone.

She felt strangely calm. Or was it numb? "Okay."

"Bad news is that he is out. Got out after eighteen months for good behavior. Apparently, he's a shit human being but a model prisoner."

"The good news?" she asked through cold lips.

"He has a girlfriend. Good thing about that is that once an abuser focuses on another person, they rarely go back to a previous relationship."

"God help her. Bad news?"

"Before I tell you this, know that it isn't going anywhere. Nothing is going to come of this. There is no way, okay?"

What could be worse than him being out of prison eight and a half years early? A horrifying thought slimed its way through her fog. "Ian," she whispered.

Wyatt sighed. "Yeah. He asked his lawyer about getting visitation. The lawyer shut him down. Told him it would never happen. I spoke to the lawyer. He reported the request to the Department of Social Services. Your case is sealed. But it has been flagged for extra precautions. There is absolutely no way. His parental rights were severed. That is extreme. Okay? I only told you so you'd know the truth. He doesn't know what your new names are. The lawyer said he called Ian 'the baby' and doesn't even know if it's a boy or girl. Ian is safe."

She forced herself to breathe. Slow. Deep. In. Out. The idea of that monster even thinking about her baby made her want to snatch up Ian and run far, far away.

"You okay?" Wyatt asked softly.

"Yes. It's hard to hear. You said there was more good news?"

"As of today, I checked right before I called you, he is still in Wisconsin. He has to meet with his parole officer in person every other day and call in on the off days. He's not missed a single report in since getting out."

"So he's out there. Wandering around free."

"And being watched carefully. The parole officer and I spoke. He was aware of the history. My contact upped his commitment to keeping tabs on this guy."

"So, you think I'm safe?"

"I can't say that with any certainty. But it does look like he's moved on. He's doing all the right things. Hopefully, he'll keep on doing them. I'll keep in touch with his parole officer. He promised me he'd let me know if he had a failure to report."

Mickie nodded and swallowed down the lump in her throat. "Thank you, Wyatt. I appreciate this. I really do. I probably can't pay you all at once, but if you send me a bill, I can pay a little at a time."

"There's no bill. You're a part of the Crew. That makes you practically family."

She slumped in the chair. *I don't even think I'm an employee anymore.* "Thank you, Wyatt. I mean it. And tell Sadie thanks for me, too. You guys have been amazing. I appreciate it."

She ended the call and sat staring at the ceiling for a long time. She didn't have the energy for any more drama. There was a light knock on the front door and she let her body slump even more. *No more, day, okay?* But the day wasn't finished with her, she realized, as she looked through the peephole. Josh.

She opened the door a crack. "Yeah?"

He held up a pile of papers, index cards carefully balanced on top. "You left these."

She opened the door and snatched the papers from his hands. "Thanks," she said before shutting the door in his face.

"Mickie, open the door. I wasn't finished."

"I am," she said, sliding the chain lock in

place. A brave declaration from someone whose heart was pounding and legs trembling.

After a long pause, she heard a sigh. "Okay," Josh said. "I'll have one of the guys bring over your paycheck tomorrow."

"Okay."

"I'm sorry."

There was nothing she could say to that. She was sorry, too. Sorry and embarrassed and furious at herself.

IT FELT STRANGE, the next morning. To hear the guys arriving for work while she sat at her kitchen table, waiting for Ian to finish his breakfast. She sipped coffee and fingered the growing stack of index cards. She'd finished the entire pathophysiology syllabus and notes the night before in an attempt to stop thinking the thoughts that had been running circles in her mind.

"Momma?"

She smiled up at Ian. "What, honey?"

"Sad?"

She forced a smile. "No, baby. Momma is tired. You done? Ready to go play?"

She felt like a fugitive, peeking out the windows before maneuvering Ian's stroller out the front door. She didn't want to bump into any of the guys. Didn't want to have to explain… anything. *Ugh. What a fool I made of myself.*

She looked down, sending her hair cascading over her cheeks, hiding her face as she hurried down the sidewalk.

After getting Ian settled in his classroom, she sat down with the director to talk about the temporary job. She filled out all the proper paperwork. Was told a background check would be done and if that came back okay, she could start immediately. She shook the woman's hand, thanked her and walked out into the heavy heat of the day. She looked around. She didn't want to go home. Sit there with Josh right next door. The guys coming and going. And not be a part of it.

She wandered over to the USC campus and practiced finding her way around. Finding a shady bench, she sat down and pulled her phone out of her backpack. She scrolled through the few contacts she had. Tiana. Josh. The day care. It was a depressingly short list. She found Diane's number. She was the single mom looking for a roommate. Mickie shook her head. She was regretting the decision to stay where she was now. She wanted to get as far away from Josh as possible. An aching lump rose in her throat. Why? Why had she let herself believe they might have had something? Why had she completely overlooked any clues about him?

She dialed Diane's number. No answer. She left a message. Now what? She called Tiana.

"I'm sleeping."

"It's after three."

"So? I worked last night."

"Sorry. Go back to sleep."

"What's going on?"

"I'm stupid." Those were the only words she managed before dissolving into tears. She lowered her head, hiding behind her hair, and wiped at her eyes.

"No, you aren't. What happened?"

Mickie couldn't speak. She swiped at the tears and took a deep, gulping breath. "I made a fool of myself." The tears wanted to come harder now. She held them back with sheer will. She was in public. She didn't sit in public and cry. She stood and began walking toward home. Yes. Walking was better. Passing people made her keep the facade in place. *Nothing to see here. Move along.*

"Let me guess. This involves Mr. Blue Eyes next door."

"Yes. There was something there, Tee. I swear he felt it, too. I went to him…"

"Geez, Mickie."

"I know. I told him that I knew neither of us was in a place where we could…but maybe we didn't have to let it go completely."

"And he said what?"

"He said he almost hit his girlfriend once. Put

his fist through a wall. He said he'd never put anyone in that place again."

Silence.

"Tee?"

"Hold up. I'm confused. He said what?"

"That when he was younger, he was violent toward his girlfriend. That his father beat his mother. And he wouldn't put any other woman in that position."

"Well. That's...interesting."

"Huh?"

She stopped in front of a house with a low brick fence around the front yard. Mickie sat down there. She really didn't want to go home but she couldn't sit on campus and cry all day, either.

"It's interesting. Most abusers would never admit that they were at fault. They always make it the other person's fault."

"Oh. Tee, how did I let this happen again? How did I fall for one of them *again*?"

"I don't know. Only you know that, Mickie. There are warning signs. Things that when you look back, you recognize as a pattern."

"I told you I can't look back on that. I can't."

"That's fine. But here's some tough love for you, Mickie. If you want to move forward, you're going to have to look back. If you want to protect yourself in the future, you have to know how and why you got into that relationship. Come on, what'd you do? Ignore this in all your psychology classes?"

Mickie looked up through the branches to the heat-dulled blue sky. "I don't know if I can, Tee. I really never want to think about it again. If I could pay to have it taken out of my brain, I would." A movement caught her eye and she glanced over to see an orange-and-white cat disappear through a gap in the fence. "I feel so ashamed."

"Well, as the valedictorian of my graduating class who walked across the stage carrying her one-year-old, I feel your shame. But let me tell you something. Shame is a good thing sometimes. The pain of it makes us change. So you can let that shame sit at the bottom of your soul and burn a hole right through or you can grab it up by its slimy little throat, look it in the eye and evict its ass. Move on. Do better."

Mickie couldn't help but smile at the imagery. "How'd you get to be so smart?"

"My momma didn't raise a fool. You have a decision to make, Mickie. Face it or have it poison every relationship you try to have."

"Cheerful thought."

"It's not a thought. It's a fact. Now, you okay? Do you need me to come over?"

"No. I've been whiny enough. I'm taking steps."

"But make sure those steps are leading somewhere. Not merely running away."

Mickie ended the call with a sigh. Tucking her phone back in the backpack, she looked over the low wall for the cat. It was long gone. Maybe she should get a cat instead of a dog. Less work. *Maybe you're trying to distract yourself. Maybe you should go home and stop hiding here.*

SHE WASN'T HOME ten minutes before there was a knock on her front door. A confident knock, not the tap Josh had given the night before. She stood on tiptoe to look through the peephole. DeShawn. She didn't want to talk to him, either, but he had her money.

"Hey," he said when she opened the door. He held up an envelope. "Josh asked me to give this to you."

"Thanks," she said, reaching for it.

DeShawn lifted it high above his head. "Not until you tell me what's going on. I just got back from Charleston. Something happened while I was gone. Don't lie to me."

"Nothing's going on. I got a job at Ian's day care. It's temporary until school starts, but it pays more. The end."

"Why is Josh hiding in his office like a kicked puppy? Why wouldn't he look me in the eye when he asked to me to give you this? Why, in fact, is he not giving this to you himself?"

Mickie crossed her arms against her chest and glared up at DeShawn. "And why, since you seem to be all about the whys this afternoon, is any of this your business?" She held her hand out, palm up, making give-it-to-me motions with her fingertips.

Shaking his head, DeShawn lowered the envelope. "Josh is my friend. Something happened. If I was a betting man, I'd say he has feelings for you. Real feelings. He has some sort of martyr thing going on where he's decided he'll never fall in love or have a family because of some messed-up shit from when he was a kid. I've seen him blow off women before."

Mickie stared up at him, her mouth hanging open. DeShawn gently placed the envelope on her palm. "You know about that?"

"I know about his parents. I know about that woman he hooked up with. What Josh doesn't see is that he isn't that eighteen-year-old kid anymore. He's holding on to this distorted vision of himself because he doesn't want to let anyone get too close. I think you blindsided him and he's pushing you away as hard and fast as he can."

She dropped her gaze to the envelope balanced on her palm. She took a corner and held it between her hands. Her name was written across the front in Josh's scrawled handwriting. "He's pushing and I'm running," she said under her breath.

"What's that?"

"Nothing. Thanks, DeShawn. You were a good friend while I was part of the Crew. Good luck with the army, okay?"

He caught the door as she tried to close it. "No. It's not okay. Josh is my best friend. He's over there hurting."

"That's not my doing. I went to him. I made a fool out of myself, DeShawn. I told him I thought we had something here. That maybe now wasn't the best time for either of us, but I begged him to give it a try. And he pushed me away. Told me no. To my face. No."

Pressing her lips together, Mickie drew in a long slow breath and stared at her toes. Her heart thudded in her chest. When she felt she had her emotions under some sort of control, she looked back up at DeShawn. "I'm sorry he's hurting, but that is his doing, not mine."

Letting go of the door, DeShawn caught her hand in his and gave it a gentle squeeze. "I'm sorry. It's just..."

Mickie forced a smile. "Yeah, I know. I've seen it. You Crew people are pretty tight. I'm glad I got to be a part of the family. If only for a little while."

He let go of her hand and pointed a finger at her. "You'll always be part of the Crew to me. Don't you forget it."

JOSH HAD HAD about enough of this day.

"This better be business," he said as he picked up Sadie's call.

There was a millisecond of silence. "I'm your damn boss. There. That was business. Now what is wrong with you?"

"There are several things wrong with me right now. Take your pick."

Silence hummed in the air. Then some rustling and a door shutting. "What's going on?"

"I can't deal with you right now, Sadie. Seriously. I can't, okay?"

Josh could picture Sadie's face as she wrestled between big-sister bossiness and fellow foster-survivor understanding. "You can't *deal* with me?"

"No. What do you want, Sadie?"

"Well, I was going to ask you about Kim, but obviously, you aren't in a mood for that."

"This is exactly what I'm talking about. It's the middle of the day. I'm working. You call me and start digging around in my personal business. Stuff you know hurts like hell and then you get pissed when I don't want to talk about it."

More silence. He let it play out. They'd played

this game before. She'd cave. She always caved when she was wrong.

"I'm sorry. You're right. I'll stop putting my nose in your business during work hours. But I reserve all rights to hound you after hours and on weekends."

"Thank you."

"So what else is going on? Because you've dealt with me nagging you about Kim for a long time. Something else is bothering you. Mickie?"

"She's gone."

"Gone? Explain."

"I told her the truth."

"You what?"

"I let it go too far. I went too far."

"Meaning what? You love her? She's in love with you? What is it? Are you going to make me drag this out of you one sentence at a time?" She dropped her voice, reminding him of the nights they'd spent telling their secrets. "Talk to me."

He rubbed a hand across his eyes. "Yeah. Even the kid was growing on me. Man. It came out of nowhere. She's so amazing. Not to mention what she's been through. But she's moving forward. Determined. Strong."

"Reminds me a lot of you," Sadie said quietly.

"I'm nothing like her. Sadie. Her ex beat her bad enough to put her in the hospital. Almost killed her and the baby. She's been living on the run ever since. I don't even think Mickie is her real name. She deserves way better than me. And I certainly don't deserve her."

"What did you tell her?"

"Like I said, the truth. I told her that I'd almost hit the woman I said I loved, and I will never put another woman in that position. That whatever there was between us didn't matter. I told her to go."

"But you didn't hit her. You hit the wall. If you're going to be down on yourself, at least be honest. There, in the heat of the moment, in your rage, you still were able to stop from hitting Ruby and turned your anger to the wall." Sadie's voice was soft but there was a thread of steel winding through her words. "You don't even see it, do you? That boy who was with Ruby doesn't even exist anymore. That boy and his potential for violence actually died that night. What you did in that moment was reject the path of anger and violence. You've dedicated your entire life since that night to healing yourself."

"No," he said, his voice ragged. "I liked it. When I saw the fear in her eyes, I liked it."

"That was the boy who'd been pushed from foster home to foster home, powerless all his life. Yes, he probably did like feeling some power. But in your heart, the core of you who are and always have been, Josh, you rejected that. You did, or you wouldn't have stopped. You would have given in."

Closing his eyes, Josh shook his head. *She doesn't get it.* He let out a breath. "Sadie, I can't explain this to you..."

"Was Mickie afraid?"

The question hit him like a slap in the face. "What?"

"When you told her that you were some sort of woman-beating monster. Was she scared?"

His head was pounding and he wanted to end the call. Stop thinking about this. "Yes."

"How did you feel about it?"

"Sick to my stomach. Ashamed. Every bad thing you can think of, Sades, that's how I felt, okay? Can we stop pouring acid in this now?"

"Yes. We can. But I want you to consider your reactions to each incident very carefully. You already know the truth. You aren't a monster. You're afraid to love. Exactly like I was."

Ending the call, he tossed the phone down so hard it skittered across the desk and fell to the floor. He slumped back in the chair and stared at the ceiling. *Damn it. Why's she always right?* He'd clung to the myth of himself as a monster for so long now. It was comfortable. It was convenient. He, like Sadie, had had to put up walls around his heart for self-preservation. It had only taken one or two moves between foster homes to teach him that lesson. You don't let yourself get attached. You don't let yourself get comfortable. Or feel at home. Because it hurt when the people you thought cared for you packed up your clothes in a paper bag and put you in the social worker's car for the drive to the next family.

And he'd been very good at clinging to the myth. Very good at using it as a shield against the world. His life had been a series of shallow sexual relationships and long periods of celibacy. Seeing Sadie happy and settling down with a ready-made family had brought clarity to him. He was lonely. Tired of keeping up the pretense that he didn't want the same things everyone else did. A woman to love. A family. A partner in this crazy world.

And Mickie was everything he'd ever wanted. Strong. Smart. Funny. Independent as hell.

And he'd pushed her away. Scared her by using her past against her. *You're such a prick. You don't deserve her.* He rubbed at the ache in his chest and cleared his throat. *Nothing you can do about it now. Let her go. It's for the best. She'll never trust you now anyway.*

He powered up the laptop and opened a clean document. His fingers found the keys. Dear Kim. He sat staring at the blinking cursor for a long time. *Just write it.* Slowly, he began to hunt and peck out letters.

When he was done, he read back over the words and nodded before printing it out. He tucked the letter into an envelope and put it in the desk drawer. He'd leave it there a few days. Read it again later. Decide if he was ready to send it. It could be her decision. They could take it slow. He didn't have to dump everything on her all at once. The smile that began faded when he heard Mickie's front door bang shut. He moved to the window to watch her pushing an empty stroller down the sidewalk. Going to pick up Ian from day care.

Peacefulness faded into a sad ache as he watched her leave. Soon, he would hear the familiar sounds from next door. Mickie's voice, soft and sweet. Ian talking at full volume. Cooking sounds. Bath time and story time.

He pressed his forehead against the windowpane. He wanted to have that. The boring routine of family life. Work. Home. Love. Mickie had knocked all his defenses aside without even knowing and walked right into his heart. And now that Sadie had exposed his excuses as the flimsy shams that they were, he had nowhere to hide. He'd thrown it all away for a lie he'd been telling himself for years.

CHAPTER TWENTY-ONE

MICKIE ALMOST IGNORED the phone vibrating on the counter. Ian was banging two toys together and she'd managed to snatch the frozen lasagna from the oven about two seconds before the smoke detector would have gone off. She glanced at the number and everything inside her went cold. It was her mother's home number. It must be something horrible if she was calling from home.

"What's wrong?" she blurted out as she answered.

"Hopefully nothing. We had a break-in today."

Leaning against the counter, Mickie tried to calm her runaway heart. She'd thought someone had died. "At the house?"

"Yes. My laptop and some jewelry were the only things taken but the whole house had been searched through."

Fear prickled along the edges of her arms and stirred at the base of her spine. "What did the police say?"

"Not much. They dusted everything for prints. They know about everything."

"Okay. I had a PI look into things. The situation has changed."

She smiled at Ian as he held up a block for her to see. Sliding down, she sat on the floor. At this moment, she'd give the last twenty years of her life to put Ian on the phone and let him talk to his grandmother. But safety came before hearts' wishes.

"So soon?"

"Unfortunately. But it's being monitored very carefully."

"Momma! Look, bwok! One bwok! Two bwok!"

"Is that…?"

"My babysitting gig? Yeah."

"Talking."

A silence fell. A silence Mickie wanted desperately to fill with every detail of Ian's life and his growth and all the amazing things he was doing and learning. Her throat throbbed with unshed tears. The pain was laced with a strong dose of anger. Why were they the ones who had to suffer? Part of her wanted to say to hell with it, throw off all pretense and live her life in the open. But one look at Ian's innocent brown eyes squelched the impulse. She had to keep him safe.

"Thanks for the update. I'm sure the police

will get to the bottom of it. I need to get back to work."

"I understand. Love you."

"Love you."

She ended the call and lightly banged her head off the cabinet. *Was this ever going to end? A laptop and some jewelry?* Her parents weren't well off by any stretch of the imagination, but if someone was going to break in, why leave the TV? The desktop computer her father used? The hunting rifles he kept in a locked case in the den? She turned the phone over and over in her hands. Maybe she should call Wyatt and tell him about this. Maybe he could call the parole guy and have him check into it.

"Hungee, Mommy. Me hungee."

She hauled herself to her feet with a sigh. She'd been hungry, too. Before the phone call. "Okay, little man. Dinner is ready."

For Ian's sake, she needed to pretend that everything was fine. Hiding her fears and doubts from him, putting on a smiling face, came so easily to her now that she half believed it was true. What-ifs were forgotten while she got him through dinner, through play time, through bath time and story time. It was when she tucked him into bed with a million kisses, when she turned off the lights and pulled the door to his room almost closed, that the fear came back.

Not even her stack of study cards could distract her from her disquiet. Finally, she picked up the phone. Put it back down. He'd done her a huge favor for free. The parole officer would notify him if anything changed. Wyatt would call her. If there was anything to tell, he would call her.

She opened the file for the next class. Nutrition. Flipping through the syllabus and Tee's notes, she didn't feel the sinking horror she'd felt when looking through the pharmacology notes. Progress. Pulling out a blank index card, she uncapped her favorite Sharpie pen. What if the parole guy didn't know about the break-in at her parents' house? *That's not something the police would do, is it? They wouldn't tell the parole guy, would they?*

Wyatt answered on the second ring. "Mickie. Everything okay?"

"Yeah. I'm sorry. I didn't mean to call so late."

"You didn't. What's going on?"

"I got a call from my mom. There was a break-in at their house this morning. Thief stole her laptop and some jewelry. She told the cops… everything, and they are supposed to look into it. I didn't know if that was something the parole guy would hear about."

"Only a laptop and jewelry? Was there anything else of value left untouched?"

"My dad has five or six hunting rifles in a

locked case. It has a glass front and they are completely visible. The house had also been gone through."

"Mmmm..." Wyatt said.

"Is this bad?"

"Sorry, I was jotting down some notes. Let me call the PO and make sure he knows about this."

"So, is this bad?"

"I don't know what this is, Mickie. Try not to worry. As of today, he's still in Wisconsin. That is a long way away. Okay?"

"Okay," she repeated back through numb lips.

"Keep your doors and windows locked. Have your phone charged and on you at all times. Keep your wits about you. It's probably nothing."

"But it could be something?"

"It could. Is there anything on the laptop that could lead to you?"

"Not that I know of. We use a blind mail service for snail mail and an app for email that is supposed to hide the IP address. Pay phones for phone calls."

"But she called you from her cell or landline?"

"Landline."

"Okay."

"Is that bad?"

"Mickie. Take a deep breath. I'll look into all of this. Try not to worry until we know if we have anything to worry about."

"Okay. I'll try."

"I'll call you as soon as I know anything, okay? Day or night. But keep your phone close, okay?"

"Okay. Thank you again. You're being so generous."

THE NEXT MORNING, Mickie still hadn't heard anything back from Wyatt. "No news is good news, right?"

"Right!"

She sighed and poured more coffee. Sleep had been elusive through the night. *At least Ian agrees with me.* Stifling a yawn, she sipped coffee and watched as Ian picked through his breakfast. He had the spoon down pat. Cheesy grits made it from bowl to mouth without a drop. Maybe she should keep him home from day care today.

There was a constant undercurrent of unease running through her. Ghosts of the past or a mother's instinct, she couldn't tell. Keith was not a burglar. Nor was he a computer expert. He'd been a bouncer at a strip club and a low-level drug dealer. Not that he'd told her that. Security was what he'd told her he did for a living. She rolled her eyes at her gullibility. She could easily imagine him showing up at her parents' house and trying to scare some information out of them. But breaking in? Stealing the laptop? And hacking in to locate IP addresses? That seemed beyond his capabilities.

A day locked up in the house alone seemed to guarantee nothing but a cranky Ian and an exhausted mommy. But that unease still sat at the bottom of her gut. Maybe the day care would let her help out for the day. Then she and Ian would be together behind locked doors with an emergency alarm wired directly to the police department. She shook her head. *You're being a coward. You promised yourself. You promised Ian you wouldn't cower in fear and miss out on having a life.*

Her phone vibrated and her heart rate went soaring. Snatching it up, she let out a sigh of relief. It was Diane, the single mom who wanted a roommate.

"Hey," she said, forcing herself to sound normal. "Thanks for calling me back."

"Sorry it took so long to get back to you. We were visiting my parents in Rock Hill. I'm also sorry to tell you that I found a roommate already."

"Oh. Okay. Darn. I'm sorry, too. Sorry I couldn't commit sooner. If it falls through, let me know, okay?"

"Will do."

Well, there goes that plan. She ended the call

and sighed, leaning forward on her elbows and covering her face with her hands. Thing is, she didn't want to move. She liked this place. She liked the neighborhood. It was quiet. Safe. School and day care were both a short walk away. It was on the bus route for when the weather got bad. If only it wasn't right next door to Josh.

Ian had finished his grits. "Done, Mommy," he said, holding the empty bowl out to her.

"I see that. Good job. Drink your milk now."

She got up to rinse out the bowl. She shook her head. *Nope. We're going to run business as usual today. Play hooky.* "Whatcha say, Ian? You want to stay home today? Hang out with Mommy? We can go to the library and get some books and movies? Does that sound like fun?"

"Fun!"

The fear would never go away. She'd learned to live with it. But she never went anywhere without being hyperaware of her surroundings. She never entered a room without hesitating in the doorway and checking out who was inside. Out in public, there was a spot between her shoulders that always felt like there was a target on it. Sometimes the fear was barely a whisper. Sometimes it sat on her shoulder, as it did now as she maneuvered the stroller down the sidewalk.

Luck was on her side today. They hit the library just as the children's reading hour began.

Ian took his spot in the circle and Mickie was able to try to relax at a nearby table. Her heart just about burst with love as she watched him sitting with the other children. Innocent to the dangers in this world. He was turning out to be a good kid. By the time she finished nursing school, he'd be ready for pre-K. She'd buy a small house in a good school district. A new car. A puppy. A big puppy that would grow up to be Ian's best friend. All she had to do was keep herself focused on that goal. Maybe she should get a book about dog breeds. She wanted one that was good with kids, protective without being aggressive, and…

Her phone buzzing in her backpack startled her from the light doze she'd slipped into. Panicked, she looked around, seeking out Ian. He still sat in the circle, but the story hour was coming to an end. The call went to voice mail before she could catch it. She waited until Ian came running to her.

"All done?" she asked.

"The bunny founded his home," Ian told her with all the seriousness he could muster.

She scooped him up and balanced him on a hip. "That's awesome. Let's get these things checked out and we'll go home for some lunch, okay?"

Once they left the library, Ian settled happily into the stroller. He'd been demanding to walk more often, but the closer to nap time, the more willing he was to ride. She took her phone out as she pushed the stroller toward home. Her heart sunk. Wyatt.

She didn't bother to listen to the voice mail. She immediately called back. "Sorry. I was in the library and couldn't answer. What's up?"

"Where are you right now?"

Fear turned her insides to ice. "Walking home. About three blocks away." She stepped up her pace.

"Okay. Still don't need to hit the panic button, but Keith missed his phone-in contact today. His parole officer met with him at the usual time yesterday, which was at noon. He was supposed to call in before ten this morning."

"So he could have been gone for almost twenty-four hours now," Mickie said. *More than enough time to drive from Wisconsin.*

"Yes. Like I said, let's not panic yet, but I think we need to get a safety plan in place. Do you have anyone you can stay with for the next few days?"

Tiana came to mind. And so did the old fear of putting innocent people in harm's way. It was one of his most frequent threats: that he knew where her parents and her friends lived. "Um. Maybe. I'd have to check."

"What about Josh? Or one of the Crew? Josh

is right next door. Could you stay with him? Or maybe he could stay at your place?"

"I don't think that's necessary. He's right next door."

And yeah, not to mention that it wasn't going to happen. The shame she felt throwing herself at him outweighed her fear at the moment.

"Okay. Go home. Lock up. Sit tight. I'll let Josh know what's…"

"No. I'll tell him."

"Will you?"

She crossed her fingers. "Yes."

"I'm not sure you will, Mickie."

"I will. When it's necessary."

Wyatt's heavy sigh was clear through the phone. "If that's how you need it to be."

"It is."

"Give me a few hours. I'll call you back. In the meantime, if you even think something is wrong, call Josh. Call the police, promise me."

"I promise."

Ending the call, Mickie pushed the phone into the front pocket of her jeans. Wrapping icy fingers around the stroller's handles, she lifted her head and straightened her back. "Let's make a quick run by the grocery store, okay, Ian? We're going to need snacks."

She was hunkering down. This was familiar. When she'd been released from the hospital after the beating, she'd lived in her old bedroom for more than three months. Trips to the kitchen for food or bathroom were terrifying ordeals. Once she'd been diagnosed with PTSD and put on medication along with therapy, she'd put her life back together. Then came the incident at the hospital. She knew what she needed. Supplies. Lock down. Hunker down. Wait it out.

Later today or tomorrow, Wyatt would call. Keith would have been found drunk or high, shacked up with some meth head he'd met at a bar. Maybe tossed back in jail for violating parole. And the paranoia would recede and she'd get back on track. Work. School. Living.

CHAPTER TWENTY-TWO

THE TRIP TO Sumter and Mr. Gathers' farm was much more pleasant now that he knew where he was going. It also gave him a place to be this weekend instead of listening for the sound of her voice through the walls. Josh revved the bike up to that magic moment where he and the road were one. He could forget about Mickie. Forget about how empty the past few days had seemed without her at the kitchen table, answering phones and flipping those index cards. There was no thought beyond the next few feet of blacktop. Leaning into long, slow curves. Lush green fields passing in a blur. Small moments caught. A small boy waving from a porch. A hawk swooping low over an overgrown field.

Mr. Gathers was waiting on the shady front porch as Josh puttered up the long driveway. He parked the bike under the branches of the same massive oak tree that shaded the porch and stashed his gear.

"Mr. Gathers," he said, greeting the old man as he came down the porch steps.

"No need for all that. Just call me Nate. Everyone does."

They sat on the porch in the rocking chairs, sipping iced tea and making small talk about the crops and the heat for a while. A deep peace settled over Josh as he rocked. The sound of the wind in the trees, the occasional high shrill of a cicada and the faint swoosh of a car as it passed by on the highway were soothing in a way he would never have expected.

Nate put down his glass on the little table between the chairs with a clink. "I have a confession to make," he said.

Josh smiled as he looked over. "Yeah?"

"I do. When you were out here last time, you caught me off guard."

"Sorry about that," Josh said. He had shown up completely unannounced. "I was grasping at straws at that point."

Nate waved off the apology. "No, no. Not that. Well, yeah, that. But what I mean is that I didn't tell you all the truth."

"About my parents?"

"No," Nate said with a slow shake of his head. "See, I've met your sister."

The words sank in slowly. Josh stared at the man, feeling slow and stupid. The whole world seemed to freeze for a moment. He shook his head slightly to jump-start his brain. "You met her?"

"Couple years ago. In fact, she sat right there in that very same chair you're sitting in now."

Josh looked down and rubbed the palm of his hand along the arm of the chair. "I don't understand. She was here?"

"I'm sorry I didn't tell you when you were here, but like I said, you took me by surprise. Her daddy brought her here. She was, oh, eighteen or nineteen around then."

"Wait." Josh held up a hand. "So she knows about—about our parents?"

"Yes, she does. Her parents had told her bits over the years and they were telling her that last hard truth. They came out pretty much for the same reason you did. Trying to understand what happened."

Josh rubbed a hand across his mouth. Trying to grasp the enormity of this information. Nate seemed to understand this and quietly set his chair to rocking. He thought about the letter in his desk drawer. *She knows. This changes everything.* His thoughts seemed to scatter. He knew he should say something. Ask some questions. All he could think though was *she knows.*

"You okay over there?" Nate asked after a few minutes.

"Yes. I think so. Pretty shocked."

"I'm sorry I didn't tell you before now. But I didn't know—"

"No, no," Josh said, interrupting. "I understand. I kind of showed up out of the blue. You had no idea if I was who I said I was or if I was… whatever."

Or if I was like my father. Those were the words he'd tripped over. Nate had been a cop all his life. He surely knew how the world worked. The cycle of abuse and abusers from one generation to the next. No, he didn't blame the man for not telling him about Kim that first day.

"Exactly," Nate said pointedly but not without a hint of humor. "But when I did know who you are, I needed to make things right. I had to tell you."

"I understand." Josh blew out a cleansing breath. "Wow. I don't know what to… What's she like?"

A raging curiosity swept over him now that the initial shock had passed. His sister had been right here on this very porch. It seemed unreal and overwhelming at the same time.

Nate took a slow slip of his tea. "Well, son, I could tell you all about her. Or you could find out yourself."

Frowning at the smiling old man, Josh leaned forward. "I don't understand."

"After I…knew who you were," Nate said with a smile, "I talked to her father."

Everything inside him went still and quiet. "You told them I had been here?" he asked through numb lips.

"Yes, I did."

"And?"

"Your sister is here. She wants to meet you right now. I didn't know if you'd be ready so I was trying to ease you into it."

Josh was on his feet, looking around. "She's here? Where?"

Nate stood with a chuckle. "I'm guessing that means yes."

"Yes. That means yes."

He could barely contain the feelings that were crashing within him. Excitement. Joy. Relief. He had to restrain himself from running down the porch steps. After all these years. After all his agonizing. She'd come to him.

"Come on, then," Nate said.

Josh followed him through the house to the back porch. As they stepped down on the small patio there, Nate pointed at the path between two fields of tobacco. "If you follow that path to the end of the field and go left, you'll see a line of trees and a pond. She's waiting down at the pond."

Looking out over the green fields, Josh spotted the stand of tall trees. Kim was there. So close after all these years. He stood rooted to the spot, though, shifting his weight from foot to foot, unable to take that first step. Nate's hand closed gently on his shoulder.

"Go on, son. It's going to be okay."

"What do I say?"

"I'd start with hello, but that's just me," Nate said with a grin.

It made Josh laugh, which seemed to break the paralysis that held him in place. Taking in a deep breath, ignoring his suddenly pounding heart, he walked across the small lawn to the fields. Once out from under the sheltering oaks, the sun was hot on his skin. He slowed his pace, still trying to believe this was real. Everything seemed hyperreal. The sun too hot. The green too green. There was a fecund, slightly sweet smell in the air. The smell of a farm? City-boy Josh didn't know.

At the end of the field, there was another path to the left. Turning, he saw the line of trees ahead and the greenish brown glint of a Low Country pond. He remembered Sadie's walk to meet her mother. Or rather confront her. He hadn't realized the extent of Sadie's bravery until this very moment. As excited he was to finally find his sister, part of him wanted to turn around, get on his bike and ride away as fast and far as possible. Because once it became real…

He stopped. A young woman was sitting on a bench next to the pond, tossing something into the water, causing circular ripples. His heart was about to pound out of his chest and a trembling made him stuff his hands in his back pockets. *That's Kimmie. Right in front of me.* He tried to call her name but his mouth was suddenly dry and he only managed a strangled croak. Then she looked over.

And smiled.

He stood staring at her. She was taller than he expected. Maybe Sadie's height. Her dark hair was up in a ponytail full of ringlets that made him smile.

She began to walk toward him and he made his feet move. They stopped a few feet from each other.

"You look like our mother," he said.

"Really? You remember her?"

Her voice was sweet and kind. She sounded exactly how he imagined a schoolteacher should sound. "Not really," he said. "I remembered right when I saw you." He stepped closer. Her eyes were blue, like his. "I can't believe you're really here. I've been looking for you for a long time."

And then, she was in his arms. He wasn't big on hugging people, but she'd thrown her arms around his shoulders and it had seemed like he needed nothing in the world more than to hold on to her. Everything went away. This was his sister. She looked like him. They had the same blood in their veins. The same past. Tears stung at his eyes.

When she stepped back, they both wiped at their eyes. She laughed. "Wow. This is crazy, huh?"

"That's a good word. I feel like I'm dreaming."

She took his hand. "Come sit down. I have a million questions."

They settled on the bench. Josh saw a bag of cracked corn on the ground. "You were feeding the fish," he said.

"He's got some bass in there. So tame he can probably net them out of the water." She threw a handful on the water and there was a flurry of circular ripples. "Did I call you Yoss?"

He laughed. "Yes. Used to drive me crazy. One of my clearest memories is of holding a jar of grape jelly and pointing at it. You'd say 'jelly' and I'd point at myself and you'd say 'Yoss.'"

She smiled but it dimmed quickly. "I don't remember anything other than that. When I was about fifteen, my parents told me about you. They didn't know much. That you existed. They didn't know that until a few days after they got me. The social worker didn't tell them. It wasn't in the paper, but it was on the news. They contacted the social worker to tell them they would take you, too, but nothing ever came of it."

"Yeah. I was moved around a lot. I had 'behavioral issues.'" He made finger quotes around the words.

Kim gave him an incredulous stare. "Ya think? They should have been worried if you hadn't had issues."

Shrugging, Josh threw a handful of feed out to the fish. "I managed."

"Do you remember that night?"

He brushed the corn dust off his hands. "Yeah."

"You don't have to talk about it if you don't want to. I'm trying to understand."

"No. It's okay." He tilted his head back to look up at the sky through a lush canopy of green. The familiar knot of dread, fear and anger tightened in his gut. "I was five, so I only remember little bits. Just moments. Like looking at a picture."

"I understand."

"She had a code. Our mother. She would yell out 'Jesus save us all' and when I heard that, I was supposed to get you and take you outside if it was daytime or to one of our rooms if it was nighttime."

Kim's hand slipped into his and she squeezed.

"That's horrible, Josh. Thank you for protecting me."

He returned the squeeze. "It seemed just normal to me at the time. I didn't know anything different."

"She was going to leave him. That's what Mr. Gathers told my dad."

"He told me that, too. I didn't know. I'm assuming that's what pushed him over the edge." He rubbed his free hand across his mouth. "I remember how hard it was to get you out of the crib, you were getting so big."

He stopped for a few deep breaths. Another memory surfaced. When he'd set her on the floor, she'd taken his hand. Like now. He looked down at their hands then up into her eyes. "I took you to the closet and hid under a pile of clothes."

Her pupils were dilated until he could only see a rim of blue. "He was going to kill us, too, wasn't he?" she whispered.

"I think so," he whispered back.

She leaned against him and he brought his arms around her. Holding her. Like all those years ago. It was surreal. Kim snuggled against him. The breeze off the pond cooled his face. The sound of a fish breaking the water from time to time. If he had had time to think about what their first meeting would have been like, he'd have thought it would be awkward. He thought they'd feel like strangers. And maybe that was yet to come. Right now, they were both survivors of the same nightmare.

He rubbed her shoulder. "But look at you now. All grown up and teaching school."

She shifted away and wiped at her eyes. "Yeah. It's amazing, I love my kids. What do you do, Josh? Do you live in the Charleston area still?"

"No. I moved to Columbia a little while ago. Have you heard of the Cleaning Crew?"

Her eyes widened. "The all-guy cleaning service? Yes!"

He grinned. "I'm setting up and running the new branch in Columbia."

"You're one of the Crew?" Her voice raised a couple of octaves in her excitement.

"I was the first Crew member," he said with a grin. And realized exactly how proud he was of that fact.

"Shut. The. Front. Door! I used to tease my mom about that all the time. That I was going to get her a year's worth of house cleaning by the Crew. She is going to flip out."

After their laughter died down, he nudged her with a shoulder. "I need to tell you something."

"Good? Bad?"

"Neither, really. A full-disclosure kind of thing. A little while ago, I hired a private investigator to find you. And he did. So I know a little about you. That you teach second grade. That you're getting married soon."

"Why didn't you get in touch with me?"

"I was going to do that. I wrote you a letter. It's in my desk back home. I was going to read it again on Monday and make myself mail it to you."

"I don't understand."

"Kim," he said seriously. "I didn't know what you knew about our past. All my life, all I wanted to know was that you were safe. And happy. And I knew that. Then I wanted to know you but was afraid I'd ruin your life."

She looked down at her feet. Reached into the bag of corn and tossed some to the fish. "Still protecting me after all these years."

He hadn't thought of it that way and let out a short bark of a laugh. "I guess. I'm not… Let's just say I didn't have the upbringing you did, Kim. I barely graduated high school. If I hadn't found Sadie and became part of the Crew, I don't know what would have happened to me."

"But you found her. The Crew became your family? They must have if you're still with them after all these years? Are you married, Josh? Do I have any nieces or nephews?"

"No, I'm not married. The Crew is family, though. My boss, Sadie, grew up in foster care. I think of her as my big sister. She's getting married soon and will have a stepdaughter. So I'm sort of an uncle."

"Good. Because I want to have four or five kids. Want them to have lots of cousins because let me tell you, being an only child sucks."

"You're not an only child anymore," he said.

"And you've got real family to add to your heart family."

He smiled at that. Heart family. Much nicer sounding than family of choice. He tucked that away to tell Sadie. *Sadie. She is going to lose her mind.* "Sadie has some half siblings. She's building a relationship with them. I'd like to do the same with you, Kim."

"Why do you think I'm here? Ever since Mr. Gathers called me last week, I've done nothing but research this. Reunification of siblings."

Mickie and her index cards appeared in his mind's eye and he had to cover his mouth with a hand to hide his grin. But Kim had said that about research with the exact same tone of voice that Mickie used when she talked about those damned cards.

Kim turned her head and caught his grin. "What? Is that weird?"

"No. You reminded me of someone."

"I like to know things. That's what I do when I'm worried or nervous. I research."

"Were you worried or nervous about meeting me?"

"Nervous. I wanted you to like me. I wanted you to remember me."

"I could never have forgotten you, Kim. You're my baby sister. I may not know the you you've grown up to be, but I loved that fat little baby girl."

She stared at him until a blink sent twin tears coursing down her cheeks. He was pretty shocked by his words himself. They'd rolled out without thought. He reached out and took her hand, grasping it tightly for a moment. "Tell me about your research."

She wiped the tears away. "It's basically what you said. Separated siblings remember the children they used to be, but as adults, they bring entirely new selves to the relationship. Your boss has it right. Let's do this slowly. Get to know each other."

"How do your parents feel about this?"

"They were hesitant at first, not because of you, but because they didn't want it to upset me if things didn't work out. Now they are happy. And feeling rather guilty about not being more insistent with following up on adopting you, also."

He shook his head. "They shouldn't. Tell them I said thank you for taking you and giving you a good life. That means more to me than they will ever know. What about your fiancé?"

"Scott. He's a little bit geeky. So, he's not going to invite you over to watch a football game. But if you can tell a DC villain from a Marvel villain, you're gold."

"Not an expert, but I know Batman is DC and Spider-Man is Marvel."

She gave him a double thumbs-up. "Gold."

"You two doing okay down there?"

They turned at the sound of Nate's voice. He was making his way toward them at an easy pace.

"Y'all been out here a spell. Thought I'd check."

Josh and Kim stood. "Yes, sir," she said. "We're doing just fine."

"Well, come on back up to the house. I got some barbeque on."

Josh scooped up the bag of corn feed and put his arm around Kim's shoulders. "That's a coincidence. I'm starving."

A FEW HOURS LATER, after gorging on barbeque, sweet tea and laughter, Josh hugged Kim goodbye. They'd exchanged phone numbers and email addresses, and had plans to meet again the next weekend. He hugged her close and grinned for the selfie she insisted on taking. He pulled on his leather jacket and strapped on his helmet, feeling lighter and happier than he had in years.

He'd pushed the bike on the ride down as a means of distracting himself from his own dark thoughts. Now, he pushed it out of sheer joy. To feel the rush. He remembered taking Sadie for a bike ride after she'd met her mother. Her triumphant scream as they tore down a back road at not-going-to-say miles per hour. He understood it all now.

Slowing the bike, he pulled into a gas station at the edge of the interstate. He dug his phone out of his jacket pocket and held it up. *Good. Got a signal.* He typed out a message to Sadie because he didn't want her to hear the joy in his voice yet. He wanted to see her face.

Hey. Near town. What are you doing?

Not more than a minute later, his phone vibrated in his hand.

God. Please. Save me.

He grinned.

What's going on?

Shopping for maid of honor and bridesmaids dresses with Lena and her mother. They might kill each other.

She sent another text as he was composing a reply.

Make up an emergency. Save me!

Tell them I need you.

Do you?

Tell them. 45 minutes. Your place or Wyatt's?

Mine.

He tucked the phone away with a smile and cranked up the engine. Even better. He liked Wyatt and loved Jules, but this felt like something for only him and Sadie right now.

It was more like an hour by the time he turned the bike into the Cleaning Crew driveway and parked. Stripping off his gear, he looked up at the building with a wave of nostalgia. This two-story brick box of a house had been his home for so long. He'd been there when Sadie bought it. He'd helped her clean it up, fixing up what they could and supervising contractors when they couldn't. All the while, it was only the two of them, cleaning houses from sunup to sundown. Then they hired DeShawn. Then Molly.

He walked around to the back, where he was

greeted with a volley of barks that would have been intimidating if he hadn't known the giant goofball dog behind them. "Jack," he said, leaning over the fence. "It's me. Knock it off."

Jack gave a few more barks, but his tail was wagging his entire back end. Josh opened the gate and stepped through. Jack jumped up, putting his paws on Josh's chest. He ruffled his hands through the dog's thick black-and-white fur, wincing at the doggy breath being blown in his face.

"Miss me, boy? Yeah?"

Jack dropped to all fours when Sadie opened the back door and skipped down the steps. Josh turned to her. She looked worried.

"What's wrong?" they said in unison.

"You," she said. "What's wrong with you? You texted me you needed me. That's usually bad."

He grinned and pulled her into a hug. "No. I said that for you to use an excuse to get away."

"Oh, for Pete's sake. I've been worrying my brains out. Come on upstairs. Why are you in Charleston?"

He held off answering until they'd crossed the kitchen and went up to the second floor that Sadie had turned into an apartment. Being back here made him homesick but it also made him determined to build something for the Columbia Crew that felt just as much like family. Like home.

He pulled his phone out of his pocket and tapped through to the selfie Kim had taken. She'd sent it to him. "I wasn't really in Charleston. Up in Sumter."

Sadie frowned as she plopped on the couch and propped her bare feet up on the coffee table. Grabbing a glass of wine from the side table, she looked over at him. "Sumter? Is that where that cop you went to see is?"

"Yep."

She cocked her head and pointed at him, her finger making a swirling motion. "Your face. What's going on?"

"Mr. Gathers asked me to come see him today."

"Oh? Did he have more information for you?"

"He had a surprise for me."

He handed her the phone. She took it and glanced at the screen. Then the frown came back as she focused on the picture. "Is that…?"

She appeared to be holding her breath as she looked back at him and set down her wineglass. He let his grin tell her.

"That's Kim?" she whispered.

"Yes. I met her today."

"Josh!" she squealed and threw herself at him, bear-hugging him tight. "Oh. My. God. I can't believe this! Finally!"

She looked back at the phone. "She looks like

you. Same hair. Same eyes. Tall. I never pictured her being this tall."

That got him. "I never thought you thought about her."

"All the time. I wanted this for you, Josh. It went well, then? She knew…everything?"

"Yes. And yes. It was amazing, Sades. She's amazing. Nate is amazing. Everything is amazing."

She stared at him before laughing. "You are almost giddy. I've never seen you like this. Tell me everything."

By the time he was finished telling her "everything," it was too late to ride the bike back to Columbia. Josh pulled off his jeans and flopped back on the guest bed. He was still buzzed from the day. His thoughts turned to Mickie. He looked at his phone. Eleven o'clock. Not too late. He typed in a message.

Everything okay there? I'm in Charleston overnight.

He added DeShawn's phone number with directions to call him if she needed anything. His thumb hovered over the send button. Why was he still doing this? He'd pushed her away. Forced her away. But part of him still…*what*? He hit Send and tossed the phone down beside him on the bed. *What are you doing? It's over. You made sure of that. Leave her alone.* He climbed under the covers and turned the light out. Sleep was what he needed. Here under Sadie's roof. Home. Where he felt safe.

The phone glowed to life. Rolling over, he tried to ignore it. But curiosity got the better of him and he reached back, groping, and found it.

All quiet on the Western front.

He frowned at Mickie's text. What was that supposed to mean? He sent a thumbs-up and put the phone face-down. He needed to let that go. If his heart could get that message, that'd be great. He fell into a deep sleep, full of dreams. Searching through abandoned homes, looking for something. What, he didn't know.

CHAPTER TWENTY-THREE

MICKIE HEARD THE motorcycle roar up the drive and around back to the storage shed, where Josh kept it locked up. Relief flooded her. She'd been awake most of the night, jumping at every sound and shadow, after she got his text that he was in Charleston. Yeah, she had the police and De-Shawn wasn't too far away, but having Josh right next door gave her some peace of mind.

Because she was about to lose her mind. Still no news on Keith. He'd gone missing. His parole officer had issued an arrest warrant for violation of parole. He had also notified the Columbia police department and they'd send an officer to see her. They would increase patrols in the neighborhood. She was grateful they were taking it seriously, but she also knew that unless they assigned a cop to follow her 24/7, she wasn't really safe.

She wanted to ask Josh if she could borrow his car because she really needed to get to the grocery store and didn't feel comfortable walking with Ian right now. But then he'd want to know why and she was too tired to explain. Walking around the kitchen, she opened cabinets and peeked into the fridge, taking inventory. She could hold out until tomorrow. But she needed to feed Ian something besides Cheerios and Goldfish crackers. Plus the diaper supply was running low.

Just do it.

"Come on, grumpy man," she said as she hauled Ian up on her hip. "Let's get this over with."

She went out the back door and crossed over to Josh's back door. The vertical blinds were open and she could see him in the kitchen. Sadness washed over her as she watched him for a moment before rapping on the glass.

"Hey," he said, sliding the door open as he turned and saw them. He looked at Ian. "Hey, little man, what's up?"

"Can I borrow your car? I need to go to the grocery store and it's too danged hot to walk that far."

"Good timing. I was about to head up there myself. We can go together."

Narrowing her eyes, she stared at him. "Together?" she asked.

"I was going up to the Publix."

"The last time we talked, you were pushing

me out the door, telling me to go away. Now you want to go grocery shopping together."

The flash of guilty shame in his eyes made her regret the tone of her voice, if not the question.

"I'm sorry. I shouldn't have done that. I've been in a bad place the last few weeks."

"Yeah, well me, too. Welcome to life, Josh. It's a never-ending series of bad places."

"Wait. What does that mean?"

She pressed her lips together. She was getting angry. Because she was scared and she hated being scared. But even so, she didn't need to be taking it out on Josh. There was enough blame on both their sides to go around.

"Nothing. I'm sorry. I've been trapped inside with a cranky toddler. I'll get the car seat. Thank you."

After she got Ian properly secured in the back and climbed into the front seat, she shook her head. Last time she'd done this, she'd been in the same mental state. Angry, frustrated and exhausted. Josh adjusted the AC so the center vents were aimed at the backseat. She leaned against the window, grateful for the blast of cold air on her face. She was going to have a heatstroke by the end of the summer.

"Why did you text me last night?"

"Huh?"

"Last night. You texted me."

"I didn't plan to be out of town overnight. I know… Hell, Mickie. I understand how few options you have. I wanted to make sure you had DeShawn's information just in case."

She stared out the window as she wrestled with that confession. She wanted to be angry. Tell him she didn't need him watching out for her, but that was pretty stupid considering she was using him to get safely to the grocery store and back. She wanted to beat herself up for not being able to do better for Ian than this precarious existence, but she didn't have the mental energy for that.

Josh pulled into the parking lot and found a parking spot. As Mickie unbuckled her seat belt, he put a hand on her wrist. "Mickie, wait a second. I want to say something."

"Josh, please, not today."

"Yes. Today. I'm sorry I pushed you away like that. I'm sorry I hurt you. I told myself that I was doing it for your own good, but really, I was trying to punish myself. I think you are an amazing person, Mickie. If I could go back and fix everything so we could at least be friends, I would."

She studied his face. "What's changed?"

"A lot. I found my sister and, in the process, I learned a lot about myself."

She grabbed his wrist. "You found her? It went well?"

He nodded. "Yeah, it did. Nothing I feared was real."

"I'm happy for you, Josh. Really, I am."

"Up! Up! Up!" Ian yelled from the backseat.

"Okay, dude, we're coming," Mickie said, popping open the door.

Josh came around as she let Ian free from the car seat. "Ready to do some shopping, little man?"

Mickie settled Ian on her hip. "Have you ever been shopping with a toddler?"

"Can't say as I have."

She laughed. "Well, you're in for a real treat."

HE CAME AWAKE with a sudden start and slight confusion. He'd splurged on a small grill at the grocery store. He had grilled up hamburgers while Ian and Mickie splashed in the small pool. *Friends*. They were trying. Having a cookout on a hot summer day, pretending everything was okay. But it wasn't okay. They couldn't be friends. He'd felt it. They were both acting. He needed to stop lying to himself. The euphoria of meeting Kim was wearing off and he could see he'd let his guard down. It was over. He and Mickie were over. He had to face that. Make her see it.

A long day in the sun with an energetic toddler must have wiped him out more than he'd realized. No wonder Mickie was on the brink of exhaustion all the time.

He ran a hand across his eyes. The movie had ended. Netflix was asking him what he wanted to watch next and as he fumbled for his phone to see what time it was, a loud pounding came from outside. He sat up, now very awake. The pounding resumed. Along with an extremely loud voice.

"Open this goddamn door, Samantha! I know you're in there. That's my kid. You ain't got no right to keep my kid from me."

Josh stood. Slowly, carefully. His body and mind slowed. The hyperawareness of adrenaline kicked in. It was coming from Mickie's front door. Her monster was here. Three quiet paces brought him to the peephole at his door, but he couldn't see anything. The pounding on her door was replaced by what sounded like kicking. As he turned to get his phone to call the police, another sound, much quieter, caught his attention. A tap on the glass of his kitchen door.

He rushed to the kitchen and opened the door. Mickie held Ian close as she rushed inside. "It's Keith. He found us." she whispered. Her face was pale and her blue eyes filled with terror. Ian was thankfully still sleeping.

"I know," he whispered back. He pressed his phone into her hand. "Go to my bedroom and lock the door. Call the police. Do not come out until I get back."

"Don't go out there, Josh. You don't know what he's capable of."

"I'm not going to argue with him. I'm going to try to stall him, buy some time for the cops to get here."

"Please, Josh, don't go out there."

Touching Ian's soft curls with one hand, he leaned in and kissed her forehead. "Go. Now. Call the cops."

Maybe it was because he'd faced this monster as a small child or maybe it was because of the level of terror he'd seen in Mickie's eyes, but he was slightly surprised when he opened his door and stepped out on to the small porch. He'd expected a giant of a man. A huge hulking beast. But the man beating on Mickie's door was anything but. He was slightly built, bordering on skinny. Maybe five-eight. The guy looked over at him.

"This isn't any of your concern, man."

Leaning against his closed door, Josh crossed his arms. "Maybe not, but you're waking up everyone in the neighborhood."

Keith turned away and resumed banging on Mickie's front door. "That's my kid in there!"

Everything in Josh went cold, silent and still. Ian. He wanted Ian? *No way that's going to hap-*

pen. Josh pushed off the door and walked to the sidewalk between the two apartments. "Hey, dude. Listen. I don't know what your problem is, but it's time to move on. Get out of here. Now."

Whirling away from the door, Keith stormed over to go chest-to-chest with Josh. "Think you scare me, big man? Think I won't go through you to get to my kid? That's my kid. Mine."

Still feeling curiously detached, Josh tilted his head to the side as he considered the man's eyes. They were his father's eyes. Full of black rage that blotted out any rational thought. Like an animal in a cage, lashing out at anything that came near. Sadie was right, he realized. Even with Ruby, he'd never had that rage.

"Yeah, well, that's what lawyers are for. This isn't going to help."

"The hell with lawyers and the hell with you. This ain't none of your business."

"Oh, it's my business, all right. You woke me up. That makes it my business."

In the distance, he heard the brief wail of a police siren. A solitary *whoop*. Probably clearing a busy intersection. Then silence. They were coming in quiet. That was a good sign. Except Keith seemed to recognize it, too.

"Bitch called the cops on me?"

"No, that would have been me," Josh said,

hoping to keep Keith focused on him. He needed to keep him here until the cops arrived.

"You called the cops?"

Josh shrugged. "You're out here, beating on my neighbor's door. Waking me up. Screaming and yelling."

"She stole my kid. Took it. Judge cut off my rights. They won't even tell me shit about my own kid."

"Like I said, that sounds like a problem for a lawyer."

"Lawyers don't care!"

Right. Maybe because you tried to kill the kid by beating his mother half to death. Josh felt a stir of anger. He purposely clenched and released his fists. As much as he'd like to put a fist right through this guy's face, he needed to keep him here, ranting and raving until the cops arrived. He flicked a glance to the street. Which should be any second.

Stall him. Lie to him. Anything. "That doesn't seem fair. I know a great PI, maybe I can get him to look into it."

"Screw that. I've got my own guy. Tracked her lying ass right down to this very spot. I've seen her. I know she's in there. She's going to give me that kid. Tonight."

It was that last word. *Tonight*. It sent a chill down Josh's spine. He stood straighter, squared his shoulders, shifting his feet apart. An aggressive stance. That was not going to happen. And where were the cops?

A sneer crossed Keith's lips. "You going to stop me, big guy? Think you're going to play hero? I got news for you." He reached behind him and a gun appeared in his hand. A gun that was pointed directly at Josh's face. "Now whatcha going to do, hero man?"

Josh unclenched his fists and held out his hands, palms up. "Come on, man, the cops are almost here. Let's not do it like this."

"I'm going to do whatever it takes to get my kid. Cops or no cops."

They each saw the police cars converge from opposite ends of the street. Silent, no lights. Josh immediately stepped back from Keith and raised his hands high above his head. He had no desire to be shot, not by this ass or the police.

The next few minutes were a confusing, loud blur of shouted instructions. Four cops were pointing guns at them. Josh stretched his arms higher so the hem of his shirt cleared his pants and turned around slowly so the police could see he didn't have a weapon.

"Drop the gun!" a cop yelled. "Drop it!"

"Get down on your knees!" another yelled.

Josh complied, awkwardly falling on his knees while keeping his hands high.

Somewhere in the continuing commands for Keith to drop his weapon, there was one to lace his fingers behind his head. As he moved to do this, there was a loud pop followed by an instant explosion in his left upper arm. He'd been hit in the arm once by a powerful line drive off the bat of a kid who went on to play professional ball. This felt similar. The force also knocked him off his knees, facedown in the grass.

He shot me. Everything grew dim as the pain hit him. Shouted voices. More gunshots. Quiet. Then rough hands turned him over. A cop. Josh could see his lips moving, but couldn't hear the words. *Shock. You're in shock.* He rocked his head from side to side, trying to snap out of it.

"He's not the one!"

Mickie's voice pulled him back to the here and now. Cops talking. Radios blaring. Neighbors coming out on their porches. He twisted to look at Mickie. "Go back inside! Don't come out here!"

She stood on the porch. "Officer. He was trying to help me. I know him."

"Go back inside, Mickie."

An officer went to Mickie and led her into the apartment. Relief flooded him. He tried to sit up, but the officer at his side pressed a hand against his chest. "Stay still. The ambulance is on the way."

"He's trying to get to her kid."

"He's not going to try to do anything anymore."

"What? Is he dead?"

"I believe so."

"He shot me."

"Yeah. Luckily for you, his aim is off. Instead of your head, he hit your arm. How's it feel?"

"Like I got shot."

The *whoop* of the ambulance covered up the cop's laugh. As the paramedics were getting him on the gurney and tending to his arm, Mickie came out on the porch again, this time holding Ian.

"Get him back in the house," Josh yelled at her. "Don't let him see this."

Mickie pulled Ian close so he was facing away. "Are you okay? Josh, I'm so sorry."

He forced a smile for her. "It'll be a better story than the bar-fight scar. Call DeShawn. He's going to have to take over for a few days."

"Where are you taking him?" Mickie asked.

"He'll be at Palmetto," a paramedic answered.

WHY IAN WASN'T crying through all this, Mickie didn't know. He was usually very grumpy if he woke up during the night. He clung to her, silent, his big brown eyes looking around at all the faces. Again and again, she told the police through numb lips the entire story. Spelling out certain words even though she didn't think Ian would understand. But who knew how much he remembered?

She tried to keep her voice calm, hoping it would keep Ian calm. None of it seemed real. Keith was dead. Gone. She should feel something about that. Sad. Happy. Relieved. Something. But there was nothing. She wanted to stop talking to policemen. She wanted to go to Josh. She wanted to know if he was going to be okay. To tell him how sorry she was.

"I need to make some phone calls," she said to the fourth officer who wanted to talk to her. She still had Josh's phone, so she used that. First, she called DeShawn. That was when the tears came. Even then, she let them roll down her cheeks. She managed to get out enough information to get him on the way to meet Josh at the hospital. Then she called Wyatt. He could tell Sadie and give the police the information he had.

When she'd handed Josh's phone to the waiting officer, she pulled her phone out of her back pocket and called her mother.

"It's over."

"What do you mean? Are you guys okay?"

"Yes. He found us, but I got away. The police shot him. But my neighbor got hurt."

Her legs began shaking and she collapsed on

the couch. Silent tears still streamed down her face. He almost killed Josh.

"It's really over?"

"He's *d-e-a-d*, Mom."

There was a hiss of breath. "God have mercy on his soul."

Mickie felt the first tinge of anger. "God can toss him in the pits of hell for all I care."

Ian patted at her face. "No cry, Mommy."

"Hey, Ian," Mickie said brightly. "Want to talk to your granny?"

"His MeMe," her mother amended.

Mickie held the phone up to Ian's hear. "Say hello."

"Ya-lo. Momma. I firsty."

"Let me get him settled and all this finished with the police and go see if Josh is okay. We'll have a much longer talk tomorrow."

THE NURSE AT the triage desk couldn't give her any information. She'd borrowed Josh's SUV, sure he wouldn't mind, to drive to the hospital. DeShawn wasn't in the waiting room, so she texted him. A minute later, he came out to find her.

"How is he?"

"Could be worse. Bullet went straight through, broke the bone. He's going up to surgery to have the bone fragments cleaned up and the arm set.

No major blood vessels hit. Nerve damage is going to be iffy, but he can move his fingers and wrist, which the doctors say is a good sign."

"Can you get them to let me see him before he goes to surgery? Please?"

"Sure. Let me talk to them and I'll come back and sit with little man here so you can talk alone."

As she walked down the halls of the ER, passing doors and curtained areas where people were living out possibly the worst day of their lives, her heart pounded. She couldn't stop her hands from shaking and her insides felt like a quivery, squirming ball of snakes. It was all starting to catch up with her and she was going to have to get home to her stash of Xanax soon. Before she slipped into a full-out panic attack.

She found the right cubicle and peeked through the curtain. Josh lay back on the gurney. Pale, his eyes closed, an IV running through a tube into his good arm and a thick bandage on his left arm. Tears stung at her eyes. This was all her fault. Her clenching fist made the curtain rustle on its metal rings and Josh opened his eyes.

"Hey," he said huskily.

She quickly crossed to the bed. "Josh, I'm so sorry. I'm sorry, so sorry." She closed her fingers gently around his left hand. She lost her battle with the tears and they streamed down her cheeks. "This is all my fault."

"No," he said. His right hand wobbled as he reached out to her. "Don't cry. Where's Ian?"

"DeShawn is babysitting in the lobby. Josh. He tried to kill you! I can't… I shouldn't have… I should have stayed in my own place and called the police. I shouldn't have involved you."

"Hey. Hush." He blinked and refocused on her face. "I'm on an ass-load of drugs here, Mickie, so I'm going to say this once. Not your fault. You did right to get Ian to safety before he broke into your apartment. I made the decision to go stall him. I was the one who screwed up. I should have stayed with you and Ian until the police got there."

She wiped at her eyes. He was right. If it hadn't been for Ian, she would have stayed where she was and called the police. But the idea of Keith even seeing his son filled her with a horror she didn't want to think about. He'd planned to kill her and take Ian. She pressed her lips together and looked down at Josh's hand, his fingers intertwined with hers.

"I love you," she blurted out.

"Mickie…don't."

"No. I love you, Josh. I know why you tried to push me away, but I also know it isn't true. I know exactly how Keith manipulated me. How he forged that instant connection with me. I knew I was being lied to and manipulated. But I was too young, too stupid, too scared to do anything about it. You are nothing like him. And I think you know it."

She paused, her heart pounding, and searched his face. He'd closed his eyes against her words. She leaned forward and kissed him lightly on the lips. Then the cheek. "I love you, Josh. If you aren't ready for that, I understand, but I want you to know. It has nothing do to with tonight. I've loved you for quite a while now."

She let go of his hand and stepped back. He opened his eyes and the hopelessness she saw in them almost broke her heart. He shook his head ever so slightly.

Her heart did break then. She stood looking into those dark blue eyes until a nurse flung back the curtains.

"We're ready to roll you up for surgery now, Mr. Sanders." She turned to Mickie. "There's a waiting room on the second floor. Take the elevator in the waiting room. We'll take good care of him for you, honey."

Mickie nodded numbly as she stepped back out of the way. Turning, she fled the room. In the waiting room, she gave DeShawn directions to the OR waiting room. A few minutes later, she sat in the SUV trying to decide what to do next. The idea of going home, walking past the police tape...*and oh, my god, what if the body is still there?* She dug the phone out of her pocket.

"Tee? Can we sleep at your place tonight? Yes. I'll explain when I get there."

Ian was asleep in his car seat before she figured out how to get out of the hospital parking lot. Her head throbbed as she drove to Tee's apartment. She needed a drink.

This was the worst and the best night of her life mashed together in the biggest mess imaginable. She was free. But a man, no matter how awful, had lost his life. Josh never even wanted to see her face again. Her heart ached for the poor police officer who'd had to take a life. Even though it had been justified, it couldn't have been easy. All because of her. She hit the steering wheel with the palm of her hand. "Damn it. Damn it. Damn it."

TIANA WAS WAITING for her. "What's wrong?"

"Everything," Mickie managed to say before breaking down again. Surely she would run out of tears soon.

"Momma sad," Ian said.

"I see that," Tiana said as she took Ian from Mickie's arms. She motioned at the couch with her chin. "Go. Sit. Begin drinking wine." She produced a sippy cup and handed it to Ian.

"Let's get you off to bed, little one. It's way past your bedtime."

Mickie curled up in the corner of the couch and grabbed the glass of wine waiting for her. She wiped at her eyes. She was here and safe and Ian was being taken care of by someone she trusted. Now that she knew it was really over forever and that Josh would be okay, the tears stopped and the shaking began. It started in her legs and spread to her arms.

Tiana came back in the room and after taking one look at her, spun on her heel and went back the way she'd come. A moment later, she reappeared with a blanket and tucked it around Mickie. She sat down and pulled Mickie into her arms. "You're safe now," she whispered.

Mickie snuggled down into the blanket and the embrace. Tiana didn't ask any questions. Just held her. Slowly, the shaking stopped and she sat up.

"Rough night?" Tiana asked archly as Mickie reached for the wine.

"You could say that," Mickie replied. And laughed. Not the good laughter but the bordering-on-hysterical kind. Tiana got up without a word. When she returned, she held a pill bottle in front of Mickie's face.

"This what you take?"

"Right now, I don't care. What is it?"

"Xanax. Point two five milligrams."

Mickie held her hand out and Tiana placed a pill in her palm. Swallowing it with a healthy swig of wine, Mickie looked up and smiled at Tiana's expression.

"I know, but screw my liver tonight. It'll regenerate. Eventually."

"It's your liver," Tiana said as she sat down. "What's going on?"

"Keith's dead. Josh is in surgery."

"Hold up. What? Who's Keith?"

Mickie filled her in on the details. She felt detached from the story now. Maybe it was the Xanax kicking in or maybe it was because it was about the tenth time she'd had to tell it.

"Lord," Tiana said as Mickie finished. "Now I need wine." She took the glass from Mickie's hand and drained it.

"Hey."

"I don't even know what to say to you. I can't be happy a person is dead, but I'm glad you're permanently rid of him and the shadow he cast across your life. Josh is going to be okay?"

"Yeah. The doctor said there could be nerve damage, but Josh could move and feel his fingers, so that was a good sign. Time will tell."

"You can see your family again."

Mickie smiled. "Yes. That's the best thing to come out of all this mess. Ian can have grandparents." The pill and the wine were kicking in. She was exhausted.

"Come on, let's get you to bed," Tiana said. "I put Ian to sleep. You go sleep with him and I'll take the couch."

Mickie pulled Tiana close for a tight hug. "Thank you for picking my name."

"Still mad you ain't a man."

CHAPTER TWENTY-FOUR

"SADIE?"

She looked up from the paperwork spread out on Mickie's desk. *Mickie's desk.* He had to stop thinking like that. "Yeah? Whatcha need?"

"I need you to go home."

A frown crossed her face. Josh had long grown immune to that glower that worked so well with some of the Crew members. "What?"

"Go home. You're annoying me. You're scaring the new guys. I'm fine."

Her eyes swept down the cast that encased his arm from shoulder to elbow. "You don't look that fine to me, Josh."

He pulled out a chair and sat across from her. "Sadie. Go home. Really. I'm good. I'm off the narcotics. Tylenol and Motrin are all I need for the pain. It's my left arm and I'm right-handed. I can't sit around all day doing nothing. I can do the paperwork. I can do the phone work."

Sadie pushed back in the chair. "You're serious."

"Yes, I am. Thank you. Thank you for coming

to stay with me. I really needed you last week. But I've got it." He held up his left hand and wiggled his fingers. Rotated his wrist. "The docs are saying no nerve damage. All I have to do is wait for the cast to come off. Some PT to rebuild the muscle. Go home, Sades. Go back to Wyatt and Jules. I know they miss you."

She nodded. "Okay. I get it. I know you're okay. But when I think that we could have lost you..."

"Stop it. No what-ifs, okay? He missed. The cops didn't. Mickie is free. She and Ian are safe now. I'd take another bullet for that."

"Have you told her that?"

He stared hard at her. But she was as immune to his glares as he was to hers. "You are in love with her, Josh. Admit it."

"Listen. Sadie. I hear what you're saying. Yes, I get it now. I'm not my father. I never will be. That thing with Ruby, you're right. I was in control. I didn't let the rage take over. I was able to stop myself. And I knew I had some growing to do. I had to leave that anger and pain behind me. But Mickie needs one hundred percent certainty that it will never happen again."

"Josh," Sadie said her voice softened. She leaned across the table and held out her hand. He took it in his. "There is never one hundred percent of anything in any relationship. All you can do is wake up every morning and try to do your best."

"I know. But it's not only her in this situation. I'd be risking her and the baby."

"You're so full of it," Sadie said, pulling her hand from his and standing up. "I'll go. But you need to stop wallowing around in this crap, Josh. I mean it. You aren't one bit worried about them. You're still a scared little boy who doesn't believe he is worthy of love. I know because until I gave Wyatt a chance, I was exactly the same. Jump, Josh, just jump in. Go tell her."

He crossed his arms and refused to respond. She brushed past him with a big sisterly pop on the top of his head. He jerked his head away. He hated it when she was right. He hated it more when she knew he knew she was right. He'd spent the week since being released from the hospital listening at walls. The living room and kitchen were the best places to listen in on life next door. He liked to think what he was hearing was a happier Mickie. A Mickie who could pursue all her dreams without fear. And Ian could grow up safe and loved. He couldn't see how he fit into that picture.

He pulled the company laptop toward him. The screen was open to the scheduling of the next week's cleaning appointments. It all had to be redone because he was out for at least another two weeks before he could start light duty. He one-finger pecked at it until he felt Sadie's hand squeeze his shoulder.

"I'm all packed up. I know it's time to go. But I liked having someone to take care of."

He stood and gathered her in his arms for a strong hug. "Big sis, I know that. But go take care of Jules and Wyatt. They need you as much as I did."

She pushed back and looked up at him with a wobbly smile. "And now we'll have Kim. Do you think I can invite her to the wedding? I know she doesn't know me, but we'll be one big weird-ass American family, right?"

"I'll talk to her about it."

"And Mickie? You going to talk to Mickie?"

He nodded to appease her. "I'll think about it."

She let out a snort laugh. "Dude, that's all you've been thinking about. I can see it in your eyes. Go over there. Tell her you love her."

"Don't tell me what to do."

"Don't be a whiny baby ass."

"Just because you've gone all soft, doesn't mean I will."

She returned his smile. It felt good to fall back into this sibling bickering. "Okay, baby brother. Call me if you need me."

He helped her carry her suitcase to her car and waved as she drove away. He loved Sadie like the big sister she was to him, but boy did she get on his nerves.

As he walked back up the sidewalk, he saw a flicker of the curtains in Mickie's living room window. His steps slowed but he walked straight back to his apartment.

Work only partly distracted him. Things had stabilized and the addition of new customers had slowed to a manageable pace. The new guys were doing well. He had DeShawn for a little longer. He needed to keep it all together. He needed to stop thinking about Mickie, standing pale but brave in the ER, her lips on his. Her words. *I love you.* She didn't know what she was talking about. She'd suffered a traumatic night. He was the one looking at this clearly. Logically. She needed to go to school. Hell, what she needed was to go back home. To where her family could help her with Ian. She had a family to go home to. A family who loved her.

And yet. And yet. He listened for every rustle, every sound from next door. Hearing the lilt of her voice pierced his soul. The sound of Ian's laughter made him smile. *You want to be a part of it.* He shook his head. *Finish up this paperwork. Get the guys checked out for the day. Get tomorrow's schedule firmed up.*

He was heating a TV dinner when he heard a sound from next door that he'd never heard before. Music. Loud music. Upbeat. Over the music, he could hear Ian shrieking with laughter. A picture rose in his mind of Mickie and Ian, dancing together. He left the microwave beeping.

She answered his knock, her face flushed and a smile that felt like the warmth of a fire on a cold winter's night. "Was the music too loud? I'm sorry."

"No," he said.

Her smile faltered as she looked at the cast on his arm.

"Don't," he said.

"Don't what?"

"Don't stop smiling, Mickie. Do you know how beautiful you are when you smile?"

She smiled then, but it was shy. That she didn't know how beautiful she was stabbed at his heart.

"I love you, too."

She went still. Her ice-blue eyes, wide and wary, met his.

He reached up and traced his fingers along the curve of her cheek. "You should go home, Mickie. To your family."

She shook her head slowly. "No. I can't. It's a small town. Everyone knows what happened to me. There, I will always be poor Samantha, the victim. Here, I can be Mickie, the survivor. Here I can stand on my own two feet. The only thing that's changed is that my parents can now be a part of our lives. And I'd like that to include you, Josh."

He stepped across the threshold and shut the door behind him. He pulled her close in a gentle embrace, dipping his face into her hair, taking in her fragrance. "I'd like to be."

Her hands slid around his shoulders and fisted in his curls. She leaned back to look in his eyes. "You can."

He wanted to kiss her. Wanted to finally let go and give in. But the doubt lay like a stone at the pit of his stomach. "Can I? Fully? No doubts?"

"Josh. There's no guarantee in life. I love you. I trust you. I want you to be part of my and Ian's lives. That's all I can say."

"That's what Sadie said."

"What did she say?"

"There was no one hundred percent."

Mickie nodded. "Only trust and hope. Trust and hope, baby."

He kissed her then, pulling her as close as he could. He never wanted to let go, afraid it would all be a dream. Her love. The peacefulness he felt in her embrace. He pulled her lips from his when he felt the wetness on her cheeks. "What's wrong?"

"Nothing. Nothing is wrong. I'm happy."

He pressed his forehead to hers. "Me, too," he whispered.

"Josh!"

They jumped apart and stared at Ian, who stood in the kitchen doorway, dressed in a diaper and holding a sippy cup. He must have thumped his hand on the volume of Mickie's iPod a few times, because the music was louder and the kid was shaking to it. It was something poppy and sassy. Josh knew he'd heard it a thousand times before, but hadn't a clue what the song was called or who sang it. Who cared? He was happy right here, right now.

"Baby man!" Mickie cooed. "You did it!"

"Josh! Dance."

Josh watched as Ian flailed his arms and twisted at the waist. Josh laughed, nodded his head in time with the beat and mirrored the little guy's movement. "Yeah, little man. I'll dance with you. And your momma."

Mickie put her hands over her mouth to hide her laugh, but Josh slid over and bumped her hip with his. "C'mon, Momma, dance," Josh said.

She smiled, put her arms around his shoulders, looked him in the eyes and began to move. "Yeah," she said. "Let's dance."

* * * * *

Be sure to check out the first book
in Janet Lee Nye's
THE CLEANING CREW *miniseries,*
SPYING ON THE BOSS,
available now from
Harlequin Superromance.

And look for the next story in
THE CLEANING CREW
from Janet Lee Nye,
coming in April 2017!

LARGER-PRINT BOOKS!